RAVES FOR
THE ROOSEVELT MYSTERIES

"A SERIES THAT'S FUN!"
Library Journal

"PERFECTLY WONDERFUL!"
New York Daily News

"LIGHT, BRIGHT, AND DELIGHTFUL!"
UPI

"CHARMING!"
AP

**"THE FIRST LADY COMES ALIVE . . .
GREAT READING!"**
Indianapolis News

**"MOVE OVER SAM SPADE,
LEW ARCHER, AND MIKE HAMMER!"**
Houston Chronicle

"A DELIGHT!"
Los Angeles Herald Examiner

"BRILLIANT!"
Seattle Post-Intelligencer

ELLIOTT ROOSEVELT

MURDER IN THE BLUE ROOM

AVON BOOKS ◣ NEW YORK

AVON BOOKS
A division of
The Hearst Corporation
1350 Avenue of the Americas
New York, New York 10019

"A Thomas Dunne book"
Copyright © 1990 by Elliott Roosevelt
Published by arrangement with St. Martin's Press, Inc.
Library of Congress Catalog Card Number: 89-77677
ISBN: 0-380-71237-7

First Avon Books Printing: June 1992

AVON TRADEMARK REG. U.S. PAT. OFF. AND IN OTHER COUNTRIES, MARCA REGISTRADA, HECHO EN U.S.A.

Printed in the U.S.A.

RA   10 9 8 7 6 5 4 3 2 1

To my wife, Patty, and my mother, Eleanor,
with love,

The Author

1

I left my heart at
    The Stage Door Canteen.
I left it there with
    A girl named Eileen.
I kept on dunkin' doughnuts,
    Till all she had were gone.
I kept on dunkin' doughnuts,
    Until she caught on.

Mrs. Roosevelt smiled and allowed her head to bob a little in rhythm with the music from the car radio.

The date was Friday, May 29, 1942, and she was on her way back to the White House from a brief visit to an elementary school in Bethesda. The children had been assembled in the central hall of the school—the building having no auditorium—and she had sat on a small wooden platform with the principal and several teachers and watched a little boy and girl solemnly explain how to extinguish the hot fire of an incendiary bomb, should one ever fall through the roof of their home.

"Not with water," the little girl had piped. "Water will make the bomb explode. You pour *sand* on it. Sand."

And the little boy, who had lugged a bucket of sand across the platform, then struggled to fit the bucket and dump its contents of damp sand over the sheets of crumpled red and orange paper that represented the bomb and its fire.

"That's why we must all keep . . . We must all keep buckets of sand in the attic. To put out bombs."

Then, Mrs. Roosevelt had spoken briefly, saying that even children could so some things to help their country win the war—and of course every one of them was to urge their parents to keep buckets of sand in their attics.

"We all know it is almost certainly *not* going to happen—that a Nazi plane flies all the way to our country. But if it *should*—"

In fact, she disliked the policy of frightening little children with instruction about putting out incendiary bombs, or how to take shelter in the basements of their schools if bombers should appear overhead; but her voice was daily drowned out by well-meaning people of Civilian Defense, not to mention the radio fare that children heard daily, plus the short instructional films that preceded movies.

War.

Everything was changed. It seemed *everything* was changed. Even the streets of Washington. Automobile traffic was light on the streets, lighter than she had ever before seen it. The buses and trolleys were crowded. Jammed. The sidewalks were thronged with hurrying people, many of them men in uniform. Young women wearing slacks, something not often seen on the sidewalks of Washington even six months ago, strode purposefully and unselfconsciously through the pedestrian traffic.

A week before, she had written in her "My Day" column:

Ever since I mentioned slacks in my press conference the other day I have been receiving offers from various firms to send me slacks which are becoming to the middle age, dumpy figure which some of us past middle life have to endure. I am much impressed with everybody's kindness, but I really have never found the need for these garments; though one picture of a kind of double, divided skirt does seem to me rather practical and cool.

Mrs. Roosevelt would have liked to get out and walk. She would have liked to have closer contact with these crowds, to try to gain a sense of how they felt and what they thought. But she couldn't. She couldn't even drive her own car. The Secret Service, whose attentions she had often playfully eluded before, now insisted firmly, with the backing of the President, that the First Lady could not leave the White House unguarded. Assassination of a First Lady was unlikely, they said; but *kidnapping* . . .

Besides, the President had told her, driving around in her little blue car with the top down, recognized by people in the streets, would not be circumspect. Gasoline was scarce and rationed. Civilians got four gallons a week. Tires were even scarcer.

Sugar was rationed, too. So was coffee. Talk was that meat and canned goods would be rationed within a few months. And butter. And even shoes.

It could well be, because there were scarcities. Clothing was becoming scarce, for example. Stores sold out of basic items, like men's and women's suits. Silk and nylon were in extremely scarce supply, which meant there were almost no women's stockings in the stores. Also, cigarettes often sold out, as did liquor. And if something went wrong with an electric toaster, a vacuum cleaner, a washing machine, a refrigerator . . . if it couldn't be repaired, the owners would likely have to do without for the duration of the war. Posters read:

USE IT UP.
WEAR IT OUT.
MAKE IT DO,
OR DO WITHOUT.

"Don't ya know there's a war on?" was a watchword, heard everywhere. It was the rationalization for every failure, whether caused by the war or not.

Every citizen knew there was a war on. There was surprisingly little grumbling. The citizen who had to elbow his way into a crowded bus every morning and evening, instead of driving the handsome Buick that sat at home in the garage with an almost-empty tank, did not complain; the stranger sitting next to him on the bus might have lost a son. War meant sacrifice. Loss of comfort and convenience was only a small sacrifice.

The Allies had suffered defeat after defeat since December 7. It seemed the Germans and Japanese had advanced on every front. Only three weeks ago General Wainwright had surrendered the last of the American forces in the Philippines. The British had lost Malaya and Singapore, the Dutch their entire colonial empire in the East Indies. Australia was threatened with invasion. In Africa, Field Marshall Rommel was pressing the British forces back toward Egypt. Though the Germans had failed to force the surrender of the Soviet Union in 1941, the fighting there was deep inside European Russia, and the Russians were suffering heavy losses.

It was strange, and immensely encouraging, Mrs. Roosevelt reflected, how Americans remained grimly optimistic that they would win the war, in spite of the succession of defeats that had not been kept secret from them. A ghastly song often heard on the radio was "The Japs Don't Have a Chinaman's Chance." Another one, even worse, was "We're Gonna Find a Feller Who Is Yeller and Beat Him Red White and Blue." Better was "Praise the Lord and Pass the Ammunition."

A pair of minor victories had raised American spirits.

On April 18, sixteen American B-25s, medium bombers, flying off the carrier *Hornet,* had bombed Tokyo. The raid did little damage but succeeded admirably in doing what the President had wanted it to do: boost American morale. The officer who had commanded the raid, Lieutenant Colonel James Doolittle, was an instant hero, as were all his men. Less than three weeks later an American carrier task force won what could at least be claimed as a victory, the Battle of the Coral Sea.

The President's spirits, too, had been lifted by those small victories. He remained ebullient and confident. His burdens were heavy, though; and Mrs. Roosevelt had noticed the toll they were taking of his energy. And today, May 29, he confronted an enigma and an irritant. They were serving a small state dinner at the White House this evening, and it did not promise to be a pleasure.

> *I will go back to*
> > *The Stage Door Canteen.*
> *I will go back to*
> > *The girl named Eileen . . .*

Mrs. Roosevelt returned to the White House by way of the West Wing. She wanted to speak to the President for a moment if she could, before she went in to speak with Mrs. Nesbitt about the arrangements for dinner.

Grace Tully sat outside the Oval Office now. Missy LeHand had suffered a stroke last year and was convalescing slowly. "The Duchess," as the President called Grace Tully, had worked as Missy's assistant for years, and now she capably performed Missy's secretarial duties.

"Is there any word about 'Mr. Brown'?" asked the First Lady.

"Not as yet," said Grace.

"Does the President have a moment?"

"I'll check."

A moment later she entered the Oval Office. The President was sitting behind his desk, wearing an old gray suit she had often told him she wished he would discard. He was smoking a cigarette in his black holder. As she sat down, he lifted his pince-nez off his nose and put it aside on his desk.

"Harry will be in presently," said the President.

"Is there any news?" she asked.

The President flipped through a stack of papers and extracted one, which he handed to her. It read:

Former Naval Person to President Roosevelt   28 May 42

> Your visitor will press hard for "Sledgehammer," as he did throughout his discussions here. As I am sure you will anticipate, he is most forceful and blunt in his conversation. It is quite difficult to like the man, though I believe our private conversations achieved good progress in mutual understanding, though they did not alter his demands or diminish our resistance to them.
>
> I will send Dickie next week, to explain more thoroughly my views of the impossibility of "Sledgehammer" in 1942. Our emphasis must be on "Torch," which is achievable. "Sledgehammer" is not and could prove a costly fiasco.
>
> In the meantime I must regretfully report that the convoy bound for Murmansk, carrying supplies for the Soviet Union, has been under constant attack from Nazi aircraft flying from Norway, and out of thirty-five ships, five merchantmen plus a destroyer have been lost.

Mrs. Roosevelt handed the document back to the President. She had seen these missives before and knew that "Former Naval Person" was Winston Churchill, who in calling himself by that term referred to his former position as First Lord of the Admiralty.

" 'Sledgehammer' is . . . ?" she asked.

"A cross-Channel invasion," said the President. "That's why 'Mr. Brown' is coming—to argue that we and the British must open a Second Front in Western Europe in the summer of 1942, to relieve the pressure on the Red Army. 'Torch' is of course the North African operation we hope to mount in the fall."

"And 'Dickie' is, I suppose—"

"Lord Louis Mountbatten," said the President. "So I'm to get 'Mr. Brown' this week and 'Dickie' Mountbatten next week—the first one to argue that we must invade France immediately, even if it is a costly fiasco as Winston suggests, the other one to argue that it will *be* a costly fiasco."

"What if the Russians are forced out of the war?" asked Mrs. Roosevelt.

The President shook his head. "It would free so many German divisions that the British would certainly lose Egypt and the Suez Canal, to start with. We could not even think about a cross-Channel invasion in 1943 or '44. The war will go on far longer."

"Is a Russian collapse possible?" she asked.

"That's what we are going to find out."

From a window, Mrs. Roosevelt watched the arrival of two black limousines, preceded and followed by Secret Service cars, bringing "Mr. Brown" and his party to the White House.

"Mr. Brown" was Vyacheslav Mikhailovich Molotov, Foreign Minister of the Soviet Union, traveling incognito. He was arriving from London, where he had spent the past week conferring with Prime Minister Churchill and British diplomatic and military leaders. He had been met at the airport by Secretary of State Cordell Hull and by Maxim Litvinov, Soviet ambassador to the United States. Those three men, plus two who were conspicuously Soviet bodyguards, climbed out of the first car.

Mrs. Roosevelt was intensely curious about Molotov, stared hard at him from her window, and saw a man grim of visage and solid as a hammer, which was what his name meant. He was square-jawed, with a thick, drooping, iron-gray mustache and a flat nose that looked bashed in. He wore a pince-nez much like the President's, except that his all but disappeared in the flesh of his face. He had a gray felt hat jammed down on his head. His suit fit him ill and was rumpled besides. His legs were short and bowed. To have said he resembled a bulldog would have slandered the bulldog.

As she watched, his eyes darted all around, nervously, as if he felt it necessary to reconnoiter any ground on which he found himself.

Litvinov, who had himself been Soviet Foreign Minister for many years, was deferential to the thickset, heavy-handed Molotov. The courtly, white-haired Cordell Hull regarded the two with unconcealed distaste, as if he dirtied his hands by having to associate with two murderous Bolsheviks.

The second limousine brought another man who could be nothing but an agent of the Soviet secret police—formerly called the CHEKA, now called NKVD—plus two timid-looking young men, probably the interpreters, and two husky young women whose function in the party was obscure.

The President did not come out to greet his visitors but waited for them in the Oval Office. Harry Hopkins came out to welcome them. He led Molotov, Hull, one of the interpreters, and one of the bodyguards into the West Wing. The rest of the Russian party were invited into the house by Lieutenant Donald Pettengill, a young naval officer assigned to the White House as assistant to the President's naval aide.

Mrs. Roosevelt hurried up to the second floor. The Russians were to be housed for their visit in the guest rooms in the east end of the floor, and she wanted to stop by their rooms to greet them and see that they were comfortably settled.

She waited until they had been introduced to their rooms and their luggage carried in, then went down the long center hall to welcome them.

"Welcome to America," she said to one of the bodyguards, not knowing who he was but seeing in his bearing and in the way he was directing the others that he was a man of some authority. "Welcome to the White House."

The man turned and stared at her solemnly for a moment. Then he said, "No Anglisky. No Amerikisky. *Vi govoritye po-Russki?*"

She smiled, taking care to show as friendly a smile as possible. "No, I'm afraid not," she said.

The Russian allowed a faint smile to show on his face—enough to display a mouthful of gold teeth. Then he turned up the palms of his hands in a gesture suggesting that any further attempt at conversation was futile—and turned his back and walked into the room across the hall.

She got a glimpse of what was going on inside that room. Another man and the two women were conducting a quick, nervous, and very thorough search. They were opening every door, every drawer. They had already stripped the bed. And now the man who had spoken in the hall began to pull the pictures away from the wall, for a suspicious look behind each of them.

Mrs. Roosevelt decided this was a good time to retreat to her office and think about other problems. Winston Churchill had sent warning that the Soviet party was eccentric.

How eccentric was to come to her attention within the hour, when Mrs. Henrietta Nesbitt, the official housekeeper, arrived to complain.

A severe woman in a severe black dress, Mrs. Nesbitt reported strictly to the First Lady and no one else. She supervised the White House kitchen chiefly, but her authority extended to all the housekeeping departments. The Russians, she said, were testing her patience. "To begin with, they demand all keys to the rooms they will occupy. They want promises that no one else has a key to any of those rooms."

"Take care of the matter in a very simple way," said Mrs. Roosevelt with a faint smile at her humorless employee. "Give them keys, tell them those are all the keys there are, and let it go at that."

"*Lie* to them?" asked Mrs. Nesbitt indignantly.

Mrs. Roosevelt nodded benignly. "Yes," she said. "And be a little skillful at it, if you can."

Mrs. Nesbitt stiffened with indrawn breath. "They insist that no one shall enter their rooms but them. No one. No maids, no ushers—"

"Lie to them," said Mrs. Roosevelt again. "Give them any assurances they ask for."

"Uh . . . Would you like to know what they are carrying in their bags?"

"Do we know? So soon?"

"Yes. We do. One of the Negro girls saw them unpacking for 'Mr. Brown'—who is, I suppose, Mr. Molotov, that evil Communist from Moscow—and saw what he had in his bag. We needn't worry about feeding him. He's brought his own food—a big loaf of black bread and a huge, greasy sausage—as if he doesn't trust us not to poison him. Plus a horse pistol!"

"A what?"

"A *gun!* A great big pistol," said Mrs. Nesbitt, spreading her arms to suggest the size of the pistol the maid had described. "Where do they think they are?"

"In a den of capitalist vipers," said Mrs. Roosevelt. "But don't worry about it. Just do the best you can with dinner, according to our plan, and hope it will all turn out all right. I remind you that Mr. Molotov's country is tying down at least a hundred German divisions our boys might otherwise have to fight. We can tolerate a good deal in the circumstances."

"Politics," grumbled Mrs. Nesbitt.

The President's usual evening schedule had to be amended to suit his Russian visitors. He liked to sit down at the end of the day in the sitting hall—the living room of the family quarters—and mix martinis and enjoy casual conversation with whoever happened to be in the White House. His usual companion these days was Harry Hopkins. Louis Howe, who had been his great and longtime friend, had been dead six years now. Missy LeHand, who had shared his cocktail hour with him for twenty years, was not able to attend anymore. Grace Tully joined him often now, instead. And there were others . . . though more and more often, there was no one. But tonight—

Tonight, formal cocktails for the Soviet Foreign Minister and the Soviet Ambassador. Then dinner. No bed tray tonight. Tonight, dinner—not in the State Dining Room but in the smaller private dining room across the hall, which was quite big enough for the party that was gathering.

Cocktails were served in the President's study on the second floor, the oval room above the Blue Room. The windows overlooked the Ellipse and the Washington Monument. Shortly the blackout curtains would be closed, but when the small party gathered for cocktails the sun had not set, and the great obelisk of the Monument was in view, catching the orange light of the setting sun.

"Washington is a beautiful city," Maxim Litvinov said in English, nodding toward the windows.

The interpreter translated for Molotov—the comment had been for Mrs. Roosevelt, not so much for the Soviet Foreign Minister—and Molotov gazed out the windows for a brief moment and perfunctorily nodded.

The President had not yet arrived. Mrs. Roosevelt was in the study. She had explained to Molotov, through the interpreter, the meaning of the ship models and naval prints with which the President had decorated this room. Molotov had seemed to react to that. Czar Peter the Great, he had said, had taken great interest in naval matters.

Hull then said something, and the time the interpreter took to translate Hull's remark and Molotov's response had allowed Mrs. Roosevelt's attention to wander from the words being spoken.

Molotov. Yes. He was the one who had signed the treaty with Hitler in 1939, the treaty that had freed Hitler from the threat of Russian intervention when he invaded Poland. Everyone had seen the photographs of Molotov, amiably exchanging pens with Joachim von Ribbentrop, the German Foreign Minister.

The man who stood beside her now and spoke a word in labored English was far better known in the world than Vyacheslav Molotov. Maxim Litvinov had been Soviet Foreign Minister during the highly publicized international conferences of the 1920s and 1930s. When he was relieved by Stalin it was widely assumed it was because he was too civilized a man to speak for the Stalinist régime in international conferences. He had been a figure in Geneva for twenty years. Chubby, with thinning gray hair that stood wildly above his dome in spectacular curls, Litvinov was as close to a professional diplomat as any man the Soviet Union had managed to produce. He spoke his country's radical views in practical, unproletarian words. Many people liked him who detested Stalin, Molotov, and the rest of the Soviet gang.

"They talk of nothing," said Litvinov to Mrs. Roosevelt. Since Litvinov had been dispatched to Washington she and he had met occasionally—both of them cautiously: he lest he seem too close to the wife of the capitalist President, she lest she seem too cozy with the notorious Communist ambassador. "Is about everything but what counts."

"And that is . . . Mr. Ambassador?"

"The second front," said Litvinov. "Is could be my country defeated this summer."

She nodded. "I hope you will make the point strongly to the President," she said.

"Yes. We make that point," said Litvinov. "No question. We make that point."

The door to the President's bedroom opened, and Franklin D. Roosevelt was wheeled into the study, pushed this time, not by his valet but by Grace Tully. It was perhaps an occasion for black tie, but the President knew his Soviet visitor had brought no such clothes with him, so he and Hull wore dark-blue suits.

Until the President arrived, no one had begun to drink.

A steward now began to offer cocktails. The Russians, Mrs. Roosevelt noticed, had brought their own—vodka—which was guarded by one of the NKVD men as if he expected the capitalists to try to poison the Commissar of Foreign Affairs.

The President had an eye for this, too. "What is that you are going to drink, Mr. Foreign Minister?" he asked.

The translation took a moment. When the answer was returned, the President grinned and said, "Perhaps I've something to learn. Let's drink a toast in *your* liquor, Mr. Foreign Minister."

When this was translated, the Russians were for a moment nonplussed. Then Molotov smiled and nodded and muttered a command to the bodyguard who held the bottle. The man reluctantly poured vodka into seven glasses. In so doing he emptied the bottle, but with the assistance of the steward he offered vodka to the President and Mrs. Roosevelt, Molotov, Litvinov, Hull, and Hopkins. None was offered to the interpreter, the bodyguard, or Grace Tully.

Mrs. Roosevelt looked skeptically into the glass that had been handed her, her nose catching the volatile fumes off the clear liquid that was not diluted by so much as an ice cube.

Vyacheslav Molotov raised his glass and barked out a toast, which the interpreter hurried to repeat in a voice mimicking the hearty tone of the Foreign Minister. "To President Roosevelt! To Comrade Stalin! And to the enduring friendship between our two great leaders and our two great peoples!"

Molotov smiled his satisfaction at the toast and translation, then tipped back his glass and emptied it. The President did the same, as did Litvinov and Hopkins. Hull sipped from his glass. Mrs. Roosevelt sipped from hers and blinked back tears as fumes off the fiery liquid filled her mouth.

"And now, Mr. Foreign Minister, since we seem to

have drunk up all your vodka, let our next toast be a favorite drink of mine.''

Molotov listened to the translation, then nodded agreement. The steward, who had been carefully instructed, began to mix a big shaker of martinis, enough for the company. The bodyguard looked on with unconcealed skepticism and suspicion. Molotov, too, watched—though with interest and no apparent suspicion. When the steward dropped an olive into each stem glass, the Commissar of Foreign Affairs chuckled and said something to the interpreter.

''The Comrade Commissar wishes to know why these fruits are placed in the drinks,'' said the interpreter.

''For flavor,'' laughed the President.

The interpreter translated, and Molotov smiled and responded, speaking at some length.

''The Comrade Commissar says it was a custom in our country in old times to drop a jewel into drinks, in the thought that it would absorb any poison that might be there. He wonders if this custom is not an American image of that old Russian custom.''

''If there is any poison in the glass,'' said the President, grinning, ''the olive will certainly absorb it. On the other hand, as the Commissar will observe, I always *eat* my olive after I finish the drink.''

While this was being translated, the steward carried a tray of glasses around. Grace Tully accepted a martini. The interpreter and bodyguard did not. Mrs. Roosevelt smiled and nodded at her glass, showing that she had not finished her vodka. Neither had Hull, but he put the vodka on the tray and accepted a martini.

''To Premier Stalin,'' said the President, raising his glass. ''And to what Prime Minister Churchill has called our grand alliance.''

Molotov drank the martini as he had the vodka, tipping the glass and taking it all at a gulp. He smiled and watched the President. The President, who had taken only a sip from his glass, dipped in his fingers, extracted his olive, and ate it. Molotov tipped his glass, let the olive roll into his mouth, and chewed it thoughtfully.

Lieutenant Donald Pettengill, wearing dress-blue uniform with white gloves, entered the study and stepped to the President's side to hand him a telegram. The President frowned for a moment over the message, then nodded and handed it back to the officer. Pettengill nodded in response to something the President softly said to him, then hurried out of the room.

Mrs. Roosevelt glanced at her watch. She moved to the President's side and quietly suggested it would be well to go down to dinner.

"He's warming up," said the President. "Let's let him warm up a little more."

"Mrs. Nesbitt was instructed to serve at—"

"I cannot conduct the difficult diplomacy of this alliance for the convenience of Henrietta Nesbitt," said the President. "She will have to accommodate herself to *my* schedule."

Twenty minutes later a buzzer sounded in the Cross Hall on the first floor, alerting the household staff that the President and his party were on their way down to dinner. A second Russian bodyguard, who had been checking out the dining room, scurried around the corner and succeeded in reaching the private stairs to the second floor before any of the official party came down.

Foreign Minister Molotov and the bodyguard accompanied the President in the elevator. Everyone else came down the main stairway. Lieutenant Pettengill waited in the elevator lobby and took charge of guiding the President's wheelchair into the private dining room on the north side of the White House.

The dinner was not grand. No musicians played. Suspecting that their Russian guests had not eaten roast beef in England and had enjoyed nothing of the kind at home for a long time, the President had yesterday sent down explicit instructions to Mrs. Nesbitt that standing ribs were to be served and she was to see to it that the roast beef was *rare,* not cooked to the point of being inedible the way she usually did it. He had ordered fresh vegetables, too, whatever she could find in the markets—knowing how scarce fresh vegetables were in wartime Europe. Red wine was poured, and champagne.

Conversation was awkward, because everything said to Molotov and everything he said in reply had to be translated by the interpreter who hovered behind him. The President tried to keep the talk light, but the Commissar of Foreign Affairs had something on his mind—

"The Commissar wishes to know if the United States has a supply of poison gas."

The President glanced at Hull, then at Hopkins, then said that poison gas was outlawed by the Geneva Convention.

When Molotov had heard this translated, he shook his head firmly. "The Commissar says that the Geneva Convention has not discouraged England from making and storing a large supply of gas bombs."

"What is the point of the question?" asked the President.

Molotov spoke at some length, as the interpreter took notes. Then the interpreter said—"Comrade Stalin is concerned that the Nazis may be preparing a poison-gas offensive in the southern part of our country. If they should, would the United States use poison gas against Germany? Our country has no stock of gas and would have to rely on our allies to provide it."

"I really haven't thought about it," said the President.

Molotov spoke at length again, and the interpreter said— "Mr. Churchill has given Comrade Stalin his assurance that the British government will regard the use of poison gas against the Soviet Union in the same light as if it had been used against Great Britain and will retaliate accordingly. The Foreign Commissar would like to carry home a similar assurance by the United States.''

''We will discuss it with General Marshall tomorrow,'' said the President.

When his food was before him, Molotov ate heartily, with obvious pleasure, and conversation ceased. The President made a few comments about the progress of the war in the Pacific, but Molotov seemed hardly to hear the quiet voice of the interpreter in his ear.

They did not linger in the dining room. Forty minutes after they had come in, the President suggested they return to the West Wing for an hour or so. They could talk around the Cabinet Room table, he said, and their coffee could be served there. Molotov nodded.

Mrs. Roosevelt did not go upstairs immediately. She went down instead, to talk with Mrs. Nesbitt about tomorrow's arrangements.

''They've *all* got guns,'' said Mrs. Nesbitt. ''Revolvers. Even the women have them. But . . . I can tell you something. The two women can speak a little French. They tried talkin' it to me. I couldn't make out a word of it, of course; but I recognized it was French. So . . . *You* can talk to them maybe. And so can somebody else. Whoever speaks French.''

''I'll try it if I get a chance,'' said Mrs. Roosevelt.

''Well . . . They eat. They're hungry. They know how to eat. They're not eating their sausages and black bread, either. We can hope they take some baths, too, since they're sleeping in our beds.''

A few minutes later Mrs. Roosevelt went back upstairs. She did not take the elevator but walked up the private stairs in the west end of the house, meaning then to walk along the hall, up the main stairs, and into her office for a few minutes before retiring to the private quarters.

Walking past the door to the Blue Room she heard distraught voices inside. Curious, she stepped into the doorway.

Two Negro ushers stood in the Blue Room, one weeping, the other trying to comfort him. Lying on the floor, face down, was a young woman—silent and very likely dead.

2

"Miz Roosevelt! Ma'am I din' touched her! As the Good
Lord be my witness, I never touched her!"

Mrs. Roosevelt frowned at the frightened, tearful young
black man, not yet quite comprehending that he thought
he was all but certain to be accused of—Well, accused of
what? Was the woman on the floor dead?

"Has anyone called the Secret Service?" she asked.

"Yes, Ma'am," said the other usher. "I done called.
Man said he be right up."

"Then . . . Then we shall wait. You haven't touched
her?"

"No, *Ma'am!*"

"I mean, to see if she's alive."

"No, Ma'am. She ain't moved. She's *dead!*"

It looked likely. Her blood, running from her head,
stained the floor. And it was true that she was not moving,
not even to breathe.

She was young, as Mrs. Roosevelt guessed. A golden-
blonde. She was dressed in dark-blue slacks with a match-

19

ing dark-blue jacket. A handbag lay just beyond her out-stretched right hand.

The frightened usher trembled. "Ma'am, I—I never touched her. I never . . ."

"Has anyone suggested you did?"

The usher shook his head. He ran his nervous hands down the front of his maroon usher's uniform, over the brass buttons, the yellow piping.

"Then—What's your name, anyway?"

"Martin," said the usher. "Martin Langhorne."

"He's a good boy, Ma'am," said the other usher. "Been workin' here almos' three years."

"Very well, I—Ah, Mr. Deconcini."

A Secret Service agent came through the door. He was a man she knew well, Dominic Deconcini (she had pronounced his name correctly: Dee-con-CHEE-nee), the agent who had worked with the unfortunate Gerald Baines on the investigation of the murders in the White House pantry. He was a handsome young man, with sharp, fine features, a swarthy complexion, and dark penetrating eyes. She knew of him also that he was a reserve officer in the United States Marines and had applied to be relieved of his duties with the Secret Service so he could enter active duty with the Marines and go to war.

"Mrs. Roosevelt . . ." he said. "What—"

"I am afraid the young woman is dead," she told him. "And I am also very much afraid she didn't die by accident."

Deconcini frowned at the young woman lying on the floor. He knelt beside her, took her wrist in his hand, and felt for a pulse. He shook his head.

"She's been dead for an hour," he said. "Let's get a doctor in here to look at her, but—Well, it won't do any good. Lufton—" He was talking to the more senior usher. "—Get on the telephone. Call the doctor to the Blue Room. Call the White House police. Go on now. Hurry!"

"Do you have any idea who she is?" asked Mrs. Roosevelt.

"I'm afraid I do. Uh . . . I'm going to turn her over, Ma'am. You may not want to see."

She did not retreat or turn her face away, but he tried to put himself between her and the body before he turned it over.

"Ohh . . ." breathed Deconcini. He shook his head. "I know who she is . . . was."

"She works in the White House, doesn't she?" asked Mrs. Roosevelt.

"Yes. In the press office, for Steve Early. Her name is Emily Ryan."

With the young woman turned on her back, the cause of her death was entirely apparent. Her head was crushed above her right eye. Quite obviously, she had been struck by a heavy object.

"You found her?" Deconcini asked the usher, Langhorne.

"Yes, Suh. I come in, turnin' off lights around the house. That's what I was s'posed to doin', turnin' off lights . . . and *there she was!* Dead . . . Already dead, like you say."

"Yes," said Deconcini. "Her blood is coagulated. She's cold. I expect the doctor will agree she has been dead for some time."

"Martin," said Mrs. Roosevelt to the usher. "Do you know who the people visiting the White House are?"

The young black man shook his head emphatically.

"Come now, Martin. Guess. Who do you think they are?"

"I think—I think they Roo-shians. I hear that's what they are."

"All right. And do you understand that it's a secret that they are here? That it's a war secret?"

Langhorne nodded.

"To be more definite about it, Martin," said Deconcini, "people can go to jail for revealing wartime secrets, just like they can if they work in a defense plant. You understand?"

Langhorne nodded, with more emphasis. "My daddy," he said. "He done gone up to Dee-troit, to work where they make tanks. An' he come home, he tell what the sign on the wall say. It say—

WHAT YOU DO HERE,
WHAT YOU SEE HERE,
WHEN YOU LEAVE HERE,
LET IT STAY HERE.

An' I know what that means."

Mrs. Roosevelt smiled. "All right, Martin," she said. "That the Russians are here is a secret. Also, the fact that Miss Ryan was killed here tonight is a secret. We will find out who killed her. But you must not tell anyone about her. Do you understand?"

"What I see here, it will *stay* here," the young usher promised.

A uniformed officer of the White House police entered the room. "Officer Grayson, Ma'am, Sir," he said. "Your orders, please?"

Deconcini looked up with a bemused smile at the brisk efficiency of the chubby blond policeman. "Keep everybody out of this room and away from the door," he said. "Regard what you see here as a defense secret."

"Yes, sir."

The physician on duty that night, Doctor Ronald Sharp, arrived next. A thin, handsome young man, he wore a wooden leg, and it was difficult for him to kneel beside the body. The leg squeaked as he manipulated it with the involuntary skill of long practice, and he managed to get down to a level where he could press a stethoscope to the chest and listen for any sound of life from the silent, unmoving corpse. He shook his head.

He frowned over the wound on the head and again shook his head. "The cause of death is obvious enough," he said. "Of course, there will have to be an autopsy."

Doctor Sharp looked around and, seeing nothing else,

took a white handkerchief from his pocket and lay it across the face and the staring blue eyes.

Deconcini squatted and leaned toward the young woman's handbag, which lay on the floor where it had been just beyond the reach of her outstretched hand before he turned her over. It was an ordinary sort of handbag, black leather, with a zipper across the top. The zipper was open. Deconcini leaned closer and squinted into the handbag.

"Uh-oh," he said grimly. "The case just got more complicated."

Taking a mechanical pencil from his inside jacket pocket, he pushed it through the trigger guard and pulled a small, short-barreled revolver out of the handbag.

"How'd she get *that* into the White House?" asked Officer Grayson.

It was a nickel-plated Iver-Johnson revolver, with black rubber handgrips—.32 caliber, five-shot. The five chambers were loaded.

"How'd she get that into the White House?" asked Grayson again. "We don't allow—"

"And *why?*" asked Mrs. Roosevelt. "Why would she be carrying a pistol?"

"Maybe she anticipated the attack that killed her," Deconcini suggested.

"Then why in the White House? And in the Blue Room? What was she doing here? How did she get in here?"

"A lot of questions," said Deconcini. "A mystery, hmm? A murder mystery. You have some experience with them."

"A bit," said Mrs. Roosevelt modestly. She looked at Doctor Sharp and spoke to him. "What has happened must not come to the attention—of . . . Well. You know who is here, don't you?"

"Vyacheslav Molotov," said the young doctor.

"He and his party must not learn there has been a violent killing in the White House," said Mrs. Roosevelt. "They are quite paranoid enough as it is. And so the newspaper men must not be allowed to find out. Do you understand? *Must not."*

"You can depend on *my* discretion," said Doctor Sharp.

"Of course," she said. "Then . . . We're going to need help, Mr. Deconcini. Part of the investigation will likely have to be carried on outside the White House. The President will not want John Edgar Hoover involved. Nothing is secret when that man sees a chance to make a headline. I think—I think we might call in Captain Kennelly. You know the captain, don't you? D.C. police? I have confidence in his discretion."

"I'll call him," said Deconcini.

Captain Edward Kennelly was chief of detectives for the District police. He was a tall, red-faced, white-haired Irishman and spoke with a pronounced brogue. Mrs. Roosevelt had worked with him before, more than once. He brought to criminal investigation something the Secret Service did not bring. The assigned task of the Secret Service was protection, that is to say, preventing crimes. Kennelly's job was the investigation of crimes in fact committed. What was more, his jurisdiction extended further than Deconcini's. The Secret Service had nationwide authority to protect the President and others, but it had very limited authority to make arrests, commit suspects to jail, and all the rest of the process of criminal investigation.

He knelt over the body, which still had not been removed from the Blue Room, though it was now almost midnight.

"Not your blunt instrument," he said. He glanced at the doctor. "Do you agree?"

Doctor Sharp wanted to avoid the painful process of kneeling again, so he bent over and peered down at the huge wound on the young woman's forehead. "Yes," he said. "Her skull was crushed by something with a well-defined corner."

Kennelly put a pocket-sized measuring stick to the wound. "Say an inch and three-quarters . . . by a little more, almost two inches. The two edges meet at right angles. She was struck by something square. That is to say, it had a square corner.''

''But not like the corner of a cube,'' said Doctor Sharp. ''Notice that the wound is in essence wedge-shaped—that is, deeper in the angle. She was hit with the corner of something sharp but not square.''

''I would suggest,'' said Mrs. Roosevelt, ''that the object with which the young woman was killed was very likely something the killer picked up in this room. It is unlikely, is it not, that he came here carrying the murder instrument?''

''On the theory that . . . ?'' asked Kennelly.

''If,'' said Mrs. Roosevelt, ''the killer came here expecting to murder Miss Ryan in this room, would he have not brought a weapon? A knife? A bludgeon? Obviously not a pistol, because of the noise. But . . . It seems to me she was probably struck by something in this room. And very likely something that remains here.''

She began to look around the room. Within a minute she was pointing at a heavy brass candlestick sitting on the mantel before a mirror. It was one of a pair.

''Don't touch it,'' said Kennelly. ''Fingerprints—''

Mrs. Roosevelt put her face close to the candlestick. It had a square base, with small square feet on each of the four corners. Projecting beyond the body of the base, they were wedge shaped.

''I shall be surprised if we don't find traces of blood on this object,'' she said.

Kennelly stepped to the mantel, took a small folding magnifying glass from his pocket, and examined the base of the candlestick. ''And traces of hair,'' he added. ''On the side now turned toward the wall.''

Mrs. Roosevelt shook her head. ''Horrible,'' she said. ''Bludgeoned to death.'' She sighed. ''A horrible way to die.''

''Struck once, I should think,'' said Deconcini. ''That's all it took.''

"By a powerful man, then," Mrs. Roosevelt suggested. "Powerful enough to have caused her death with one blow."

"By a man she faced," said Kennelly. "She was struck on the front of the head, not on the rear."

"And she didn't scream," said Mrs. Roosevelt. "Or, if she did, no one heard her."

"We'd have heard," said the young usher. "She scream in here, we'd have heard in the usher's office. Besides, they was people in the dining room."

"People in the hall, I'd think," said Deconcini. "There had to be people around, with an important diplomatic dinner in progress."

"With an important diplomatic dinner in progress," said Mrs. Roosevelt, "this young woman entered the main floor—presumably from the West Wing. She—"

"Rather informally dressed," observed Kennelly after another glance at the body.

"Actually," said Mrs. Roosevelt, "young women are wearing slacks to work these days, even in the White House. It is, uh . . . Well, they say they have to save back their skirts, their more *appropriate* clothes, because as those wear out they can't buy any more."

"I suppose next they'll start wearing blue-denim jeans on the streets," said Kennelly.

"Well . . . Perhaps. But—"

Mrs. Roosevelt sat down, a little weary, in one of the blue-upholstered armchairs around the periphery of the Blue Room.

"There is not much left to do tonight, Ma'am," said Deconcini. "Doctor Sharp and I can arrange to have the body removed. The autopsy may tell us something. Tomorrow we will have to question a lot of people."

"While our thoughts are focused," said the First Lady, "let's do take a moment to organize a theory of what happened. It will help to ask the correct questions tomorrow."

"She was murdered," said Kennelly, "by someone she knew. Otherwise there would have been some outcry."

"She could have been surprised here," Mrs. Roosevelt suggested.

"I don't think so, with all due respect," said Kennelly. "In the first place, she was struck from the front. In the second place, she was in a part of the White House where she shouldn't have been—which means almost certainly that she came to this room to meet someone."

"Or she met someone outside and they ducked in here for privacy," said Mrs. Roosevelt.

"Very well. That's certainly a possibility. And in the third place, she was carrying a gun in her purse. I don't think she surprised a burglar. Or—you will forgive me—a would-be rapist."

The First Lady stared thoughtfully for a long moment at the body, its face now covered with Doctor Sharp's handkerchief. "Before Mr. Deconcini turned her over, her hand was outstretched toward her purse. As though . . . as though it had fallen when she was struck and she were reaching for it. What's more, it was open."

"The pistol," said Deconcini. "She was reaching for the pistol."

"Yes. Almost certainly. But what was she doing here? With a pistol? Who did she encounter? And who killed her?"

Mrs. Roosevelt looked in on the President in his bedroom before he went down to the West Wing for the morning meetings with Vyacheslav Molotov. Grace Tully was already with him as the President sat up in bed and ate his breakfast. He was dictating some short memoranda to her. The little black Scottie, Fala, scampered around the room, chasing bits of toast and bacon the President tossed to him, then hurrying back to the bedside to beg for more. The bed was littered with newspapers, telegrams, and notes. The President's working day began in bed.

The brevity of his memos were a source of amusement

to his staff—occasionally of concern when they did not understand them. He dictated one to Grace Tully just as Mrs. Roosevelt entered the room—"H.S. Okay. But make it fifty. F.D.R." Mrs. Roosevelt understood that H.S. was Henry Stimson, Secretary of War; and Stimson would understand what was okay except that the number was to be fifty. Most members of the staff thought the President meant to be efficient. Others suspected he intended his memos to be cryptic, so no one but the recipient would know what was meant.

"I have something unfortunate to tell you," said Mrs. Roosevelt.

The President lifted his coffee cup. His jaw twitched faintly, perhaps because his unspoken thought was that his wife too often was the one to bring to his attention small irritations that interfered with his concentration on weighty problems.

"There was a homicide in the White House last night," she said. "In the Blue Room. Probably while we were having dinner across the hall. The victim is a young woman who works for Steve Early. Her name is Emily Ryan."

Grace Tully gasped. *"Emily!"*

"I won't trouble you with details, except to say that Mr. Deconcini and Captain Kennelly have the matter fully under control. The Russians don't know it and need not discover it. The press need not know it."

The President's face was hard. "You've handled these matters before, Babs. And with some skill, too, though I've tended to laugh about your detective work. I don't need to tell you how important it is that we keep the matter entirely secret."

"I'll give it close attention," she said.

"It couldn't have been one of the Russians, could it? I mean, the man who killed her."

Mrs. Roosevelt shook her head. "That seems extremely unlikely. But I can't promise it was not."

"Deconcini and Kennelly . . ." said the President.

"And Doctor Sharp. Plus a couple of the ushers."

"Grace and I," the President added. "And Steve Early will have to be told. But keep the circle as narrow as you possibly can . . . at least until Molotov and his staff are on their way back to Moscow."

Half an hour later the President entered the Cabinet Room for the morning meeting with Foreign Minister Molotov. For this meeting the American delegation of the President, Secretary of State Cordell Hull, and Presidential Assistant Harry Hopkins was augmented by General George Marshall, Chief of Staff, United States Army, and Admiral Ernest King, Chief of Naval Operations. Molotov and Ambassador Litvinov represented Premier Joseph Stalin. Molotov's two interpreters sat behind him and Litvinov. This morning the President also had his own interpreter, Professor Samuel Cross of Harvard.

"I should be very grateful," said the President to Molotov, "if you would brief us on the military situation on the Russian front."

Molotov began to talk. The interpreters scribbled hastily. When he stopped one of them translated, and he waited impatiently. As soon as the translation stopped, he hurried on.

"The Comrade Commissar wishes to say that the season for a Fascist offensive is on us. That is to say, the summer season. The Red Army has carried out some successful operations in the south, but the Fascists have now recovered almost all of what they lost to those operations. They seek now to consolidate themselves in the Ukraine and to capture the oil fields of the Caucasus. If they succeed, they will add to their assets the immense food-producing capacity of the Ukraine and the oil of the Caucasus, which will immeasurably strengthen the capacity of the Fascists for waging war. The question is—Can the Soviet forces hold against the overwhelming onslaught the Fascists are expected to launch within the next few weeks. The answer is—That is doubtful."

General Marshall frowned hard, his face dramatically

showing concern but also skepticism. He knew what Molotov wanted. He had expected the Russian would make his case, not just strong, but *too* strong.

Molotov went on—

"I cannot promise you, and Comrade Stalin cannot promise you, that the Red Army can hold against the enormous numbers of men and machines the Fascists will hurl against it this summer. If the Americans and English do not invade France this summer, thereby drawing off forty or fifty Fascist divisions, the Soviet Union may well lose the Ukraine, the Caucasus, Leningrad, Moscow . . . and the war. So—Can I tell Comrade Stalin you are preparing a second front?"

The President nodded at General Marshall.

"You may tell Premier Stalin that we are preparing a second front," said Marshall.

"To be opened in 1942?" asked Molotov through the interpreter.

"I think we can say we will open a second front this year," said the President. In his mind, the invasion of North Africa would be a second front.

Marshall hastened to clarify. "It must be understood that we cannot move an army across the English Channel until we have enough shipping—invasion barges and so forth—to carry the army and its supplies. Also, we must have air superiority over the Channel and the beaches. Otherwise the invasion could be a fiasco."

Molotov looked at him coldly. He spoke sharply. It was obvious when the interpreter translated that he was softening the tone—"The Comrade Commissar says that even what the general terms a 'fiasco' would draw off enough Fascist divisions from the Red Army front to prevent a Fascist victory."

"An ill-prepared invasion could cost America and Britain a hundred thousand casualties," said Marshall.

Molotov again spoke sharply, and again the interpreter softened his statement—"The Comrade Commissar says if you don't take that risk, the Soviet Union will undoubtedly lose ten times that many men."

Dom Deconcini sat down in Mrs. Roosevelt's office. He had the rumpled look of a man who had not been to bed. In fact, he hadn't; he had shaved in the bathroom in the West Wing, using a razor he had borrowed from a staff attorney; and he was still wearing the clothes he had worn yesterday.

"The basic facts," he said. "Emily Ryan was twenty-eight years old. In one sense, we are fortunate. There is no mother or father who have to be informed. She was reared in an orphanage here in the District. She lived in a boardinghouse on K Street. She has worked in the Executive Wing, for Steve Early, since 1936. She was a competent stenographer and typist. Unfortunately, that's about all we know."

"Someone knows a great deal more, quite obviously," said Mrs. Roosevelt. "Obviously she had friends. A personal life. And—"

"And some reason for carrying a gun," said Deconcini.

"How did she get into the first floor of the White House?" asked Mrs. Roosevelt. "I thought the premises were strictly guarded."

"She had access to the West Wing, where she worked. So she was on the grounds. She was already inside the tightest element of White House security. To come through from the West Wing into the ground floor, she would have had to pass the police desk in the hall there. To come around and in the South Portico, she would have had to pass another police desk."

"In a window, then," said the First Lady.

"They are locked," said Deconcini.

"Well, then . . . the President has asked me to work with you and Captain Kennelly. Where do we start, Mr. Deconcini?"

Deconcini shrugged. "With Kennelly maybe," he said. "He may have the autopsy report by now."

Half an hour later they entered D.C. police headquarters through a rear door and were escorted directly to the spartan office of Captain Edward Kennelly. Mrs. Roosevelt had seen it before. The captain's desk was of scarred oak, his oaken swivel chair squeaked shrilly whenever he turned or leaned back in it, and his desk and windowsills were littered with dusty bulging files, empty cups and saucers, ashtrays, and dead flies.

Mrs. Roosevelt declined with thanks the coffee Kennelly offered, but Deconcini accepted. A uniformed officer went off to bring it.

"Well, we could use Sir Burton on this one," said Kennelly, referring to the Scotland Yard detective Sir Alan Burton who had worked with them on the pantry murders. He had always called the man Sir Burton, and neither Mrs. Roosevelt nor Sir Alan had ever had the heart to correct him. "It's gonna be a real mystery."

"Do you have the autopsy report?" asked Deconcini.

"Yes," said Kennelly. "Doesn't say much we don't already know." He flipped over the typewritten pages. "She died of 'a massive fracture of the frontal bone of the skull, approximately four centimeters above the supraorbital ridge and four centimeters to the right of a line running vertically from the center of the nasal bone.' It goes on to say that the force of the blow drove fragments of bone into the frontal lobe of the brain. The autopsy man—and I can vouch for him; he knows what he's talking about—says the blow that caused death was 'delivered with great force.' "

"Are there other bruises on the body?" asked Mrs. Roosevelt. "I mean, are there any marks suggestive of a struggle before she was struck the death blow?"

Kennelly shook his head. "Nope. The report goes into that in some detail. No bruises anywhere. Uh . . ." He ran his finger down the typewritten sheets. "Nothing unusual in the bowels or bladder. She smoked heavily but had not been drinking. She was sexually, uh . . . well, the word here is 'experienced,' but the condition of her private parts indicate she'd had no sex within the twenty-four hours before she died. She was in overall good health.''

''And had a life expectancy of another forty years,'' said Mrs. Roosevelt sadly.

''No one has claimed the body,'' Kennelly said.

''Who knows she's dead?'' asked Deconcini.

''The people at her boardinghouse,'' said Kennelly. ''We brought in her personal possessions, from her room. Obviously we didn't tell anybody how she met her maker.''

''Speaking of personal possessions,'' said Mrs. Roosevelt. ''Where are the clothes she was wearing?''

Captain Kennelly nodded toward a paperboard carton sitting on a filing cabinet. ''Want to look at them?'' he asked.

''Please.''

The clothing the young woman had been wearing was modest and inexpensive—the dark-blue slacks and jacket, a white cotton blouse, a pair of white rayon panties, a brassière, and a pair of high-heeled black shoes. The blouse and the front of the dark-blue jacket carried stains of dried blood.

''Here's something,'' said Kennelly. ''Look at this bloodstain on the back of the jacket. What's that suggest?''

Deconcini nodded sardonically. ''Our murderer wiped the blood off the candlestick on the back of her jacket.''

Kennelly nodded. ''That's how I read it. A cold-blooded killer.''

''Has the candlestick been checked for fingerprints?'' asked Mrs. Roosevelt.

''Yes,'' said Deconcini. ''And there are two sets of smudged fingerprints on it. What would you care to bet they belong to maids or ushers?''

''I wouldn't take that bet,'' said Kennelly. ''My guess is, we're dealin' with a cool customer.''

''Even so, you are of course checking,'' said Mrs. Roosevelt.

"We are checking," said Deconcini.

The First Lady lifted the shoes from the box. "Oh, dear," she said. "This is really too much like Sherlock Holmes. Look—"

She was pointing out that the soles and heels of the black high-heeled shoes were brown with dried mud.

"She worked in the West Wing," said Mrs. Roosevelt. "Surely she didn't work around the office of the Press Secretary to the President all day, wearing muddy shoes!"

"Well . . ." said Deconcini quietly. "We talked about how she got into the White House from the Executive Wing. That mud suggests she went out on the grounds, maybe into the rose garden."

"Then in a window," said Mrs. Roosevelt.

Dom Deconcini nodded. "Yes. And carrying a pistol in her handbag."

3

"I am sorry, Ma'am, but I don't think you want to see this person."

Captain Kennelly referred to a young woman who had made such a fuss at the desk outside that Kennelly had felt compelled to go out and see her, even though the First Lady was in his office.

"She claims the body," said Kennelly. "She says she's entitled to it."

"When you say she is hysterical, Captain Kennelly, are you saying she is just generally hysterical or is legitimately hysterical to have learned that Miss Ryan is dead?"

"Oh, I'd guess . . . Well, it could be either way."

"Why does she claim she is entitled to the body?"

"She says she's her sister."

"The sister of an orphan?"

"Well . . . there seems to be some reason—"

"Let's talk to her, Captain."

The young woman said her name was Peggy Shearson. She was in her early twenties, from the look of her—a tall, slender, handsome blonde, her jaws working hard and fast on her chewing gum and her eyes wide and angry. She wore her gray skirt at what was called the "patriotic length"—well above her knees, which saved fabric that was in short supply.

"No, I ain't her sister, strictly speakin'. But I'm as close to family as she ever had—and she was to me, too," said Peggy tearfully. "Her an' me, we was at that orphan asylum too damn long, and we was the only pair of girls that didn't hate each other. An' hate the ol' witches that run the place, too. When she got out, she promised me she'd get *me* out as soon as she could. An' she did, too. So we lived in the same boardin' house, an' . . ."

Peggy Shearson covered her face with her hands and wept.

Mrs. Roosevelt stepped behind the girl's chair and put a hand on her shoulder.

Peggy looked up. "My *God!* You're Miz *Roosevelt!*"

The First Lady frowned first at Dom Deconcini, then at Captain Kennelly. She shook her head. "Emily was your friend," she said softly.

"Well . . . yes. *Yes!* My friend . . . All the friend I ever had, too. An'—"

The First lady kept a hand on the girl's shoulder. "Peggy . . ." she said. "Do you know how Emily died?"

Peggy sobbed. "No. . . . Not exactly," she whispered. "But it wasn't of no damned pneumonia."

"Someone killed her, Peggy," said Deconcini sympathetically. "Somebody who knew her. Maybe you can help us find out who."

Peggy Shearson turned up her head and looked over her shoulder at the concerned, obviously caring face of Eleanor Roosevelt. "Why *you* got somethin' to do with it?" she asked. "Did . . . Was she . . . ? In the *White House?*"

"Why don't you help us?" asked the First Lady.

Peggy Shearson dropped her head into her cupped hands and sobbed. Mrs. Roosevelt's thought was that it was gratifying at last to hear someone weep for Emily Ryan.

* * *

Returning to the White House and checking her schedule, Mrs. Roosevelt found she had a luncheon appointment. She was to share lunch with Mr. Gene Tunney, former world's heavyweight boxing champion. Some newsreel cameras would be set up on the lawn after lunch, and Tunney was expected to make a statement in support of the war effort. It was one of those public-relations duties the President himself would have attended to if he'd had ten minutes. As it was, the First Lady was expected to cover the moment.

She sat down at a table in the private dining room with Tunney and with her close personal friend Lorena Hickok, who had expressed admiration for the famous boxer and asked to meet him. The luncheon was brief and the conversation light.

"What do you think of Mr. Barrow as a boxer?" asked Mrs. Roosevelt of Tunney.

"I'm sorry? Who?"

"Mr. Barrow. Joseph Louis Barrow. I received him, too, here at the White House, one day some years ago."

"Oh. *Joe Louis*. Oh, yes. A fine boxer."

While they were eating the newsreel cameras were set up on the lawn. Mrs. Roosevelt and Tunney came out and gave some minutes to the cameramen who needed to take sound levels and set their cameras for the news event.

Finally, the cameras rolled.

Mrs. Roosevelt spoke first. "We are pleased to welcome to the White House today Mr. Gene Tunney, whose name I am sure is known to all of you. Mr. Tunney has dedicated himself to the war effort, particularly in the field of physical fitness, which I am sure everyone realizes is essential to victory. Mr. Tunney has an important message for Americans."

Tunney spoke. "Thank you, Mrs. Roosevelt. I'd like to take a moment to speak to young men who want to serve their country. In this time of emergency, physical fitness is all-important. Men who are called on to be soldiers, sailors, flyers, and marines—but also men who are called on to work on our farms and in our defense plants—need every ounce of their physical strength. I'm calling on all American men to live healthy lives while this war lasts. Eat the right foods. Get plenty of sleep and fresh air. Lay off smoking and drinking for the duration. And men, you will all do a great service for your country if you practice sexual continence until the war is won. Nothing saps a man's strength like the sex act, particularly too much of it. Right now, your country needs you to be at the peak of physical force, so I'm asking you to give up that kind of thing until this war is over. Do it for your country. Thank you.''

In her office half an hour later, Mrs. Roosevelt and Dom Deconcini met with Lieutenant Donald Pettengill, the young naval officer assigned to the White House.

"You were outside the dining room when the official party came down to dinner last night," Mrs. Roosevelt said to him. "Are you aware that a murder was committed in the Blue Room either during the dinner or maybe shortly before?''

Pettengill had a reputation in the White House—indeed, everywhere he had ever been—for being an exceptionally handsome young man, though some observers found his appearance flawed and didn't think him handsome at all. He was tall. His hair was straw-blond, as light as the late Jean Harlow's—and his eyebrows were all but invisible against his pale complexion. His eyes were pale blue, beneath overhanging brows and under high cheekbones that half hid them. He carried himself rigidly erect—ramrod-stiff some said—and his smile was withheld for special moments. This afternoon he was wearing his white summer uniform.

"Yes, Ma'am. The fact of the murder is . . . uh, not generally known but has been , . . rumored.''

"It never happened, Pettengill," said Deconcini. "Nothing happened in the Blue Room last night. Now—

You were on duty in the hall outside. What did you see? Or hear?''

"Sit down, Lieutenant," said Mrs. Roosevelt. "Be comfortable. And do tell us, what did you observe, if anything?''

"I observed nothing, Ma'am," said Lieutenant Pettengill. He sat down and still managed to hold himself stiff and erect.

"Do you know the identity of the person who was murdered?'' she asked.

"I have heard it was Miss Ryan, who worked for Mr. Early.''

"Yes. Now—She somehow managed to enter the White House from the West Wing, carrying a loaded revolver in her handbag. And somehow she got into the Blue Room. It seems likely she came through the main hall.''

"Excuse me, Ma'am," said Pettengill. "Actually, she could have come in through the Red Room, which she could have reached from the State Dining Room, and she could have reached the State Dining Room from the ground floor by the stairs or elevator that come up in the butler's pantry. Or, she could have entered the Blue Room from the Green Room, which she could have entered from the East Room. Also, she could have come in off the South Portico. I'm sorry, Ma'am, but there are various routes into the Blue Room.''

Mrs. Roosevelt regarded the solemn young man with some curiosity. Then she nodded. "Yes, of course," she said.

"Did you know Miss Ryan, Pettengill?" asked Deconcini.

"Yes, Sir.''

"Expand on that.''

"I saw Miss Ryan socially two or three times a few months ago," said Pettengill. "I took her to dinner, to a movie. That sort of thing.''

"Was the relationship, uh . . . intimate?''

"Briefly romantic, Sir. But not intimate.''

"You, as the term is, 'dated' her, then?" asked the First Lady.

"Yes, Ma'am."

"Do you know her friends, people who know her?" asked Deconcini.

"Her best friend," said Pettengill, "is—was—a young woman named Peggy Shearson, who is a waitress in the dining room at the Mayflower Hotel. They were, uh, reared in an orphanage together. They spoke of each other as sisters, though they were not sisters."

"Can you think of any reason why Miss Ryan would have been carrying a loaded revolver in her handbag?" asked Mrs. Roosevelt.

Pettengill's mouth dropped open. "She was . . . carrying a *revolver?* She—No. I can't imagine any reason why Emily would have been carrying a pistol. Unless—Well . . ."

"Go on, Lieutenant Pettengill," said Mrs. Roosevelt. "Unless what?"

"Well . . . Obviously I know nothing of the investigation. But is it not possible that the revolver was put in her handbag by the person who killed her?"

The First Lady glanced at Deconcini. "I imagine that's a possibility," she said. "I guess we hadn't thought of that."

"She wasn't the sort of person who would go about carrying a gun," said Pettengill. "She was mysterious in some ways—I suppose the better word is 'reserved'—but I can't imagine why she would have been carrying a pistol."

"Did you ever meet any other friends of hers?" asked Deconcini.

The lieutenant shrugged. "Well . . . Other people who work here in the White House. Her only *personal* friend I ever met is Peggy Shearson."

Deconcini sighed, glanced at Mrs. Roosevelt, then said—"Finally, then, the big question. Do you have any idea why anyone might have wanted to kill her?"

Lieutenant Pettengill shook his head. "I've been thinking about that pretty much constantly, ever since I heard about her death. I can't think of a reason. I can't imagine why anyone would want to kill Emily Ryan, of all people."

Mrs. Roosevelt went to the West Wing to see Stephen Early. Although Early had been associated with the President in several capacities for many years and was the President's press secretary, the personal relationship between him and the First Lady was—as she put it when asked—"correct." The fact was, Steve Early was a southerner, and Mrs. Roosevelt's sympathy for what he called "the colored" seemed to him excessive. They had exchanged some terse memoranda.

In any event, he always received her cordially, and she always spoke with him in friendly terms.

"You are aware, of course, that your secretary, Miss Ryan—"

"I've been told," he interrupted. "Actually, Eleanor, she wasn't my secretary; she was just one of the secretaries who work for me."

"It is essential that we keep all word of the murder away from the press," she said.

He nodded. "The Boss gave me that word this morning."

"At least until the Russians have left."

"Well, I can't handle it the same way I've handled the Molotov visit," he said. "So far as the visit by 'Mr. Brown' is concerned, I simply asked for cooperation. And we've had it. The boys know who's here, and it has to be one of the biggest stories of the year, but they're keeping it mum. But I can't ask them to conceal a murder. We'll just have to keep it from them. That's what I told the Boss."

"Yes . . . Well, what do you know about the young woman?"

Early shrugged. "Not much. She's worked here for a

few years. Since 1936, I believe. The only kind of employees who are conspicuous are the ones who don't do their job or make some kind of trouble. She was never the source of any problem, so I never paid much attention to her. It was 'Good morning, Mr. Early' and 'Good morning, Miss Ryan' or 'Have you finished that letter, Miss Ryan,' and 'Yes, Mr. Early.' That was the extent of *my* relationship with her. She was rarely in my office because she didn't take shorthand. She transcribed what I dictated into a Dictaphone.''

"No impressions? No ideas? None at all?''

Early shook his head, then frowned and said—''I might say, I suppose, that she was a rather . . . How shall I say? A rather *earthy* young woman. I believe the story is that she grew up in an orphanage. She was, uh . . . bold. For example, when the custom became established that young women could wear slacks anywhere, even to work in offices, she was the first secretary in the West Wing to appear in them. There were some stares at first. That didn't seem to bother her. And . . . and the short skirts—you know, above the knee—that are supposed to be patriotic because they save fabric. She took to that custom, too. You might call her trendy. Bold and trendy.''

" 'Be not the first by whom the new is tried, nor yet the last to lay the old aside,' '' said Mrs. Roosevelt with a sad smile.

"Hmm? Oh . . . yes. Well, she was the first to try the new. Like the Dictaphone. When she came here and applied for the job, she told me taking shorthand was old-fashioned.''

"What about young men?'' asked Mrs. Roosevelt.

"I know nothing of whom she saw.''

"Very well. Anything more, Steve?''

"I'm afraid not. I wish I could be of more help.''

While the First Lady was talking with the press secretary, Dom Deconcini was at Emily Ryan's desk, searching, removing items—some with a handkerchief so as not to put his fingerprints on them.

Mrs. Roosevelt came in. Emily Ryan had shared this small office with another stenographer-typist. The other young woman had left the room during the search.

There was little in the office to reflect the personalities of the two young women who worked there. Emily's desk was of gray steel, and she'd had a wooden secretary's chair. She had typed on a big black Underwood typewriter. The transcribing unit of a Dictaphone occupied much of the top of her desk. Deconcini had pulled the desk drawers open. One drawer was filled with paper—the letterhead of the White House press office, bond paper, onionskin, and a box of carbon paper. Another drawer contained a supply of pencils, paper clips, a stapler, a roll of Scotch tape, and a box of tissues.

"The only personal things are in the center drawer," said Deconcini. "I laid a few things out on top here."

In a little group in the middle of the desk lay a Ronson cigarette lighter engraved

H.D./E.R.

"And look on the other side," said Deconcini.

With his handkerchief he turned the lighter over and displayed more engraving.

$$\male + \female = \heartsuit$$

" 'H.D.,' " she said quietly. "We'll be interested in learning who 'H.D.' is, won't we?"

Also lying on the desk were three packs of Herbert Tareyton cigarettes and the silver-bars insignia of a captain in the army or marines or a lieutenant in the navy.

"Have you interviewed the other young woman who works in this room?" asked Mrs. Roosevelt.

"Not yet."

"Well, then. Let's ask her to come back in."

Her name was Alicia Robinson. She had red hair, and a pair of wire-frame eyeglasses sat atop her freckled cheeks. She wore a simple flowered cotton dress, cinched at her waist with a wide patent-leather belt. She glanced back and forth between the First Lady and the Secret Service agent, awed and apparently a little frightened.

Deconcini closed the door. Mrs. Roosevelt sat on Emily's chair, and Deconcini waved Alicia Robinson toward her usual chair.

"How long have you worked in the White House, my dear?"

"Uh . . . Two years, Ma'am."

"Long enough, then, to understand that very much of what we do here must remain confidential—confidential, that is, until the appropriate time for disclosure. This is particularly true in wartime."

"Yes, Ma'am."

"Then . . . do you know what happened to Miss Ryan?"

Alicia Robinson shook her head. "I heard . . . There's a rumor."

"Miss Ryan is dead," said the First Lady. "What is more, she was murdered."

Alicia Robinson began to cry. She did not cover her face. She just sat, still glancing back and forth between Mrs. Roosevelt and Deconcini, and quietly wept, letting the tears run around the rims of her glasses and down her cheeks.

"She was your friend," said Mrs. Roosevelt sympathetically.

The young woman nodded.

"Do you have any idea why anyone would want to harm Emily Ryan?" Deconcini asked.

"I need to ask you to identify some of these things I found in her desk," he said. "Uh—This cigarette lighter. What do you know about it?"

She stared dully at the lighter for a moment, then said— "It was hers. She kept it in her pocketbook. Why would it be here? And her smokes. Were those in her drawer? She carried those with her. She always reached in her pocketbook for a cigarette and her lighter.''

''Who is 'H.D.'?'' asked Mrs. Roosevelt.

''The initials on the lighter,'' said Deconcini. 'H.D.' and 'E.R.' We know who E.R. was, but who was H.D.?''

Alicia stood and came to Emily's desk, to squint at the lighter. Deconcini turned it over, so she could see the symbols on the other side. She took off her glasses, which had been fogged by her tears, and wiped them with her skirt. She shook her head.

''Don't know who it is?''

''No. And I don't know what these marks mean, either. I never looked at the lighter up close. I never saw what was engraved on it.''

''Do you have any idea how long she had it?''

''No, not really,'' said Alicia as she sat down again. ''I guess she had it all the time I knew her. I did notice it. That kind of lighter is not cheap, you know.''

''Okay,' said Deconcini, ''another question. What about these?'' He pointed to the silver bars. ''Know anything about those?''

''Don gave her those. Don Pettengill. *Lieutenant* Pettengill.''

''How do you know he did?''

''She told me he did.''

''Why would he give her a lieutenant's bars?''

''Well . . . I imagine it was because she asked him for them.''

Deconcini glanced at Mrs. Roosevelt. He was becoming a little annoyed with the short answers.

''Dear,'' said Mrs. Roosevelt. ''Why don't you just explain all you know about the relationship between Miss Ryan and Lieutenant Pettengill?''

''Well, Emily and Don dated. He took her out, and she really liked him. Emily was a sort of romantic-type girl, and she liked to get things like those bars from fellows she dated. Her souvenirs. I remember when she came in one morning with those silver bars in her pocketbook. She took them out and showed them to me, like she'd got an engagement ring.''

"Was it that serious between them?'' asked Deconcini.

Alicia shrugged. "I doubt it. Emily liked to play games, like she'd got every guy she ever went out with to propose to her. But Don . . . He's just a fun guy. I mean, he even dated *me* a couple times. He liked to take out every girl he met. It wasn't anything serious. I think he liked to show up at the Farragut Bar with a different girl on his arm every night.''

"When was it that she was going out with Pettengill?'' asked Deconcini.

"Well, not the last two or three weeks,'' said Alicia.''Not that I know of, anyway. He didn't come around this office like he did when he was dating Emily or me. And she didn't mention him anymore. When she got the lieutenant's bars, that was maybe a couple of months ago.''

"Was she dating anyone else?'' asked Mrs. Roosevelt.

"I suppose so. She always was. It wasn't anybody that came in here, though.''

"Did she mention anybody?''

"Well, no. But then she wouldn't. There wasn't anything to talk about unless it was somebody I knew, too.''

"Did you ever see Emily other than here at the office?'' asked Mrs. Roosevelt.

"Only once. They had a Christmas party at her boardinghouse, and she asked me to come. I went, but I didn't stay long. I met a fellow who asked me to go someplace else with him, and I went.''

"Was that the Christmas of 1941?''

"Right. Last Christmas.''

"Alicia . . .'' said Deconcini. "When Emily was killed she was carrying a pistol in her purse. Do you have any idea where she got it? Or why she had it?''

Alicia began to cry again. "No. I don't know anything about that. Why would she want to do that?''

"She must have had it in this office yesterday," said Deconcini.

"Well, I never saw it," wept Alicia. She pulled off her glasses and put them on her desk. "And, to tell you the truth, I can't hardly believe it, either."

"Describe Emily as she was yesterday," said Mrs. Roosevelt gently.

"You mean the last time I saw her alive?" Alicia sobbed.

"Yes. Please."

"She was still here when I left. About five-thirty. I usually leave the office at five-thirty, and there wasn't any reason not to yesterday. She was sitting there typing. I said good night, and she looked up and said good night, and that's all there was to it."

"Was she moody yesterday? Did you see any sign that she was brooding on anything?"

"No. She was ordinary. Really, she had sort of two personalities. When something she liked had happened, she would dance around and laugh a lot. Most days, though, she was just . . . well, ordinary. Which she was yesterday. She did her work. She talked about the weather and things like that."

Mrs. Roosevelt nodded. She could see that Dom Deconcini had run out of questions. "Well, then . . ." she said quietly. "You will remember that what has happened must remain confidential, won't you?"

"Yes, Ma'am."

"I'd like to have a list of every man Emily ever mentioned dating," said Deconcini. "Write them down as you think of them, even if all you know is a first name, even if you don't know any name at all but know where the guy worked or something like that. I'll come back for that list, say, tomorrow morning. Okay"

"Okay," Alicia murmured sadly.

When Mrs. Roosevelt returned to her office on the second floor, her secretary Malvina "Tommy" Thompson had a stack of telephone message notes for her. One of them was from Harold Lufton, the elder of the two ushers who had been in the Blue Room last night. He asked if he could come up for a moment, and Mrs. Roosevelt told Tommy to call down and tell the man to come.

Also, there was a call from Dom Deconcini. That could be something important, since she had left him only a few minutes before. She returned his call first.

"On getting back to my office," he said, "I found a call from Kennelly. I called him back. He had an interesting piece of information. He took the Iver-Johnson revolver to the D.C. police labs for a fingerprint dusting and so on. They also ran the serial numbers through their file of stolen-weapon complaints and guess what? The Iver-Johnson is a stolen revolver, stolen from a Mr. McCloud in Anacostia about a year ago. More than that. The ballistics-lab men fired a couple of rounds through it, and the bullets match ones taken from the body of a notorious dealer in stolen property—a fence—about six months ago. An unsolved murder was committed with this revolver."

"And fingerprints?" asked Mrs. Roosevelt quietly.

"Only hers. Not a single fingerprint from anybody else, either on the pistol itself or on any of the cartridges in the chambers."

Mrs. Roosevelt frowned and turned in her chair to look out the window, toward the Washington Monument. "I should not want to draw too hasty conclusions from those facts, Mr. Deconcini," she said.

"All right. I agree. Oh, and incidentally, the fingerprints on the candlestick were only those of identified White House staff—the people who polish the thing or dust around it. Since 1930 the FBI has maintained a record of the fingerprints of all employees of the White House, and the prints on the candlestick match people who work there."

"I see."

"I propose to go out and visit the boardinghouse where she lived. This evening. And you—"

"Must dine with the Russians."

"Yes. My sympathy."

"Thank you, Mr. Deconcini. Let me know what you learn."

Harold Lufton, the usher, arrived. He brought with him Martin Langhorne, the young usher who had found the body of Emily Ryan.

"We saw something last night we think you should know," said Lufton. "It maybe don't have anything to do with what happened, but it's a fact."

"Sit down," she said. "Now. What did you see?"

Lufton turned to Langhorne, who said—"One of dem Russians was prowlin' roun'. He was prowlin' *all* 'round, lookin' behind of every door."

"They seem to think that's necessary," said Mrs. Roosevelt. "As if we were going to try to kill Mr. Molotov."

"They snoop," said Lufton.

"Anyway, your point is that the Russian could have been in the Blue Room and could have killed Miss Ryan."

"Is as likely as anybody," said Langhorne. "Likelier'n most."

"Which of the Russians was it?" she asked. "Describe him."

"The one with the short gray hair," said Lufton. "I saw him too."

"God forbid!" said the President. "God forbid the man had anything to do with it. God forbid Molotov should find out or have the least suspicion."

"I don't regard him as a suspect, actually," said Mrs. Roosevelt. "I cannot think of a motive he could possibly have had."

"*I* can," said the President wryly.

"Oh yes, but surely she would have cried out. There would have been a tussle. Noise. And, in any event, such a scenario offers no explanation as to why Miss Ryan was carrying a pistol in her handbag."

They were in the sitting hall, where the President was

relaxing after the day's meetings with the Soviet Foreign Minister. He had bathed and was wearing a fresh suit, his dark-blue pinstripe; and as they talked he scanned the late editions of the newspapers.

"A bit of news," said the President almost casually. "The main Japanese fleet is at sea. It left Japan yesterday. A major operation is in progress. Admiral Nimitz is all but certain the target is Midway, but of course it could be Hawaii."

"Could it even be our West Coast?" she asked.

"Midway, Hawaii, or Alaska," he said.

"I can't help but remember that our sons are in the Pacific," she said. "Except for Elliott, who's in the European theater. I know other people's sons are there as well, but—"

"The boys aren't where this battle is going to be fought," said the President. "Our carriers left Pearl Harbor this morning—that is, this morning Hawaii time. This battle will be fought at sea. Or in the air over the sea. The Japanese fleet includes four big carriers that we know about, and maybe more. We have three—*Enterprise, Hornet,* and *Yorktown.* I don't have to tell you how much is at stake."

"Midway . . . ?"

"The *fleet,*" said the President. "If we were to lose two or three of those carriers, the Pacific would become a Japanese lake. We lost the battleships at Pearl Harbor. If we lose those carriers, we have no striking force left. The Japanese navy will go anywhere their high command wants, carrying anything they want—and we'll have no way to stop them."

"Then God grant that we win," she said solemnly.

"Yes," the President said, returning his attention to the newspapers.

A few minutes later Lieutenant Pettengill—handsome in his blue uniform and white gloves—arrived to tell the President that his Russian visitors were ready. "They've done whatever it is they do when they're alone in their rooms—

it doesn't seem to include bathing—and are ready to join you for cocktails.''

"Invite them up to the study, Lieutenant," said the President. "And tell Marshall and King we're ready for them, too."

The President wheeled himself into the study, where last night a steward had set up an assortment of wines and liquors on a small table. This time the Russians came bearing three bottles of vodka. Maxim Litvinov, even so, seemed troubled; and Vyacheslav Molotov was grimmer.

Molotov greeted the President somewhat curtly, then moved determinedly toward Mrs. Roosevelt.

"The Comrade Commissar wishes to say," said the interpreter, "that he hopes you will pay a visit to the Soviet Union sometime soon."

"I should be very much interested in doing so," she said with a warm smile.

Molotov spoke again, and the interpreter said—"The Comrade Commissar says that Comrade Stalin, too, hopes you will come."

"I am honored."

Her reply seemed to soften the face of the Foreign Minister. He nodded, and a bright reflection flashed off the lenses of his pince-nez. Then he spoke again, and the interpreter said—"You will, he hopes, regard the invitation as official. It is conditioned on one thing only, that the Soviet Union survive the German summer offensive—which it may not do unless your husband and Mr. Churchill open a second front very soon."

"Tell Mr. Molotov that he is a very persuasive man," said the First Lady.

4

Lucky Strike green has gone to war!
Yes, Lucky Strike green has gone to war.
Ye-es, Lucky Strike green *has* gone to war!

Captain Ed Kennelly irritably switched off the car radio. He stared for an instant at the crumpled white cigarette package lying on top of the dashboard. It was true that the olive-green package that had distinguished Lucky Strikes since he began smoking them as a boy was now white. So who the hell cared?

"If they keep broadcasting that, I'm going to switch to Raleighs," he said to Dom Deconcini.

The Secret Service agent laughed. "The President smokes Camels," he said. "And poor old Louis Howe smoked Sweet Caporals. I think that's what killed him."

"I guess Mrs. Roosevelt has no influence on the President about that," said Kennelly. "I wouldn't have a smoke in her presence."

"Neither would I," said Deconcini. "But it's no problem for me, because I don't smoke."

Kennelly glanced at him, curiously. "That's right, you don't. I guess you're about the only man I know who doesn't. How come you don't?"

Deconcini shrugged. "Just never got started. My brothers do, my sister . . . I just never got started."

"You're lucky, you know?" said Kennelly. "Me, I smoke two packs a day. Make it two and a half and maybe a few more. I figured this out. I pay fifteen cents for a pack, so that means I spend about forty cents a day for smokes. You know, that comes to two dollars and eighty cents a week, and *that* comes to almost one hundred and fifty dollars a year. I figured out that I could buy a nice new car for what smoking costs me every four years. I mean, with trade-in and so forth, I could be driving a new car all the time, for what it costs me to smoke."

"So why don't you quit?"

"Can't buy a new car till the war's over. Maybe I'll quit then," said Kennelly. He laughed. "Kiddin' aside, you *can't* quit."

They were on their way to the boardinghouse on K Street where Emily Ryan had lived. Kennelly had been there last night, to search the young woman's room and seize a box of personal items that he had taken to police headquarters. Now they had questions to ask.

The big white frame house was in good repair. Obviously it had been a single-family residence not many years ago. People were sitting on the porch in the last twilight, and as Deconcini and Kennelly walked up the smell of pipe smoke drifted to them.

"Good evening. Is Mrs. Bartlett at home?" Kennelly asked.

Mrs. Sophia Bartlett was the owner of the house, whom Kennelly had met last night, and the man smoking the pipe said she was inside.

"Say, you're that detective that was here last evening,"

said the man with the pipe. "About Emily. How come, if you don't mind my askin'? What happened to Emily?"

"A routine investigation," said Deconcini. "When a member of the White House staff dies suddenly, and being young, we look into it a little."

"You're . . . ?"

"The name is Deconcini. Secret Service."

"Secret Service!" the man repeated. "Mm-mm. Never met a Secret Service man before. I'm Clyde Merck. The ladies here are Phyllis Anderson and Betty Howard."

The "ladies" he referred to were two girls, neither of them twenty years old as Deconcini judged, one smoking a cigarette, the other vigorously chewing gum. Both were wearing shorts and were barefoot, and seemed glad they could hide in the fading half-light.

"Peggy Shearson lives here, too, doesn't she?" asked Kennelly.

"Yes, she does," said Merck.

"Is she home?"

Merck chuckled. "On a Saturday night? Huh-uh! Well . . . Actually, she'll be workin' till about ten-thirty. Then—Well, if she don't have a date, it'll be the first Saturday night I can remember when she didn't."

"Excuse us," said one of the two girls, and the two of them went inside the house and up the stairs.

Merck watched them until they were beyond hearing what he then said—"Khakiwacky, that pair. Y'know what I mean?"

"Not exactly," said Deconcini.

"Khakiwacky," said Merck again. "Victory girls. Anything for the boys in uniform."

"How about Peggy Shearson?" asked Kennelly. "She like that, too?"

"Ohhh . . . I wouldn't go so far as to say that," said Merck, pulling thoughtfully on his pipe and popping out a blob of smoke. "No. Just a modern girl. You understand?"

"And Emily Ryan?" asked Deconcini.

Merck shook his head. "Emily was a deep one. She was never without a date. Pretty girl like her—She never had to worry about boys wanting to take her out. But she wasn't—She wasn't like that pair there, or even like Peggy."

The door opened, and Mrs. Bartlett came out. She was a heavy woman, wearing a flowered dress draped loosely over her ample figure, and she was smoking a cigarette.

"If the police keep coming here, it's going to ruin the reputation of my house," she complained—but she complained amiably, faintly serious, not emphatic.

"I hope this is our last visit, Mrs. Bartlett," said Kennelly. "This is Agent Deconcini, Secret Service."

"So how did poor Emily die?" the woman asked. "You wouldn't be here if it was of natural causes."

"Officially," said Deconcini firmly, "she died of natural causes. Because she worked at the White House, what happened to her is a defense secret; and anybody who tells it around that she died any other way can be in trouble."

"I figure it might be just as well if I went inside and left you three to talk," said Clyde Merck, and he stood and started toward the door.

"Please stay, Mr. Merck," said Deconcini.

Merck returned reluctantly to his chair, and Mrs. Bartlett sat down in the porch swing that was suspended by chains from the ceiling.

"I have a question," said Deconcini. "Who is 'H.D.'?"

The two shook their heads.

"Emily had a Ronson cigarette lighter," said Deconcini. "It was engraved with her initials and the initials H.D.—together with some symbols suggesting a love affair. We need to know who H.D. is."

"You figure this H.D. killed her?" asked Merck.

"Clyde!" said Mrs. Bartlett sharply. "They haven't said she was killed."

"That's right. We haven't, said Deconcini. "Let's keep thinking of it that way. And the answer is no. We don't suspect H.D. of doing anything wrong. We just want to talk to him.''

''Well, I can't place those initials at all,'' said Mrs. Bartlett.

''Do you know the names of the other young men she dated?''

''The fact is,'' said Mrs. Bartlett, ''she didn't bring them here very often. Sometimes a young man would come and pick her up, but she'd be watching for him, and he wouldn't come in. And of course they brought her home. They'd sit out front in the car and talk, and he might or might not come up on the porch.''

''Men in uniform?'' asked Kennelly.

''Funny-lookin' blond fellow, almost albino you might say, in a navy uniform,'' said Merck. ''Navy *officer,* I mean. I doubt she ever dated a man who wasn't an officer.''

''There was an army major, too,'' said Mrs. Bartlett. ''Never heard her say his name.''

''Oh, yeah,'' said Merck. ''There was another young fellow used to come see her. Odd-lookin' young man. Lawyer, I think she said he was. From California. Works for the Office of Price Administration. What was his name, Sophia? He came up on the porch and introduced himself. What was his name?''

''Ohh . . . Dixon, I think it was. Dick Dixon. Now, there'd be your H.D. if he'd been Harry Dixon. But he wasn't. He was definitely Dick.''

''Yeah,'' said Merck. ''Dick. But it was more like Nickerson or Nickelson. Anyway—''

''Okay,'' said Deconcini. ''Did you notice anything different about Miss Ryan the past few days? Was she upset about anything?''

''She had a big fight with her friend Peggy,'' said Mrs. Bartlett. ''First of the week it was. Monday, Tuesday . . . Big blowup.''

''About what?''

The woman shook her head. ''Don't know. It was in

their room. You know, they shared a room. It was up there, behind the closed door. I heard 'em screamin' at each other.''

"They glared at each other after that," said Merck. "There was some bad blood between 'em. Which is strange, because they were good friends.''

"Peggy has claimed the body," said Kennelly. "She says she's going to arrange a funeral.''

"Decent of her," said Merck solemnly. "Peggy's a decent girl.''

"We should chip in and help her pay for it," said Mrs. Bartlett.

Kennelly glanced at Deconcini. The two men shared the same thought: they had heard all there was to hear from these two people.

Over dinner Vyacheslav Molotov, through his interpreter, represented the situation on the Russian front as desperate. Even if the Americans and British could not in fact open a Second Front in 1942—which he and his government did not by any means accept—they should at least announce their intention of doing so. Anything that would draw German troops away from the Red Army front could prove to be the salvation of the Soviet Union.

"Some Americans," his interpreter said for him, "decry our dedication to Marxism-Leninism-Stalinism. And yet, is there so much difference between our political philosophies? I defer to Mrs. Tryphosa Duncan Bates-Batcheller, president of the DAR, Daughters of the American Revolution— surely not a socialist organization—who said at the Fifty-first Continental Congress of that society (and I quote), 'Today in Russia, Communism is practically nonexistent.' Who could say it better?''

The President laughed. Mrs. Roosevelt laughed. And Molotov, almost for the first time during his visit, allowed his smile to spread into a grin, plucked off his pince-nez, and laughed, too.

* * *

Deconcini and Kennelly drove to the Mayflower Hotel. Dom said he had put in a long two days and would like to sit down over a good dinner. Anyway, he said, Peggy Shearson might be their waitress, if they asked for her.

Their identification got them the table they wanted, with the waitress they wanted.

"Kennelly," said Peggy Shearson. "Fancy seein' you here."

Deconcini could see why Emily Ryan's friend had been described by Kennelly as "a sexy broad with a body that ain't gonna go away." She made the prosaic brown uniform of a dining-room waitress look provocative, wearing the skirt short and tight, the bodice snug.

"Meet Dom Deconcini, Secret Service," said Kennelly.

Peggy Shearson nodded. "You guys want somethin' from the bar?" she asked.

"Sure. And then dinner," said Kennelly. "And we also want to talk to you a little. When do you get off for the night?"

"Ten, officially," she said. "But it'll be later before I can actually get out of here."

"Like to ask a few questions," said Kennelly. "Then we'll drive you home."

Peggy stood smiling at him, her hips cocked. "I got a date," she said.

"Then maybe tomorrow," said Kennelly.

"Tomorrow's Sunday."

"We're investigating a murder," said Kennelly.

Peggy shrugged. "We'll work it out," she said.

Over their drinks, then over their meal, Deconcini and Kennelly talked about the murder.

"I've got another bit of information," said Kennelly. "The Iver-Johnson revolver. The serial number shows up on another piece of paper. It was pawned in a pawnshop four months ago. D.C. law requires a pawnbroker to report the numbers of any handguns he takes in."

"Why wasn't that matched against the serial number on the stolen-weapon report filed by—What was his name?"

"McCloud," said Kennelly. "It should have been matched. It wasn't because too much time had passed between the theft report and the pawn report. For a few weeks after a theft, the serial number of a stolen weapon is kept in an active file, and the pawn reports are checked against that file. But the card file gets big and unwieldy after a while, so cards off the bottom of the stack are moved over to an inactive file."

"And the fact that the gun was used in a murder—"

"Ballistics report only," said Kennelly. "We didn't know the serial number of the pistol used to kill the fence."

"I want to talk to that pawnbroker," said Deconcini.

"So do I. But we can't till Monday. I checked the place. It's closed till Monday morning. To find out who has the license for that pawnbroker shop, we'd have to go through records in offices that are also closed till Monday. It'll cool till then. The guy isn't going to run away."

Peggy Shearson was busy. She served her tables efficiently, bustling back and forth from the kitchen and the bar. It was obvious she was a popular waitress, that many of her customers were regulars, and it was easy to guess she picked up good tips.

"Would it be worthwhile to stay around and see who her date is?" Deconcini asked Kennelly.

"Thinkin' the same thing," said Kennelly.

They used Kennelly's police identification to learn where the waitresses left the hotel at the end of their shift; and they moved the car around and waited where they could see them leave.

At 10:21 Peggy Shearson came out alone.

"Oops. Nobody meeting her?"

"I don't know, but let's get out and follow her."

"*You* get out and follow her. I'll follow you with the car. If she catches a cab or bus, two guys on foot—"

"Right," Deconcini agreed. "I'm off."

Peggy Shearson walked down Connecticut Avenue to K, then turned east. Deconcini had to keep a brisk pace not to lose her. She walked decisively, without hesitation. She shook off propositions from a pair of sailors and a marine and kept walking. Deconcini followed her for half an hour, until she walked up the steps and onto the porch of her boardinghouse.

Kennelly, who had been following a short distance behind in his car, stopped and picked up Deconcini.

"Now that's odd," he said. "No date. She was emphatic that she had a date."

"Wait a little," said Deconcini. "Maybe he's coming here for her."

Half an hour more. No date. Kennelly and Deconcini gave up.

"It'd be a mistake to give too much significance to this," said Deconcini, "but there's something odd about this evening. The way she walked out of the Mayflower, she *knew* nobody was waiting for her. Why didn't she want to talk to us tonight?"

Kennelly shook his head. "I have never been able to understand well-stacked little broads," he said.

Deconcini's night wasn't over. He returned to the White House and telephoned his wife. We don't often have a murder investigation on our hands, he told her, so you'll have to endure this, as I do. It can't last more than another day or two.

Then he checked with the telephone operator to see if Mrs. Roosevelt wanted to receive a report this late.

She did.

They sat together in the family sitting hall in the west end of the second floor. She called for a pot of coffee and a bottle of brandy.

"The President has retired," she said. "Mr. Molotov and his party will leave on Monday. The visit has been trying for the President, I may tell you. Not only has he had to tell Mr. Molotov there can hardly be any invasion of France in 1942; he has had to tell him also that some shipping heretofore devoted to carrying materiel to the Soviet Union must now be diverted to carrying essentials to Great Britain. I have a terrible suspicion, Mr. Deconcini.''

"Which is?''

"That if Mr. Molotov returns to Moscow without the concessions Premier Stalin sent him here to get, he may lose his post. At the very least. And it could be worse. I may tell you—in strictest confidence, of course, and because I know I can trust you—that Mr. Litvinov is very much afraid to be called home. Soviet ambassadors who do not achieve what Stalin sends them out to achieve are sometimes—Well . . .''

"Shot,'' said Deconcini.

"Poor Mrs. Litvinov has asked for asylum in the States. She has told me personally—and again in strict confidence—that if her husband is called home, and he goes, she fears she will never see him alive again.''

"She doesn't exaggerate?''

"Of course she does. They all exaggerate—to put the kindest word on it. But what is she exaggerating? Exaggeration must be built on a base. What does she legitimately fear?''

Deconcini reported what he and Kennelly had learned that evening. The coffee and brandy were brought in, with a few small sandwiches and some cookies. Mrs. Roosevelt took coffee only but encouraged Deconcini to have a splash or two of brandy and something to eat if he wanted it. She was well aware of the hours he had kept the past two days.

"I'd be interested to know something about that Russian who was prowling around downstairs last night,'' said Deconcini.

"His name is Potapava,'' said Mrs. Roosevelt. "Mr. Vasili Aleksandrovich Potapava.''

"How did you learn that?'' asked Deconcini, genuinely surprised.

"A word or two with one of the women who serve the

Foreign Minister,'' said Mrs. Roosevelt. ''She speaks a little French, as do I.''

Deconcini smiled. ''You never cease to amaze me,'' he said.

''There is nothing amazing about speaking a little French, Mr. Deconcini. Indeed, I had little choice in the matter. As a girl I was sent to England to school. I had to speak a bit of French if I were to eat and drink.''

''Ohh . . .''

''The kind French lady who 'imposed' her language on me was the dearest teacher I ever had.''

''In any event, you never cease to amaze me,'' said Deconcini.

''I think,'' said Mrs. Roosevelt, ''we shall be unable to interrogate Mr. Potapava. The President feels—and I must say I agree with him—that any implication that one of the Foreign Minister's servants had committed a murder in the White House would be more destructive of Soviet-American relations than the bad news Mr. Molotov has to carry back to Premier Stalin.''

''In other words, if Mr. Potapava killed Emily Ryan, the murder remains 'unsolved,' '' said Deconcini dryly.

''Precisely. The lives of tens of thousands of American men may depend on the maintenance of the somewhat fragile alliance between our country and the Soviet Union. That alliance must be preserved at—'' She paused. ''Well, not at *all* costs, but at the cost of our failing ever to discover who killed Miss Ryan, if that is what it takes.''

''Anyway,'' said Deconcini, ''I don't think the Russian killed her. Why would he? Unless we find out she was a Communist and a spy—''

''Not likely, I think,'' said Mrs. Roosevelt.

''No,'' said Deconcini. ''I can't help but think it had something to do with her personal life. I—''

''You realize the implication inherent in that, I imagine,'' the First Lady interrupted.

''Uh . . . ?''

''The implication that necessarily follows is that someone in the White House played an important role in her personal life. And I think that should possibly be the focus of our investigation. With whom, Mr. Deconcini, did she have a personal relationship?''

"Other than Lieutenant Pettengill, you mean?"

"Lieutenant Pettengill and who else? Hmmm? Whom did she encounter in the Blue Room? Why was she carrying a gun last night? Why was she in the White House?''

"And who else . . . ?'' mused Deconcini.

In the morning, Mrs. Roosevelt went to church. Returning to the White House, she found a note from Deconcini saying that the body of Emily Ryan had been taken from the morgue to a funeral home and that the funeral would be on Monday. She called the West Wing and asked if Steve Early was working. He was. He came on the line, and she suggested to him that it might be appropriate if he and she went to the funeral home and signed the guest book.

A little before one o'clock they arrived at the funeral home. Though they had intended only to sign the book and hurry away, they were encountered in the hall by Peggy Shearson.

"Nice of you to come," she said to Mrs. Roosevelt.

"Let me introduce Mr. Stephen Early," said the First Lady.

Peggy reached for Early's hand and shook it. "Nice of you, too," she said. "Emily used to speak of you."

Mrs. Roosevelt bent over the guest book on the little hallway table and signed her name.

"You must come in and see her," said Peggy. "She looks okay. They done a good job on her."

Reluctantly, Mrs. Roosevelt and Early walked into the room where Emily Ryan was laid out in a big bronze casket. The mortician's cosmetologist had indeed done a good job. They had placed a small black hat on her, set at a jaunty angle, so it covered the wound on her head. Her hands were folded over a small white Bible.

"She'll be buried in Rock Creek Cemetery," said Peggy. She sighed. "The least we could do for her is give her a first-class send-off, I figure."

Deconcini showed his identification to Gregory Dolan, funeral director.

"Please," said Dolan in the affected-solemn voice of his profession. He gestured toward a stairway.

Only when they had reached the second floor of the funeral home and entered the mortician's private office—and he had closed the door—did Dolan speak in a normal voice and abandon his set expression of funereal solemnity. He offered Deconcini a chair, sat down at his roll-top desk, and lit a cigarette. He was a man in his forties, thin, slight, balding.

"I assume, Mr. Dolan, that in your business you are accustomed to dealing with matters in confidence, completely in confidence," said Deconcini.

"Propriety is the name of the game," said Dolan in a matter-of-fact voice.

"You, uh, prepared Miss Ryan for burial?"

"Yes."

"You know how she died, then. The story has been kept out of the papers and must be."

"That point was made with emphasis before the body was released from the morgue," said Dolan.

"A defense secret is involved, Mr. Dolan. A rather sensitive matter."

The funeral director turned down the corners of his mouth and nodded. "In my line of work I see some distressing things, Mr. Deconcini. I've handled the bodies of murder victims before. I never discuss any element of what I see. Not with anyone."

"Good. Now you are going to have to make an exception. I am going to ask a question or two."

Dolan drew a deep breath. "I suppose I should ask what your authority is, what is your jurisdiction. But—" He shrugged. "I will cooperate. What do you want to know?"

"I want to know who is paying for this funeral," said Deconcini bluntly.

"Miss Shearson is paying for it," said Dolan immediately.

"How much?"

"A thousand dollars, roughly—including the cemetery plot."

"That's a year's income for a waitress," said Deconcini.

Dolan puffed on his cigarette. "I . . . I asked for the money in advance, in the fear she could not pay it. She handed me one thousand dollars in cash. Twenty fifty-dollar bills."

"With no comment as to where she got it, I suppose."

"No. Not a word."

5

On Monday morning, the last day of the Molotov visit, the Commissar of Foreign Affairs asked Mrs. Roosevelt to have breakfast with him. Because it was a warm spring morning, she arranged for breakfast to be served at a table in the colonnade between the White House and the Executive Wing, overlooking the rose garden where some of the roses were already in bloom.

This arrangement made the Soviet security men nervous, and they spent some time before the Foreign Minister came down, hurrying around the grounds, looking, presumably, for rifleman hidden in the shrubbery. When Molotov did arrive, they took up stations, one in the colonnade, the other on the lawn beyond the rose garden.

Vyacheslav Molotov appeared on time, dressed in his somewhat old-fashioned gray suit, his pince-nez sitting firmly astride his nose. His interpreter followed him at a respectful distance, and when he sat down the interpreter stood behind him.

Mrs. Roosevelt had seen no reason to have her own

interpreter, no reason to ask Professor Cross to come to the White House early. If he had come, she reflected, he would have sat at the table with her and Molotov, not stood behind her chair.

Without words, gestures sufficing, she offered scrambled eggs, bacon, toast, melon, and coffee; and Molotov happily accepted everything offered.

"I am afraid your return journey to Moscow will be somewhat dangerous, Mr. Foreign Minister," she said.

After an exchange between Molotov and the interpreter, the interpreter said—"The Comrade Commissar says that his journey will be interrupted by a second visit to London, only after which will he fly home. And that, of course, may be a bit dangerous, since it requires him to fly within the range of Fascist fighter aircraft."

"I wish him Godspeed," she said.

Molotov smiled at the translation. The interpreter said, "The Comrade Commissar says he prefers a good aircraft in the hands of a good pilot to any assistance from any mythological being."

"Since I can't help fly the aircraft, I may be able to help with my prayers," she said.

Molotov heard the translation and then spoke at some length. The interpreter said, "The Comrade Commissar thanks you for your prayers. He says that he very much hopes it will be possible for you and the President to visit the Soviet Union in the near future. He says also that he realizes how difficult it is for the President to make such a journey and that he therefore hopes it will be possible for you to come alone, if the President cannot come."

"I am honored by the invitation."

"The Comrade Commissar says our country would be honored by your visit."

"I am very much interested in the status of women in various nations. If I can come, I should be most interested in meeting with Soviet women, to learn all I can about their burdens and opportunities, which we are told are very different from what they are here."

Molotov nodded during the translation, then spoke, and the interpreter said—"The Comrade Commissar says that Soviet women share equally with men in every sort of opportunity and obligation. For example, a majority of physicians trained since the Revolution have been women, whereas very few women are doctors in the United States. Many of our most productive scientists are women. Women constitute half of all university teachers."

"But I believe," said Mrs. Roosevelt, "that I have seen photographs of Russian women sweeping the streets."

Molotov's iron face did not flicker as he heard the translation. He spoke calmly. "I spoke of obligation as well as opportunity. Women do any work for which they qualify. So, you also see women carrying rifles in infantry companies at the front. The Comrade Commissar says that equality is . . . equality."

"I am not entirely sure," said Mrs. Roosevelt, "that American women would welcome the opportunity of becoming street cleaners."

The translation—"The Comrade Commissar hopes you will come and speak with Soviet women who sweep the streets, and learn how they feel about it."

While the First Lady was sharing breakfast with the Commissar for Foreign Affairs, Dom Deconcini and Captain Kennelly were visiting the pawnshop which had reported the pawn of the Iver-Johnson revolver found in Emily Ryan's purse.

Lou's Pawnshop was on a run-down street, situated between a bar that was already doing brisk business so early in the day and a Chinese laundry. It was a typical pawnshop—the windows and the shelves inside crowded with things taken in pawn: three typewriters, some radios, two phonographs, one of them electric, some albums of records, half a dozen guitars, a saxophone, a trumpet, a banjo, a set of drums on the floor, an electric fan, some hats and boots probably taken for the price of drinks, pistols, rifles, shotguns, knives, luggage, watches, jewelry, some medals, a set of dishes, assorted silverware, an ivory manicure set, a set of jade chessmen, a sword, four almost-new tires, a box of matched carpenter tools, a dozen or so fountain pens, a shelved set of Encyclopedia Britannica, a foot-treadle sewing machine, some mantel clocks, some wall clocks, a long telescope, two barometers, half a dozen cameras of various types, two bicycles, a baby carriage containing twenty or thirty harmonicas, and a saddle. The pawnbroker sat inside a little cage, protected from his customers by a black steel mesh and dealing with them through a small window.

"Good morning, Uncle," Kennelly said to the man behind the window. All pawnbrokers were called Uncle, and the man looked up into the face of the Irish cop without a trace of reaction. "Kennelly, D.C. police."

Still no reaction. The man was maybe fifty years old. He held the unlighted stub of a cigar clenched between his teeth. He wore an old black suit that looked like something he had taken in pawn, so badly was it worn and so poorly did it fit him. He stared for a moment at the badge Kennelly showed him. Maybe he shrugged. His body was so deep inside his oversize suit that it was hard to tell.

"You filed this report," said Kennelly, handing over the half-sheet document on which the pawnshop had reported taking the Iver-Johnson revolver in pawn.

The pawnbroker nodded. He still hadn't spoken a word.

"Took the pistol from one William Franklin," said Kennelly, reading upside down the name written on the form.

Again the pawnbroker nodded.

"Sold it to who?" Kennelly asked.

The pawnbroker shrugged. "I can look it up," he said grudgingly.

"Why don't you do that?"

Chewing on his cigar, the pawnbroker pulled a ledger from beneath his counter. "Gun record," he said. "I keep better than I have to." He ran his finger down a page, then wet his finger and flipped the page over. Pulling a pair of gold-rimmed spectacles from his pocket, he set them on his nose and frowned over the ledger sheets. "Dere," he said. "I sold dis pistol to a young voman. May twenty-six." He nodded.

"Dere," he said, turning the ledger for Kennelly to read. "Miss Ruth Thompson. You see her address? Massachusetts Avenue."

"The pistol was used to kill a man, Uncle," said Kennelly.

The pawnbroker frowned and shook his head. "Vell . . . I am sorry for dot. But it is not mine responsibility, is it? Can I help vot dey do with guns dey buy? Could a dealer in *new* firearms? No. Ahh—Even so . . . Dot young voman! She could *kill?*"

"She didn't kill," said Kennelly. "The pistol you sold her had already been used to kill. It was stolen, and it was used to kill. Then it was pawned to you."

"Ahh, but I have done vot I am required to do," the pawnbroker protested, wagging a finger. "I am filing the required report, no? Wiz the serial number and the name of the man. I have no knowledge of—"

"Did William Franklin show you any identification?" asked Kennelly.

Once again the pawnbroker shrugged. "A man comes in here and vants money from an old pistol, he should have *identification?* No. He vants three dollars. He killed somebody wiz dis pistol? I doubt it. If he did, it didn't make him rich."

"I want you to look at a picture," said Kennelly. He extracted from an envelope and handed over an eight-by-ten print of the morgue photo of Emily Ryan's face.

"Dot's a *stiff!*" the pawnbroker protested.

Kennelly nodded. "Right."

"And . . . dot is Ruth Thompson," said the pawnbroker glumly. "It . . . It didn't save her life after all."

"She said it would?"

"She said a man vas t'reatening her, and she vanted a pistol for protection. So . . ."

"Did she say anything about this man who was threatening her?"

"No. Just dot he vas t'reatening her. She asked me to show her how to load it."

"Did she buy the cartridges from you?" asked Deconcini.

The pawnbroker shook his head. "Oh, no. I don't sell dot. I just show her *how* to load. I didn't have no cartridges."

"There were no fingerprints but hers on that revolver," said Deconcini. "How come yours weren't on there?"

"I see a gun, first I vipe it clean," said the pawnbroker. "I don't vant guns going around town mit *my* fingerprints on."

Kennelly sighed. "Okay, Uncle. I want you to come into headquarters and look at some other pictures. I'd like an identification of your man William Franklin. We may have a mug shot of him."

Mrs. Roosevelt sat down in the little office where Emily Ryan had worked. Alicia Robinson had come in late, but she was at her desk now.

"I gave it a lot of thought," she said to the First Lady. "I wrote down the names. I mean, I wrote down the names of the ones I know. Emily had lots of dates with men I never met, guys with names she never told me."

"She was a very popular girl," said Mrs. Roosevelt.

"Well . . . I'd like to say something about that. It wouldn't be right to call her loose or immoral or anything. She was a modern girl and had a lot of fun, but she wasn't any . . . she didn't do anything wrong, is what I mean."

"I am pleased to hear you say that," said Mrs. Roosevelt. "I hadn't thought otherwise, but I am pleased to hear you say it."

"Okay. I wrote down the name Bob Gray. I think she liked Bob Gray pretty much. He worked at the Treasury Department. 'Course, now he's down in Texas learning to fly. Joined the army air corps. He's a cadet."

"When did he enlist?"

"Uh, January. February at the latest."

"All right. Go on."

"We already talked about Don Pettengill. I . . . uh. I'm starting off with the young fellows, 'cause she did date some older men. Then there was a fellow whose name I never did catch. He's a lawyer from California, works for the OPA. We walked out of here one night, and he was waiting for her on the street. She introduced me, I guess, but I don't remember the name. We walked a little way together. I remember him saying he got his law degree from Duke University. He looked like there was some kind of shadow over him. Kept his mouth turned down a lot and walked with his shoulders hunched up. Said he was going into the Navy as soon as his commission came through. Emily went out with him a few times, but she didn't like him and put a stop to it. I think he asked her to marry him. She laughed about that!"

"A little cruel," observed Mrs. Roosevelt.

"Yeah. Particularly when the guy had an ego that needed bolstering in the worst possible way."

Mrs. Roosevelt nodded thoughtfully. "Go on," she said.

"Well, that's it for the young fellows. Then she—You know, this sounds like Emily really got around. But remember I knew her for two years. Since she didn't have a real permanent relationship all that time, of course she dated a lot of guys. Nothing wrong with that."

"Nothing wrong with that," Mrs. Roosevelt agreed.

"Okay. Then . . . well, she went out with some older men. Uh . . . I don't want to suggest it was serious with any of them. Emily was a good-looking girl, and men liked her. Okay?"

"We need not make judgments," said Mrs. Roosevelt.

"Well, then. There's a Congressman that took her out once or twice. A little fat sort of fellow in his forties, I guess. He's married, so it really wasn't serious. Emily said she was opposed to breaking up a marriage. Anyway, this

Congressman is from Illinois. Guy by the name Ev Dirksen. You ever hear of him? You oughta hear him talk. Sounds like the voice of God. He knows it, too, and chooses his words like it was God talking.''

"What are you saying, Miss Robinson? Congressman Dirksen is indeed a married man, with a daughter I believe. When you say Miss Ryan 'went out' with the man, just what do you mean?''

Alicia Robinson threw out her hands. "Just for some fun. Nothing serious. I guess they went—Well . . . I don't know. He called her here, on the phone. I answered. He wouldn't say who he was, but I'd heard that voice and *knew* who he was. Emily called him when she came up from Mr. Early's office, and she laughed for five minutes on the phone. And—''

"How did you know his voice?''

"She introduced me to him one night at the Adelphi. We didn't have any dates that night. He was with some men. He got up and came over to say hello. So I knew his voice after that. You wouldn't forget it. Like—'Oh . . . *Em*-ily. How . . . *nice* . . . to see you. Please introduce your . . . *friend.*' ''

"Miss Robinson—''

"Well, I don't know. I'm not saying they slept together. You asked me for a list of men she dated. He took her out. Maybe just to dinner. I don't know. But they were good friends. They were good enough friends to have a lot of little jokes together.''

"Anyone else?''

"There were others. I can't think of who 'H.D.' is. One of them was a guy with a lot of money. I mean a *lot* of money. She talked about that. But she wouldn't say his name. I asked, and she wouldn't say.''

"Well . . . Thank you, Miss Robinson. If you think of any more names, please let me know.''

Alicia Robinson frowned hard. "I don't want to change your opinion of Emily,'' she said. "She wasn't any loose girl. I don't want you to think of her that way. She was just a *modern* girl, who liked a good time. I think the guys she dated understood that.''

Mrs. Roosevelt sat down with Dominic Deconcini over a late lunch of tuna fish salad and iced tea. Deconcini reported on the meeting with the pawnbroker, and she told him what she had heard from Alicia Robinson.

"I . . . I do not propose we call Representative Dirksen," she said. "On the other hand, it might be well to know where he was Friday night. Some distressing ideas come to mind.''

"Like that a member of Congress might be able to get into the White House," suggested Deconcini.

"That is one of the ideas," she said.

"I am beginning to think," said Deconcini, "that we are obliged to look a bit more deeply into the character of Emily Ryan.''

"Although I dislike the implication behind the suggestion, I cannot disagree," said Mrs. Roosevelt.

"A 'modern girl,' '' mused Deconcini.

"I have to wonder," said the First Lady, "if Steve Early doesn't know more than he has told.''

"I will leave it to you to question Mr. Early," said Deconcini. "Italians are another group he doesn't much care for.''

"May I, then, assume you will cope one way or another with Mr. Dirksen?" asked Mrs. Roosevelt with a sly smile.

"Since I've never heard his name before today, I will beard that lion in his den," said Deconcini.

Mrs. Roosevelt could not question Steve Early that afternoon. He had gone to the funeral of Emily Ryan. It had seemed appropriate, since she had worked for him.

The First Lady had a long-standing appointment to inspect—for the newsreel cameras—a vehicle the army had contracted to purchase by the thousands. Warned that the inspection might be wet and muddy, she appeared in pubic for the first time in a skirt and jacket of serviceable khaki, with a cap with a Red Cross insignia.

She would have much preferred to drive herself to Fort McNair, but the rules established and strictly enforced by the Secret Service since December 1941 required that she sit in the backseat of a black Packard and be protected by armed guards.

This is the voiceover for the newsreel seen in theaters all over the country the following week—

"Mrs. Eleanor Roosevelt, wife of the President of the United States, inspects the amphibious Jeep! Here she climbs into the odd-looking vehicle, accompanied by Army Chief of Staff General George Marshall. Look out there, General! You seem to need a hand more than the First Lady does!

"Wait a minute here! What are they doing? Look at that driver! He's driving the Jeep down the bank and into the Anacostia River!

"Well . . . that's the idea. *This* Jeep is supposed to swim! The army has ordered thousands of these little amphibians, and they are supposed to carry U.S. troops across rivers anywhere in the world.

"Okay, it doesn't sink! Look at that baby go! Up over its wheels in the river, it wallows a bit, but it moves. Mrs. Roosevelt likes the ride! See her wave! Just like a ride in a motorboat. Or maybe not quite. . . .

"After a nice ride around the point, up the Washington Channel and back, the Jeep is ready to return to land. But—Uh-oh! The best-laid plans of mice and men! The driver runs ashore. But—But the amphibious Jeep won't climb the slippery bank! See that Jeep throw mud!

"Stuck! They're stuck! So, now what?

"Well, Mrs. Roosevelt knows how to come ashore, if nobody else does. Over the side she goes! Up to her knees in the Anacostia River! And now wading ashore, unabashed and laughing!

"Is the water cold? The First Lady shakes her head. A nice day for a swim, she says!

"Seriously, the army is buying thousands of these little swimmers—and usually they do better than this. But if you're watching this, boys, just remember how Mrs. Roosevelt got ashore. If she can do it, you can!"

Dom Deconcini trudged into the House Office Building, unenthusiastic about his appointment with the Congressman from Illinois, Mr. Dirksen. He did not anticipate a friendly reception, once the Congressman knew why he had come.

He was surprised. Even after Representative Everett Dirksen understood the purpose of the visit, the Congressman remained cordial.

"Yes, of course I knew this young woman," said Dirksen as he stared at the morgue photo of Emily Ryan. "Yes . . . Emily. I am *shocked* to learn of her death. I am shocked, Mr. Deconcini." He shook his head. "She was a fine young woman."

"Her funeral is this afternoon," said Deconcini. He glanced at his watch. "About now, in fact."

"Ahh . . . A tragedy."

The Congressman from Illinois was possessed of a bounty of curly hair, mostly dark but now turning gray. He was distinctly overweight, and the cream-colored double-breasted suit he affected did nothing to make him appear any thinner. He was a distinctive, even an unforgettable, man. The distinction lay in two things: first, his voice; second, the mouth from which it issued. The voice was mellifluous, honeyed. He chose his words carefully, spoke slowly, and the words rolled out in a ponderous cadence. But more interesting than that was the way his mouth formed around the words, much like the affectation adopted decades before by Georgie Jessel, with loose lips shaping sounds and allowing them to fall out like so many ball bearings crammed into his mouth and dribbling forth as they were released.

"I would like to confide a defense secret," said Deconcini. "I know you can be trusted."

Dirksen puffed out his lips and nodded dramatically. "Why, of course," he said.

"Miss Ryan was murdered."

"The photograph suggested as much," said Dirksen.

"Witnesses say that you enjoyed a rather close personal relationship with Miss Ryan," said Deconcini, exaggerating the number of witnesses who said so.

"Indeed I did," said Dirksen blandly.

"Uh . . . One that would be embarrassing to you if it were known, Congressman?"

"In what context is this question asked, Mr. Deconcini?"

"We are compelled to ask questions of everyone who had a close personal relationship with her."

"In other words, did I murder Emily?"

"In other words, did you murder Emily?" asked Deconcini.

"No. Do you believe me?"

"I . . . I can't believe *anybody,* Mr. Dirksen. I have to deal with facts, not with what I believe."

Everett Dirksen smiled. He leaned back in his chair, shook a cigarette from a pack, and lit it. "What a man believes is the most important thing about him, Mr. Deconcini. I, for example, believe in God. A couple of years ago I was on a train, on my way home to Illinois, and in my roommette I was seized with a sudden, awful pain. I thought it was a heart attack. I think in fact it *was.* I dropped to my knees and asked God to spare me. And He did. I believe he spared me because He knew I put my trust in Him. He knew I believed in Him. What a man believes is—"

"Thank you, Congressman. But that doesn't answer the question, does it?"

Dirksen smiled lazily. "You'd be surprised at the number of people for whom it answers any question at all."

"Can I ask where you were Friday evening?"

"I was at home with my wife and daughter. You can ask. But what will you ask my wife, Mr. Deconcini? Will you ask, 'Was your husband at home Friday night—or was he, as we suspect . . . ?' Actually, what *do* you suspect? Do you suspect I was shacked up with Emily Ryan that night? Or—''

It occurred to Deconcini that Dirksen did not know Emily Ryan died in the Blue Room in the White House—either that or he was a bold dissembler.

''You can damage my marriage, Mr. Deconcini,'' said Dirksen. ''Not destroy it, I think. But—''

''Congressman. I am not here to damage your marriage, or even to accuse you. Uh . . . frankly, no one lists you as a suspect in the death of Emily Ryan.''

''Oh . . . I seem to have gone overboard.''

Deconcini shook his head and sighed. ''Mr. Dirksen . . . someone known to Emily Ryan—probably a friend she trusted—murdered her by crushing her skull with a heavy bronze candlestick. I need to know who that trusted friend might have been.''

''Where did it happen, Mr. Deconcini?''

''Let's leave that fact out for the moment, Sir. Who do you know who might have—''

''No one,'' said Dirksen, his loose lips flapping. ''I can think of no reason why anyone might have murdered that young woman.''

''Someone anxious to prevent the disclosure of—''

''No,'' said Dirksen firmly. ''You mean blackmail. Emily was not that kind of girl.''

''She was,'' said Deconcini, ''what her friends call a 'modern' girl.''

''Very well,'' said Dirksen. ''I will accept that term. Yes. She was a modern girl.''

''Congressman,'' said Deconcini, ''I am willing to accept your word that you didn't kill Emily Ryan and don't know who did. What I need to know is, can you help me come up with an idea as to who—''

''No. I think not. My relationship was not so close.''

''All I need is the names of other friends of hers.''

''Men friends,'' said Dirksen.

"Men. Yes."

The congressman turned up his hands and turned down the corners of his mouth.

"How did you meet Emily Ryan?" asked Deconcini.

"I was introduced to her by Harry Hopkins, as a matter of fact," said Dirksen.

"Where?"

"In a bar. Uh . . . yes. It was in a bar called the Farragut, on Eye Street. I stopped in there for a drink one evening in . . . oh, January, I think it was. She was there. Alone. But Harry came in, greeted her, then greeted me, and introduced Emily. When I was about to leave, she was about to leave, so I offered to drive her home."

"After which, one thing led to another," Deconcini suggested.

"That is a facile way of putting it," said Dirksen with an air of dignity aggrieved.

"Sorry. Did you ever see her with anyone else?"

Dirksen crushed his cigarette in an ashtray, and adopted an impatient tone that suggested the interview had come to an end. "Mr. Deconcini," he said, "it was not in the nature of the brief relationship I had with Emily that we went to public places. You will make whatever you want of that. So I can't give you any other names. So far as her murder is concerned, if you will tell me where she was murdered then maybe I can do more than just tell you I was at home Friday evening. Maybe I can prove I wasn't where the crime occurred."

"It occurred in the White House," said Deconcini.

"Friday evening . . ."

"Friday evening."

"Well then, the crime must have been committed by someone who has access to the White House, which I certainly have not. Really, Mr. Deconcini, the question of my involvement in this case could have been settled at the beginning of this interview if you had only told me where poor Emily died."

"You are not a suspect, Congressman," said Deconcini. ''I just wanted to hear what you know about Emily and her friends.''

Dirksen stood. ''You have heard all I know,'' he said mellifluously.

When Mrs. Roosevelt returned to the White House from Fort McNair, the Russians were gone. Under the critical eye of Mrs. Nesbitt, a crew of men and women was busily cleaning and airing the rooms they had occupied.

''They didn't know how to live in a house,'' she complained. ''Filthy Communists. I wonder how they live at home.''

''Be prepared,'' said Mrs. Roosevelt cheerfully. ''I think we may have another visit from Mr. Churchill in a week or so.''

''Oh, God save me! We'll have to lay in an extra supply of soap.''

''And brandy,'' said Mrs. Roosevelt. ''Be sure there is plenty of brandy and Scots whiskey.''

''Enough to float the old buzzard,'' said Mrs. Nesbitt.

Going on up to the family quarters, Mrs. Roosevelt encountered Lieutenant Pettengill on his way to the President's study with a briefcase.

''Ah, Lieutenant,'' she said. ''I hope you have a moment.''

''Certainly, Ma'am.''

She had used towels at Fort McNair to wipe the mud and water off her legs, but her skirt remained damp and muddy, as did her shoes; and her stockings sagged. As she led Pettengill to a chair in the sitting hall, she explained to him where she had been and what she had done.

''But, Lieutenant, what I really want to talk to you about is Miss Ryan.''

''Miss Ryan?''

''Yes. We could wish that our investigation into her death would become narrower, more focused. Instead, it is expanding, like the ripples from a pebble dropped in a pond. And it has become necessary to inquire more deeply into her character, though to do so raises an implication I am *most* reluctant to make.''

Pettengill, who was wearing khakis instead of his dress blues, interlaced his fingers and frowned. "I see," he said blandly.

"Allow me to ask you something about yourself, Lieutenant," she said. "You are, I suppose, the graduate of a good college?''

"Harvard," he said.

"And your family is . . . ?''

"My father is an investment banker in Boston," he said. "My mother was a Cabot.''

"Ah. A marriage between the Pettengills and Cabots. A distinguished lineage. You prepped, I imagine?''

"Choate," he said.

"Now—Miss Ryan was reared in an orphanage here in Washington. We don't know who her parents were. Indeed, we have inquired of the orphanage, and even they don't know. I doubt that she knew herself. She did not complete high school. When she was in school, she studied typewriting and shorthand, to prepare herself to earn a living. In brief, Lieutenant—and without meaning to denigrate Miss Ryan in any way—I find myself wondering why a young man of your background would have found her company interesting. And you are not the only man of your education and background who did, apparently. What is implied is not very pleasant. Is it?''

Pettengill stroked his chin and nodded. "I understand," he said. "But, please understand, Mrs. Roosevelt, that Emily was an engaging, vivacious girl. It would have been difficult not to like her. A man, meeting her—Well, use myself as an example. I . . . I hardly knew her before I developed a fascination with her and wanted to know her better. But—But the contrast you have suggested was overwhelming. After a few dates with her, I had to accept the fact that she was . . . How shall I say it? She was not—She was not *our* sort of person.''

"I understand.''

"It makes me most uncomfortable to say it. But, you understand, I could not allow a *serious* relationship to develop."

"Yes. I entirely understand."

"Oh—And Emily was *ambitious*. She could have married anytime, to any of a dozen men who, I am sure, offered her marriage. But she wanted to marry—How can I say it?"

"Above her station," Mrs. Roosevelt suggested dryly.

"That sounds so *crass*. But maybe it describes the situation."

"Lieutenant . . . I think you did not tell me the whole truth when we discussed this before. Your relationship with Miss Ryan was in fact intimate, was it not?"

Pettengill stiffened. He sucked down a deep breath. "It was foolish of me to deny it," he said.

6

When Dom Deconcini returned from the Capitol, Mrs. Roosevelt was still sitting with Lieutenant Pettengill, still talking about Emily Ryan. He sat down with them, and shortly the elevator came up, and the President arrived, accompanied by Grace Tully and Harry Hopkins. He asked them all to stay with him for his cocktail hour.

"It's not often I have so much company these days," he said, a faintly rueful tone behind the comment. "It will be pleasant to have all this company. With—With a wife who looks like she's been shooting ducks. Whence the mud, Babs? Don't tell me. I'll read it in the newspapers."

"I should go and change," said Mrs. Roosevelt.

"You do, I'll be offended. What were you people conferring on, the unfortunate death of Miss Emily Ryan?"

"As a matter of fact, we were," said the First Lady.

"She couldn't have gotten herself murdered at a more inopportune time and place," he said as he shoved a Camel into his cigarette holder. "With Molotov here! So— Who did it? And why?"

"We have no idea, literally no idea," said Mrs. Roosevelt.

"Is there a murderer at large in the White House, then?"

"The killer had to be someone with access to the White House," said Lieutenant Pettengill.

"Except for the Russians, who was in the White House Friday night who wouldn't ordinarily have been here?" the President asked Deconcini.

"We've reviewed the logs from the gates," said Deconcini. "Except for the Russians, the only person here who wouldn't ordinarily have been here was Secretary Hull."

"You omit one," said the President.

"Who is that, Sir?"

"Emily Ryan," said the President. "How did she get in?"

"Our theory," said Mrs. Roosevelt, "is that she came in through a window. Her shoes were muddy. We suspect she made her way from the West Wing into the house proper by climbing in a ground-floor window."

Harry Hopkins, who was pouring himself a heavy bourbon and soda, asked—"Was she *ever* in the house proper? Did she have any business over here?"

"As a matter of fact," said the President, "she was in my study right here"—He gestured toward his oval study three doors down the hall—"on Friday morning. Steve Early sent the draft of a press release up for me to look at, and it was delivered by a blonde girl in dark-blue slacks. I particularly noticed the slacks. Wasn't that Emily Ryan?"

"I believe," said Lieutenant Pettengill, "she came over here with papers from time to time. I think she knew her way around among the rooms in the White House."

"Did *you* know her, Harry?" asked Mrs. Roosevelt.

"To speak to," said Hopkins casually. "I knew her well enough to say hello in the halls."

"Mr. Hopkins," said Deconcini, "have you ever been in a bar called the Farragut?"

Hopkins shook his head and dismissed the question without speaking a word.

* * *

About nine o'clock Deconcini and Kennelly entered the Farragut Bar on Eye Street.

It was nothing surprising: a bar a cut or two above the typical Washington watering hole, with the look of an old saloon that had somehow survived Prohibition. A long dark-oak bar extended the whole length of the room to the right of the entrance, affording twenty-five or more customers seats on bar stools. Others sat at tables. The décor was vaguely nautical, or naval, suggestive of the name Farragut. The lights were dim. Cigarette smoke hung heavily in the air.

The customers were mostly young. The great majority of the men were in uniform, all of them officers. Of the young women, about half wore slacks, the other half the short skirts fashion now dictated—together with padded-shoulder jackets, bright red lipstick, and smoothly coiffed shoulder-length hair.

"Something I'll never get used to," said Kennelly to Deconcini.

"What's that?"

"I guess I'm an old-fashioned guy, but when I see an unescorted girl in a bar, I have to figure she's a hooker. But obviously these girls aren't. Government girls. Work all over town. And independent as hell."

Deconcini laughed. "Catch the civilian at the bar. Toward the back."

"Oh, *God!*" muttered Kennelly.

The civilian was a man in his early twenties, dressed in an outlandish and controversial style. He wore a dark gray pinstriped suit, but the loose double-breasted jacket, with heavily padded shoulders, hung well below his hips, almost to his knees. The trousers were voluminous, baggy, but pegged at the cuff. He wore the jacket unbuttoned, revealing a dark blue shirt worn without a necktie. A key chain, attached to one of his belt loops, hung in a loop to his ankles. The officers at the bar wore their caps, so the civilian had not removed his hat, a flat, wide-brimmed brown felt.

Deconcini kept on laughing. "That," he said to Kennelly, "is a zoot suit."

"I know it," said Kennelly disgustedly.

"Next week, next month," said Deconcini, "he goes into khaki or navy blue. For now, he's got—"

"I've heard the song," grunted Kennelly.

"Yeah," laughed Deconcini. " 'I wanna zoot suit with a reat pleat, and a drape shape and a stuff cuff.' "

"Some joints, they'd assault him," said Kennelly.

"Yeah," said Deconcini. "Some joints, they would."

The Farragut was crowded, so Deconcini and Kennelly pushed up to the bar. Kennelly lit a cigarette and glanced around the room with a sharp curiosity that Deconcini took to be professional—unless Kennelly was self-consciously playing the role of Hawkshaw the Detective.

Deconcini's attention was drawn by the conversation between two young naval officers at the bar. "So, okay, so she says I should come see her family's summer home. We can have a good time there, she says. A weekend. Hey, I figure she means a weekend with her *family.* Wouldn't you figure?"

"Don't tell me," said the other office dryly, lighting a cigarette.

"You guessed it. I get off the train in Boston, she meets me, driving a big blue Buick convertible. 'Where we going?' I ask. 'Cape Cod,' she says. Cape Cod! Listen. This is the first time in my life I ever saw salt water. I may be wearing anchors on my uniform, but the most water I ever saw in one place is the Ohio River. Hank, I never before saw water you couldn't look across and see the other side!"

"So?"

"Yeah. Well, the point is, there wasn't any family there. Or anybody else. Big house on the beach. All closed up. Her father's here in Washington, doing government work, and her brother's a pilot in Hawaii, so the family didn't open the summer house this year. So, hey! *We* opened it. She puts the car in the garage, so neighbors won't see there's anybody in the house. And when it got dark, no lights in the house.''

"Bil-ly . . .''

"Yeah. For what she had in mind, we didn't need lights. I couldn't believe it! I couldn't believe I could have this kind of good luck.''

"There's gotta be a catch someplace,'' said the other officer cynically.

"Yeah . . . but not yet. We eat. Drink some beer. Go upstairs. She undresses. I swear, Hank. As God is my witness she—And she's gorgeous. A *dream!*''

"There a catch, Billy. You said there's a catch.''

The young ensign nodded sadly. "Done in by Hitler,'' he said. "Just then, just when everything . . . *Boom!*''

"Boom?''

"Yeah. Boom. A Nazi sub torpedoed a tanker something like a mile offshore. Boom. And fire. So out go boats to save the crew. Coast Guard and just private boats. And pretty soon there's a thousand people on the beach. Neighbors all over the place. They see the house is occupied. Bang on the door. 'Oh, Martha, we didn't know you were here. How nice to see you!'' Yeah. 'We just stopped by to pick up some things,' she says. And an hour later we're in the car on our way back to Boston. After which, nothin'.''

"Nothin?''

"Nothin'. She wouldn't go to a hotel. Even if she would've, what chance has a lowly ensign got of gettin' a room, what with the war? I wind up on the train, *standin' up*, all the way back to Washington.''

"War is hell,'' said the other ensign, lifting his glass and drinking whiskey.

"Right off the coast. I'd heard about it, but I didn't believe it. Right off the coast of the United States—not more'n a mile off the coast. A ship torpedoed! Guys killed! Right off the coast! That tanker burned and burned and burned. You could see the fire and the smoke . . . for hours."

"You see it sometimes off the Jersey coast. My parents try not to mention it when I'm home. But . . ."

Deconcini's thought was that this pair would serve their country better by not talking about what they had seen. But he was conscious that he was standing here in civilian clothes and decided not to say anything.

Anyway, Kennelly had just nudged him.

"Look who we got," said Kennelly.

Deconcini followed Kennelly's eyes toward the entrance. Peggy Shearson had just come in. She had braided her long blonde hair and fastened the braids up over her head, where she had also fastened a white flower. She was wearing a simple pink blouse and a black skirt. She wore open shoes with exceptionally high heels. For a long moment she stood in the doorway, looking around.

"Ho-ho," grunted Deconcini to Kennelly.

Peggy smiled happily as a man approached her. It was Lieutenant Don Pettengill, standing tall and straight, a head above nearly every other man in the bar. Peggy threw her arms around him and kissed him on the cheek.

Pettengill looked down on Peggy with an amused, tolerant smile. He patted her affectionately on the behind. She laughed and nuzzled his neck, and he led her toward a table, where the two of them sat down with another officer, a lieutenant (jg).

"Do you get the impression that those two have met before?" Deconcini asked Kennelly.

"I get the impression that Emily's funeral this afternoon did not much upset Peggy Shearson," said Kennelly. "Got any idea who the man is?"

"Oh, for sure," said Deconcini. "Lieutenant Pettengill works at the White House. He dated Emily Ryan."

"Works at the White House. Where was he when she was killed?"

"On duty at the White House. He couldn't have been very far away when she was killed."

"Well, then? There you have it. A suspect anyway."

Deconcini shook his head. "He's been a suspect all along, just because of where he was, then because he dated the girl, and also because he wasn't entirely candid at first about what the relationship was. But—Well, okay . . . *An American Tragedy,* hmm?"

"What?"

"The novel, by Theodore Dreiser. Sweet but lower-class girl falls in love with ambitious upper-class boy and lets him seduce her. So he kills her, because it wouldn't, after all, do for a man of his status to marry the likes of her."

"So there you have it," said Kennelly.

"Except for a few little things," said Deconcini. "In the first place, the girl in *An American Tragedy* was pregnant. Emily wasn't. She may have been pressing Pettengill, but he didn't have to kill her to get rid of her. In the second place, a Dreiser-type story does nothing to explain why Emily was carrying a gun. In the third place, if Pettengill wanted to kill Emily, the White House would be— it seems to me—the last place in the world where he'd do it."

Kennelly stared at Don Pettengill and Peggy Shearson. Pettengill's hand was on the girl's leg, stroking it from knee to thigh. She clutched his other hand. They were talking, laughing, obviously comfortable and happy.

"I hate to spoil a scene like that," said Kennelly, "but let's see how they act if we walk over and say hello."

Deconcini nodded. "Why not?"

They paid for their drinks and left the bar, walking together to the table where Pettengill and Peggy sat with the younger officer.

"Well," said Deconcini amiably. "Hello."

Donald Pettengill was suave. "Dom," he said. "Didn't know you came here. Nice to see you. You know Peggy, I understand. And, I don't think . . ."

"Captain Ed Kennelly, D.C. police," said Deconcini.

"Nice to meet you, Captain. This is Peggy Shearson."

"We've met," said Peggy glumly.

"And say hello to Lieutenant Foster Morris."

The younger officer stood to shake hands with Deconcini and Kennelly.

"Sit down gentlemen," said Pettengill. "Have a drink with us. Uh . . . there's a chair. And . . ."

"Thanks, but we're on duty . . . so to speak," said Deconcini.

"Working on Emily's case?"

"Right."

"Best of luck," said Pettengill. "Anything I can do, let me know."

'Lights burned at the White House. At an hour when the President would ordinarily have been in bed, probably finished with his dinner tray, and maybe listening to some music on the radio and reading, he was in his study, with Admiral King, General Marshall, and Harry Hopkins.

The President's tray was on his desk, and he had eaten, but he remained dressed and seated in his wheelchair. Admiral King had brought from the Navy Department a large chart of the Pacific Ocean.

"Two movements," said Admiral King, putting a finger on lines penned on the chart. "These three forces are going for the Aleutians. There can be no doubt of that. Mr. President, we are going to lose Attu and Kiska. We simply aren't in a position to defend them against a major force."

The President shook his head. "Losing the Philippines is bad enough," he said. "And Wake. And Guam. Losing part of Alaska—even if we are talking about islands thousands of miles from the mainland of North America—is going to be a bitter pill for Americans."

"We can hold them out of Alaska proper," said General Marshall.

Admiral King's attention remained fixed on the chart. "Another major task force is moving northeast from Saipan," he said. "There can be little question about where it's going. Midway Island, Mr. President."

"Well . . . our forces are on their way into that area,'' said the President.

"The problem, Mr. President, is that we don't know where the main Japanese battle fleet is. We know it is at sea, but we don't know where.''

"If we've guessed wrong that the target is Midway—'' Hopkins began.

"We're in big trouble,'' said the President.

As they sat staring at the chart, they heard voices in the hall outside. General Marshall stepped to the door just as Mrs. Roosevelt appeared and looked in.

"Oh . . . Crisis?'' she asked.

The President sighed. "Every hour of every day is a crisis,'' he said wearily.

"I won't trouble you,'' she said. "Mr. Deconcini and Captain Kennelly are with me. I'll take them in my office.''

The President nodded. She could see in the slack set of his shoulders and in the grayish tone of his complexion that he was worried and tired. From her glance at the chart, she knew what worried him. He had concurred in the Navy's decision to commit all its aircraft carriers to the defense of Midway. If the main Japanese fleet eluded those carriers to the north or south, nothing stood between the powerful Japanese fleet and Hawaii or even the West Coast.

It was difficult to focus her attention on what Deconcini and Kennelly had come to talk about, but she knew she could do nothing about the situation in the Pacific while maybe she could do something about a worrisome enigma in the White House. She sat down with the two men. She offered to send for coffee or something stronger. They declined with thanks.

They had already told her, as they walked through the hall together, about seeing Pettengill with Peggy Shearson.

"Lieutenant Pettengill has not been truthful, I am sorry to say,'' said the First Lady.

"Neither has somebody else this afternoon," said Deconcini. Congressman Dirksen told me that Harry Hopkins introduced him to Emily Ryan, at the Farragut Bar. Do you recall that when I asked Mr. Hopkins earlier this evening if he'd ever been in the Farragut Bar, he just shook his head?"

"Yes, I do recall that. I wondered why you asked."

"One of them is not telling the truth," said Deconcini. "Dirksen or Hopkins, one or the other."

"Which one, do you think?" asked Mrs. Roosevelt.

"I'm sorry, but I have to think it is Mr. Hopkins. The congressman was entirely forthcoming. He readily admitted he'd had an intimate relationship with Emily Ryan. That being said, why would he tell me Mr. Hopkins introduced them at the Farragut Bar if it wasn't true?"

"Maybe we should find out," said Mrs. Roosevelt decisively.

She walked down the hall and found, as she had expected, that the President's meeting was breaking up. She asked Hopkins to come to her office for a few minutes.

Hopkins sat down and lit a cigarette—being one of the few people who would in that office.

"Harry," said the First Lady. "Have you ever been in the Farragut Bar?"

Hopkins smiled. "Is it an issue?" he asked casually. He crossed his legs and relaxed.

"Not necessarily. But you said this afternoon you had never been there, and someone else says you have. I should like to resolve the contradiction."

"Who says I have?"

Mrs. Roosevelt glanced at Deconcini and Kennelly: a quick glance that suggested to them she wanted to continue this line of questioning in her own way and that they should not intervene.

"A particular gentleman says that you introduced Miss Ryan to him at the Farragut Bar," she said.

" 'A particular gentleman . . .' "

She nodded. "Has that gentleman lied to us, Harry?"

The question did not make Hopkins less comfortable. "Well . . ." he said. "Let me think. The Farragut Bar. Where is that?"

"On Eye Street," said Mrs. Roosevelt, a faint hint of impatience creeping into her voice.

"Uhm . . . and I'm supposed to have introduced Emily Ryan to somebody in this bar . . . When?"

"When was it, Harry? You tell us."

Hopkins blew an audible breath, his cheeks puffing out and then collapsing. He looked around for an ashtray. Mrs. Roosevelt didn't have one in her office, so poured some paper clips on her desk and handed him the small empty box. He flicked his ashes in the box.

"Emily," he said, "was a naughty innocent, if you know what I mean. Charming . . . Cute, really. She, uh, collected boyfriends. Innocently, you understand. I don't mean to imply that—"

"Exactly what was your relationship with her, Harry?" asked Mrs. Roosevelt.

Hopkins shrugged. "Casual. Not prurient, if that's what you're asking. I can speak confidentially in this company, I suppose. I haven't announced it, but I'm going to marry again in a few weeks. I met a wonderful girl a few weeks ago, and I'm going to marry her."

"To whom did you introduce Emily Ryan at the Farragut Bar?" Deconcini asked bluntly.

"You know," said Hopkins. "You couldn't ask the question if you didn't. So . . . okay. She was with me at the Farragut one evening, and I introduced her to Ev Dirksen, a Republican congressman from Illinois. Is he suspected of killing her?"

"Not really," said Deconcini.

"The minute he met her, Ev's eyes lit up. He wasn't subtle about it, and she saw what he was interested in, immediately. Emily had an instinct for things like that. She could play a man like a piano."

"But she couldn't play you, huh, Harry?" asked the First Lady.

Hopkins grinned and shook his head.

"You introduced her to Dirksen," said Kennelly. "Anybody else?"

Hopkins shrugged. "Anybody I saw," he said. He frowned over his cigarette because he could not put the burning butt in the little paper box Mrs. Roosevelt had supplied him. Frowning more deeply, he pinched the cigarette just behind the fire in it, dropped it in the box, and thrust his thumb and finger in his mouth. "At the Farragut, yes. Also at the Airline Bar."

"Names," said Kennelly impatiently.

Hopkins blew on his singed finger and thumb; nevertheless he immediately lit another cigarette. "At the Farragut one evening I introduced her to Major General Eisenhower, chief of the operations division at the War Department." He shook his head. "Don't go question him. He was cordial. He always is. But he didn't take to Emily."

"Who did?" asked Kennelly.

"Marv Ritchey. He took to her with enthusiasm—about the same way Dirksen did."

"Marvin Ritchey?" asked the First Lady.

Hopkins nodded. "Everybody's favorite newscaster," he said. "I think he dated her. Ask him."

"Uh, who introduced Miss Ryan to you, Harry?" asked Mrs. Roosevelt.

Hopkins drew deeply on his fresh cigarette before he smiled and said, "Steve Early. Which brings it full circle, doesn't it?"

"I'm afraid it does," she said. "So—We need not detain you longer, Harry."

Hopkins stood. "Anybody but me care for a nightcap?" he asked. "I know you won't, Eleanor, though the invitation is for you, too. I'm thinking of raiding the refrigerator."

Hopkins lived in the White House, and his late-night demands on the kitchen infuriated Mrs. Nesbitt.

"No? Well. My best. I hope you catch your murderer.

It's creepy, thinking of a murderer loose in the White House.''

It was in fact creepy. Mrs. Roosevelt went to her bedroom at the southwest corner of the second floor—it was the room next to her office, where she had just met with Deconcini, Kennelly, and Hopkins. She undressed, brushed her teeth, brushed out her hair, and pulled on a cotton nightgown. For a couple of minutes before she lay down on her bed, she switched off all the lights and pulled back the blackout curtains.

For years she had taken pleasure in the sight of the Washington Monument, illuminated until midnight but showing red blinking lights on top at every hour of the night. Since December 7, the city had been blacked out every night. Although she could see a point of light here and there—blackout violations—Washington was dark. But the blackout was futile tonight. The moon shone hard-white in a cloudless sky, and she could see the Monument, tall and gray against the black southern sky. In the distance the moon shone also on the classic dome of the Jefferson Memorial.

Eighty years ago Abraham Lincoln had stood at one of these windows at night and had seen the campfires of a hostile army on the Virginia hills only a few miles away. This generation's war was farther away but somehow no less imminent.

She threw the heavy black drapes across the windows again and turned on the lights. On the table beside her bed she had reading material waiting for her attention—reports, memoranda, newspaper articles, magazines, books . . .

Tommy had left the typescripts of four "My Day" columns. She used a red pencil and made a few changes. Then she began to look at some of the other documents. For an hour or so she read reports and memoranda, then some newspaper clippings. A little after midnight she found herself dozing, reading a while, losing track of what

she was reading, then waking and concentrating and reading some more.

At some point she went soundly to sleep. She awoke
with a start, to find her mind fastened on the murder of
Emily Ryan. It was strange. She was wide awake, alert—
and troubled. Something . . . something had been overlooked. It just wasn't possible—was it?—for a murderer to
bludgeon a young woman to death and leave no clue.

Yet . . . what had they missed? Something in the Blue
Room? Had they overlooked something in the Blue Room?

Impulsively, she pulled on her robe and stepped into her
slippers. She went out into the quiet, dimly lighted hall
and crossed to the west stairway. She walked down one
floor, then crossed the main hall to the Blue Room.

She stepped inside. For a moment she groped for the
light switches, conscious that the room was not as dark as
its blackout curtains should have made it, that the moon-
light fell pale and cold on the floor beneath one of the
windows.

Then she was aware there was someone in the room! In
the near-darkness, a shadowy figure moved toward the one
window not covered by a blackout curtain.

The window was open, and as she found the switch and
flooded the room with light, the man—for it was a man—
scrambled through the window and out onto the South
Portico. She had but a glimpse of him. He was a brawny,
menacing figure.

And in the White House! Once again, someone had broken into the White House.

7

"In the White House, Mr. Deconcini. Our security is tight enough to be a constant inconvenience, but not tight enough, it would seem, to protect the premises against intruders."

She was speaking on the telephone to Dominic Deconcini, from her bedroom early Tuesday morning.

"I notified the police and the army captain on the grounds, and neither of them found anyone. It's as if the intruder were . . . were one of them—a soldier or a White House police officer. Are you certain that tunnel is actually sealed?"

She referred to a drainage tunnel under the grounds, the one the would-be assassins had used during the Churchill visit in December. It afforded access to the White House grounds, almost under the south windows, from the street beyond the fence. It had been sealed, but—

"I'm sure it's sealed," said Deconcini. "I'll have it checked again."

"I may not, perhaps, drive my own car any more," she

said. "I may not go horseback riding in the park without a half dozen agents huffing and puffing alongside—which of course means I don't go riding now—but, Mr. Deconcini, I do feel I should be able to walk through the rooms of the White House at night and not encounter . . . whomever I encountered."

"I do agree one hundred percent, Mrs. Roosevelt," said Deconcini. "Somebody . . . Well—You understand, I imagine."

"I believe, Mr. Deconcini, the term you are reluctant to use is, somebody's ass is in a sling."

She listened to silence on the line. Obviously she had shocked the Secret Service agent.

"Uh . . . yes, Ma'am."

"Well—Not yours, Mr. Deconcini. But somebody's. And I expect the deficiency to be remedied. Will you give the necessary emphatic orders, or shall I ask the President to give them?"

"I'll take care of it, Ma'am," he said. "And I'll see if anything can be done about identifying the man who was in the Blue Room last night."

"Very well. I will speak with you later. Thank you, Mr. Deconcini."

She had spoken with Deconcini with an eye on the clock, because she wanted to listen to Marv Ritchey's radio news at eight o'clock. Now she switched on the radio.

Ritchey was sponsored by Chase & Sanborn coffee, so for a minute she had to endure a saccharine spiel about the superior taste of that brand of coffee. Then—

Marv *Rrr . . . ritchey* with . . . *news!* Tuesday, the second of June, nineteen-forty . . . *two.*

Yesterday . . . three Jap midget submarines got into the harbor at Sydney—that's in *Aus . . . tralia*—and sank an Allied warship. The Australian government doesn't want to tell us how many were killed . . . but it was more than a *few.* Bad show, Aussies! That was in your own . . . *harbor.*

The butcher of Prague, SS Something-führer Rein-hard . . . Heydrich remains in critical condition in a Prague hospital, trying to recover from a Czech attempt to assassinate him. Our *prayers* are . . . Well, where are our prayers, ladies and gentlemen? Have to think about that one.

Rumors have it that the main Jap battle fleet is loose somewhere in the Pacific . . . and . . . *our Navy doesn't* . . . *know* . . . *where!* If I lived in Hono-lulu—or maybe even in San Francisco or L.A.—I think I'd lay in a food supply in the basement. Washington, of course, is playing it all very close to the vest. As don't they always? As usual, Presy-diddle Rosenglooby is determined that the people of the U.S. of A. shall know *nothing* . . totally nothing, about what their government is doing.

Mrs. Roosevelt switched off the radio. She had heard Marv Ritchey before, more times than she might have wished. Since 1935 he had made a career, almost, of hating the Roosevelts—father, wife, and children. So . . .

So he had taken to Emily Ryan, just as Congressman Dirksen had—as Harry Hopkins put it. The First Lady had to suppress the thought that it would be amusing, and some kind of justice, if Marv Ritchey turned out to be the murderer of Emily Ryan.

Her schedule for the day included a morning meeting with some Hollywood people who were to receive awards for their efforts in selling War Bonds.

After that she was meeting with Secretary of the Navy Frank Knox to discuss some problems arising from racial segregation in the armed forces. She glanced over a letter she had received from her friend Mary McLeod Bethune, outlining some elements of that problem. The record of the Department of the Navy was not good, and she meant to have her say on the subject.

* * *

The meeting with the Hollywood people was on the lawn. The newsreel cameramen appreciated the sunlight, which they said always gave them better film footage than did artificial light, no matter how bright.

The President would say hello to the Hollywood people in the Oval Office just before they came out on the lawn, but he would not himself come out. Because Lord Louis Mountbatten was arriving today, the President was closeted with General Marshall, General Eisenhower, and Admiral King, discussing the war plans they would have to defend vigorously against whatever changes Churchill was sending Mountbatten to sell.

Mrs. Roosevelt and General Henry H. Arnold, commanding general of the United States Army Air Force, would present the plaques to the entertainers. The little ceremony would take place on the south lawn, where the newsreel cameras would have a view of the White House for background.

"Off the record, Ma'am," said one of the cameramen to Mrs. Roosevelt as they focused their cameras on her and took sound levels while waiting for General Arnold to bring the four Hollywood people out from the Executive Wing. "Off the record, have you seen all these people on the screen?"

The First Lady laughed. "Off the record, strictly," she said, "I have seen all of them—but I had to ask for some films to be brought here and run for me the other night, so I would know them and their work. I had of course seen Mr. Tracy many times and always admired his work as an actor. But—Well. I must confess I had not seen a film starring Miss Grable before, and—" She shook her head and laughed. "I'm afraid I had never seen Mr. Abbott and Mr. Costello perform. They are very amusing, aren't they?"

"Millions of Americans think so," said a reporter.

"Yes," she said. "Yes. And I do, too, now that I've seen them."

A moment later General Arnold came out of the Executive Wing, escorting Spencer Tracy, Betty Grable, and Bud Abbott and Lou Costello.

Spencer Tracy was in person as he was on the screen: self-possessed, intensely sincere, a man of powerful presence. Betty Grable, whose photo in a white, skin-tight bathing suit and high-heeled shoes was the most popular pinup in the world, was subdued and shy. The two comics, Abbott and Costello, were conspicuously nervous.

"Hope you won't mind if we clown it up for the cameras a little," the short, rotund Costello said respectfully to Mrs. Roosevelt.

"I should be disappointed if you didn't," she told him.

"Thanks," he said, and in a moment he was in character. From somewhere he produced a derby too small for him, which he set atop his head, and when he buttoned the jacket of his suit it was apparent that the suit also was two or three sizes too small.

When the cameras rolled, Bud Abbott slapped Costello alongside the neck and by expression and gesture ordered him to stand straight, look respectful, and smile. Costello mugged. Betty Grable laughed. Spencer Tracy smiled tolerantly.

General Arnold made a brief statement about the bond drives and about how the entertainment industry was supporting the war effort magnificently.

"The whole nation is grateful," said Mrs. Roosevelt, "for the many hours each of you—Mr. Tracy, Miss Grable, Mr. Abbott, and Mr. Costello—for the many hours you have voluntarily given to the War Bond drives. You and so many others in your industry have made a major contribution to the war effort. On behalf of the President, I am pleased to award you these plaques, expressing our gratitude."

When she handed Costello his plaque, he let it slip from his hands. It fell on his foot, and he jumped around, mimicking a man in terrible pain, yet a man trying not to cry out. Everyone laughed but Spencer Tracy, who smiled and nodded indulgently.

A short stepladder was produced by the cameramen, who encouraged Betty Grable to sit on it and cross her legs.

"Okay?" she asked Mrs. Roosevelt behind a hand.

"Of course."

The blonde perched on the ladder, crossed her legs, and in response to clamorous urging from the cameramen and reporters edged her skirt back to show her knees and a bit of her legs above the knees. She blushed, and the cameras rolled.

During the filming of this newsreel bit, Mrs. Roosevelt had been aware that Dom Deconcini was standing apart, anxiously waiting for the filming to end. As soon as he could, he hurried across the grass, waited for the First Lady to finish a brief conversation with Spencer Tracy, then slipped up beside her and said, "Need to talk. Something's happened."

She shook hands once again with each of the Hollywood guests, then slipped away with Deconcini.

"It's Peggy Shearson," he said when they were well out of the hearing of anyone else. "Kennelly called. Peggy's dead. Murdered."

"Oh!"

"Not very different from the way Emily died," said Deconcini. "Skull caved in by blows from a blunt instrument. Only this time it was repeated blows, as she struggled to live."

Mrs. Roosevelt took Deconcini's arm. For a moment she was literally staggered by the news.

"Where? When?" she asked in a breaking voice.

"It happened last night," said Deconcini grimly. "I'm on my way to police headquarters. I'll get all the information."

"I'll accompany you," she said firmly.

Half an hour later they entered D.C. police headquarters through a back door, met there by Captain Kennelly who had been alerted by telephone by Deconcini before they left. He had driven the First Lady in an unmarked Secret Service Ford, followed at a discreet distance by another black Ford carrying agents assigned to watch and protect the wife of the President of the United States.

Mrs. Roosevelt remained distraught as Kennelly led her through back halls and into his office. He insisted she take the chair behind his desk, a veteran yellow-oak swivel chair that he said was the only comfortable chair in the detective bureau. It was a chair in which she had sat a good many times before, and she hoped the Irish detective did find it comfortable; certainly she didn't.

"Coffee?" asked Kennelly.

He always offered coffee. She never accepted it. Deconcini usually did. This time the pot was steaming on the desk, and Kennelly poured two cups of the dark, muddy brew.

"Please, Captain Kennelly," she said. "Give us all the facts about this horrifying affair."

Kennelly nodded. "She was found this morning, about two A.M. I wasn't notified until I came in this morning. The night boys handled it like a routine homicide investigation. They didn't know about the relationship between Peggy Shearson and people at the White House. In fact, nobody knows anything about that. We've kept it confidential, of course."

"Pettengill," said Deconcini darkly.

"My first thought," said Kennelly.

"I hope we are not jumping to that conclusion," said Mrs. Roosevelt.

"No," said Kennelly. "But we know Pettengill was with Peggy Shearson last night at the Farragut Bar. We also observed that the relationship between him and her was . . . How shall we say? Friendly. No. More than that."

"Affectionate," said Deconcini.

"Good enough."

"What time did she die?" asked Mrs. Roosevelt.

"We have a bit of good luck in that respect," said Kennelly. "We *know* what time she died."

"The autopsy—"

"No. She was beaten to death with some kind of bludgeon, maybe a piece of pipe. She threw up her arms, I suppose to protect her face; both her wrists were broken. So was her wristwatch. Shattered. And it stopped at eleven-seventeen."

"Where did this happen?" asked Mrs. Roosevelt.

"In an alley about two blocks from the boardinghouse where she lived."

"What has been accomplished in the investigation?" asked the First Lady.

"We don't have the autopsy report yet," said Kennelly. "The preliminary medical investigation indicates she'd been dead two hours or so when she was found—which gibes with the wristwatch."

"You and I left the Farragut about nine-thirty, I think it was," said Deconcini. "Peggy Shearson was sitting at a table with Pettengill."

"And with that other young officer," said Kennelly. "Morris, as I recall. Foster Morris."

"I see no alternative but to regard Lieutenant Pettengill as a suspect," said Mrs. Roosevelt. "And to interrogate him. I wonder, though . . . I wonder if you would object to delaying it until this afternoon." She glanced at her watch. "I must return to the White House now. I am hostess at a luncheon for Lord Mountbatten and Ambassador Halifax. As a matter of fact, I imagine Lieutenant Pettengill will be on duty at that luncheon."

"Middle of the afternoon will be fine with me," said Kennelly. "I have a couple of questions to ask some other people in the meantime."

* * *

Dom Deconcini accompanied Mrs. Roosevelt back to the White House.

Kennelly, alone, drove out to K Street and to the boardinghouse where Emily Ryan and Peggy Shearson had lived. The owner, Sophia Bartlett, was sitting on the front porch, half obscured from the street by her collection of porch plants. She was smoking a cigarette and drinking beer from a bottle.

"Figures," she said to Kennelly. "I figured you'd be here sooner or later. The fact that I was up half the night talkin' to cops don't cut no ice, I suppose. Want a beer?"

"No, thanks. I'm on duty."

She shrugged. "So'm I—though I ain't gonna have no duty to do if my boarders keep gettin' murdered. The screechin' an' yellin' around here last night . . . Well. What can I tell you that you don't already know."

Kennelly handed her a photograph of Lieutenant Donald Pettengill—one that had been obtained from Navy files this morning. "Know him?"

"Sure. One of the boyfriends."

"Whose boyfriend? Emily's or Peggy's?"

Mrs. Bartlett tipped her head to one side and frowned. "Y' know . . . both of 'em, now that I think of it. I figured he was Emily's beau. But—Well, to tell the truth, he dated both of 'em."

"You get to know him?" Kennelly asked.

"No. He never came in, never even came up on the porch. Sometimes he had a car. He'd sit on the street and honk."

"Okay. Did you see him last night?"

"No."

"What time did Peggy go out?"

"Uh . . . 'Bout nine, I guess. Little before. She worked yesterday but came home early. She dolled herself up and went out . . . like, I'd say, between eight-thirty and—"

"Did she ever come back?"

Mrs. Bartlett shook her head sadly. "I never saw her

again after she left for the evening. I didn't know she wasn't in the house, till the cops came to the door sometime in the middle of the night.''

Kennelly arrived at the White House at three. Deconcini came out to the gate to meet him and told him Mrs. Roosevelt had decided they would interrogate Pettengill in the President's second-floor study, since the President was meeting in the Oval Office all afternoon with Mountbatten, Halifax, Marshall, and Hull.

Lieutenant Pettengill arrived in white uniform. He had, as Mrs. Roosevelt had anticipated, served as the President's naval aide this morning and during the lunch. He was relieved now because the President and the others were engaged in top-secret discussions.

Pettengill accepted a chair with a gesture of gratitude. He looked a little faded and wilted.

"This is an official interrogation, Lieutenant," said Mrs. Roosevelt gravely. "It is only fair that we tell you that."

Pettengill sighed. "I've been expecting it. I heard about Peggy."

"Why don't you start," said Kennelly, "by telling us just what you did last night, from the time Dom and I saw you at the Farragut?"

"All right. What time did you gentlemen leave? Was it, say, half-past nine? Something like that? We stayed. Peggy and I. And Foster Morris. Peggy liked to drink beer, so we ordered a pitcher of it. And we sat there and drank beer until . . . oh, I guess it was about ten. I suggested to Peggy that we leave. Which we did. Morris stayed there."

"A little early to break up the evening, wasn't it?" asked Kennelly.

"Well . . . I'm embarrassed to have to say it, but I had it in mind that Peggy and I would go somewhere else, where we could be alone. If you follow me."

"Be specific, Lieutenant Pettengill," said Mrs. Roosevelt.

Pettengill drew a deep breath and blew it out. "I . . . was not always . . . the gentleman with Peggy. I wanted her to go—please. You understand."

"So?" said Kennelly coldly.

"She wasn't in a mood for anything like that. In fact, she was testy about it, said it wasn't right to do anything like that on the day when she'd buried Emily. So . . . so I walked her home, to the boardinghouse on K Street. She, uh . . . she didn't go in, I don't think. She and I weren't talking very friendly at that point. I left her on the sidewalk in front of the house, and when I looked back she was still standing there, with her hands on her hips."

"What time was that, when you left her?"

"Say, a quarter past ten. Pretty close to that."

"Then what did you do?"

"I went back to the Farragut. Morris was still there. Still sitting at the same table. I sat down with him, and . . . I'm afraid I got pretty drunk. I don't feel so great, today."

"What time did you leave the Farragut?" asked Kennelly.

"About midnight. Maybe a few minutes after."

Kennelly sighed noisily and compressed his lips tight. "Midnight. Morris will back you up on that, I suppose."

"Morris and others," said Pettengill. "I'm something of a regular at the Farragut Bar."

"Do you have a car, Pettengill?"

He shook his head. "No. No car."

"Sometimes you picked up your girlfriends in a car," said Kennelly.

"My father's car. When he comes to Washington, I borrow it."

"You have acknowledged," said the First Lady, "that you had an intimate relationship with Miss Ryan.

Are we to understand you also had one with Miss Shearson?''

Pettengill nodded.

"Get around, don't you?" said Kennelly dryly.

"I, uh . . . I seem to make friends easily," said Pettengill.

"Young women," said Mrs. Roosevelt crisply. "And you take advantage of them."

"I don't want to seem conceited, Ma'am, but I don't really take advantage of them. I—"

"They take advantage of you," said Kennelly sarcastically.

Pettengill stiffened. "To be perfectly frank with you, Captain," he said defiantly, "I don't see how that's any of your business. Unless you are accusing me of having caused the death of Peggy Shearson, whether I seduced her is none of your business. I didn't, but I don't really feel I have to deny it to *you.*"

"Is Mrs. Roosevelt being told to mind *her* own business?" asked Kennelly.

Pettengill turned to face the First Lady. He flushed. "I'm sorry, Ma'am," he said quietly. "With all due respect, I can't see that it is a concern of yours, either."

"Apparently our interview is over," she said.

"I apologize to you, Mrs. Roosevelt. I certainly don't want to be rude to you. But it seems I am being accused— Or am I? Am I being accused of anything?"

"You were with Miss Shearson in a bar a few hours before she was murdered," said Mrs. Roosevelt. "You can hardly expect not to be asked some questions."

Pettengill glanced from one face to another. "I had an intimate relationship with both the dead girls," he said. "I did not seduce either of them. They were entirely willing, even anxious I may say. I can't argue that my conduct conformed to the highest moral principles, but I did not defile or dishonor either of them."

"I don't think we need to go into that further," said Mrs. Roosevelt.

But Kennelly did a couple of minutes later, in the hall. "I suppose you mean you didn't deflower Emily or Peggy," he said.

Pettengill's eyes flashed with anger, and between clenched teeth he replied—"Emily was deflowered before I was old enough to accomplish it."

Kennelly chuckled. "An officer and a gentleman," he said.

They could have asked Pettengill where they would find Lieutenant (jg) Foster Morris, but Deconcini and Kennelly elected not to but to inquire of the Navy Department. At four-thirty the young officer arrived at the White House.

Dressed in suntans, he was awed and formally stiff. He was young, too, very young, with an intensely innocent boyish face.

"Where did you meet Lieutenant Pettengill?" Deconcini asked him.

"We rowed together."

"I beg your pardon?"

"We rowed together, on the Harvard crew. He's a year older than I am. His family is very prominent, you know. His mother was a Cabot."

They sat in the Secret Service office on the ground floor, a modestly furnished room where the air was stirred by an old fan that rattled as it oscillated.

"Are you aware, Lieutenant Morris, that Peggy Shearson was murdered last night?" asked Deconcini.

"Yes, Sir. Don—that is, Lieutenant Pettengill—called and told me this morning."

"She died within a couple of hours after we saw you at the Farragut Bar," said Kennelly. "What we want from you is an account of the evening. Every detail you can give us."

Morris frowned. "I . . . I have a little difficulty with that," he said. "After all, Don Pettengill is a friend, a fellow officer, and all that. I'm not sure I can—''

Deconcini put his hand on the telephone. '' 'Conduct unbecoming,' '' he said darkly. ''Withholding information from the police in a criminal matter, also from the Secret Service in a matter involving the security of the White House. Now, before I put through a call to the Navy Department, do you want to resolve your difficulty, Morris? Or do I speak with your commanding officer?''

The young lieutenant's face turned glowing pink. ''I . . . I was only thinking of my obligation to—Well. Uh . . . What is it you want to know?''

''Let us suppose,'' said Deconcini, ''that you were Ernest Hemingway and you were writing a description of the scene at your table at the Farragut Bar last evening. What would you say?''

''Uh . . . okay, I got there about eight-thirty, I guess. Actually a little later, like a quarter till nine. Don was there. He had a table. I sat down with him and had a couple Scotches. We didn't talk about anything much, just the news and what had happened at the Department yesterday. And then—I guess it was about nine or a little after, and Peggy Shearson came in.''

''Did you know her?''

''I'd seen her before, with Don. But I'd never talked with her. She sat down with us and ordered beer, which she said she liked better than whiskey.''

''What kind of beer was that, do you know?'' Kennelly asked.

''No. It was draught beer, in a pitcher. With three glasses. We all drank beer then. And—well . . . What more can I say?''

''We were at the bar,'' said Deconcini. ''The relationship between Pettengill and Peggy seemed very friendly.''

''I guess it was. I mean, she was affectionate. She was vivacious and outgoing.''

''What did she talk about?''

"Nothing much. You know she didn't have much education. Worked as a waitress. She didn't seem to be up on anything much. I mean . . . events."

"But she talked," said Kennelly. "We could see her talking. Some kind of lively conversation. What was it about?"

Morris pondered for a moment. "She talked about how things would be when the war was over, now that I think of it. She said she'd always wanted to travel, go to nice places as she put it. She talked about when Don got out of the Navy they could—" He stopped.

"They could what?" Deconcini prompted.

"They could go to nice places," said Morris weakly.

"Together?"

Morris nodded.

"Did she think she had some kind of permanent relationship with Pettengill? A commitment of some kind?" asked Deconcini.

"I . . . I can't think so. I can't imagine she could have an idea like that. After all, Don—"

"Is a Pettengill," said Deconcini mordantly. "And his mother was a Cabot."

Morris smiled innocently. "It doesn't sound very democratic, I suppose, but, yes, that would be a barrier between them."

"Did she understand that?" Kennelly asked.

"I don't know."

"All right. Keep on. After we stopped by your table, then left, you did what?"

"We drank beer. She ordered a second pitcher. It was sort of jolly. She laughed a lot."

Morris stopped. His mouth hung open for a moment and he frowned and shook his head, as if remembering that the girl had laughed a lot, and now was dead, imposed a dark despondency on him.

He went on. "We'd had a lot to drink, you know. That is, Don and I had: the Scotch, now the beer. Don got sort of giggly, if you know what I mean. He showed Peggy how to play chug-a-dunk, and they laughed so much over that that they kind of made a spectacle of themselves. I was a little embarrassed. That kind of thing wasn't like Don Pettengill. Anyway, after a while, say about ten, they left.''

"That was ten o'clock?"

Morris nodded. "About. About ten o'clock."

"Then what?"

"Well, I sat there awhile, not sure what to do. I had a table and was sort of reluctant to give it up, since they were scarce. An Army officer joined me—a Major Deakins; I don't know his first name. Anyway, by this time I had gotten a little careful about how much I was having to drink. You know how it is. The room starts to revolve. So I sipped what was left of the beer. The major was trying to tell me something about how every weapon the Army used was being replaced with something new and nothing would work as well as the old weapon. I got a crash course on Springfield rifles and Garands and so on. And the first thing I know, I look up, and there's Don—back again.''

"What time, Morris?" Kennelly demanded sharply. "What time?"

Morris sighed. "Couldn't have been gone long. Make it, say, half past ten."

"For sure?" Kennelly asked "For damned sure?"

"For very sure," said Morris. "I was surprised to see him back so soon. I knew he'd expected to have a good time with Peggy Shearson last night, and if he was back in the Farragut in half an hour or so, obviously he hadn't had any good time."

"Where would he have taken her for a good time?" asked Deconcini.

"Home," said Morris.

"And where's that?"

"The Pettengills maintain flats in New York, Washington, and Palm Beach," said Morris. "Don lives in the Washington flat. It's within walking distance of the Farragut. He'd have had time to walk there and back in half an hour, easily.''

''You are sure about the time?'' asked Kennelly. ''Damned sure?''

''I couldn't be off more than . . . ten minutes, either way, if that makes any difference,'' said Morris.

''Say fifteen minutes,'' suggested Deconcini. ''He was back in the Farragut by a quarter to eleven at the latest. Right?''

Morris nodded. ''Right. Absolutely right. At the *latest*.''

Admiral the Lord Louis Francis Albert Victor Nicholas Mountbatten, known to his friends as Dickie, was forty-two years old and universally regarded as one of the world's handsomest and perhaps most romantic men. He had commanded a destroyer in the Mediterranean, and it had been sunk beneath him off Crete.

"I am a sailor, you know," he said to Mrs. Roosevelt, beside whom he sat at dinner. He spoke with the most upper-class of English accents. "My father was a sailor. He was First Lord of the Admiralty, you know. But when I sought another sea command after losing *Kelly,* Winston denied it me and gave me a desk command. I was to have had command of the aircraft carrier *Illustrious,* and when I remonstrated with Winston, what do you suppose he said to me? He asked me what I expected to accomplish with *Illustrious,* except to be sunk in a bigger and more expensive ship."

She joined in his laughter at this story, as did the President who had overheard it.

Mountbatten's official title was Chief of Combined Operations, which meant he was responsible for the kind of air-sea-land operation that would be required to mount a cross-Channel invasion. He had come to Washington to say bluntly, with absolute finality, that it could not be done in 1942—no matter what happened on the Russian front.

Discussion in the Oval Office that afternoon had been lively. General Marshall and Secretary of War Stimson had begun to believe a cross-Channel invasion just might be possible in 1942. The President had asked if a "sacrificial" effort might not be worthwhile—accepting the loss of a few units, to draw ten or twenty or forty divisions away from the Russian front. Lord Mountbatten had heard this suggestion with horror and cabled the Prime Minister that the President might be "getting a little off the rails."

"I had the honor of knowing your father, Lord Mountbatten," she said. "I was educated in England, you know, and my husband and I were there for some weeks on our wedding trip."

"Louis of Battenberg, I imagine," said Mountbatten.

"Yes. I knew your father before the war hysteria of 1914 compelled him to Anglicize your family name."

"Then did you, by any chance, encounter any of the Saxe-Coburg-Gothas?"

The First Lady laughed. "The royal family. Yes. They were still Saxe-Coburg-Gothas then."

"And Windsors now," said Mountbatten. "I'm glad, really. I am pleased. There had to be an end sometime of Germans on the British throne—even if until now we have only changed the names."

"The present king is married to an English lady," said Mrs. Roosevelt. "Their descendants will be—"

"Only a little German," laughed Mountbatten. "In any event, they don't speak German in Buckingham Palace or Windsor Castle today, as they did as long as that dotty old lady lived."

" 'Dotty old lady?' "

"Victoria," said Mountbatten. "The old dear was

'barmy,' to use the English term. The American one, I believe, is 'batty.' The dear old queen was—"

"She lived a difficult life," Mrs. Roosevelt interrupted.

"She was born barmy," said Mountbatten. "And if I said so today in London, someone would throw a rock at me."

"I should think so," said Mrs. Roosevelt. "My recollection of my years in England was that no one in your history was held in higher regard than Queen Victoria."

Mountbatten laughed happily, without restraint. "Winston," he said, changing the subject entirely, "is looking forward with great enthusiasm to his visit two weeks from now."

"We, too, are looking forward with much pleasure to seeing the Prime Minister again."

Deconcini and Kennelly had located the 'Major Deakins' that Morris had mentioned. They spoke with him in his office at the Pentagon.

"I don't know what's behind the questions," said Major William Deakins, "but without knowing, I can confirm what Morris said is true. I sat down with him in the Farragut last night and was with him when Pettengill came in and sat down with us. To be perfectly frank, I don't much like either one of those Harvard snobs; but I've worked with Morris on a plan that has to do with amphibious landings, and when I saw him and he asked me to join him, I figured it was better than standing up."

"You sat down with Morris at—?"

"Pretty close to ten-thirty," said Major Deakins.

"And when did Pettengill come in?" asked Kennelly.

"Too damned soon," said Deakins. "What . . . ? Five minutes after I sat down? Ten minutes? Like that."

"How long were you there?" asked Deconcini.

Major Deakins thought about the question for a moment. "Tell you how I have to answer," he said. "I was with them long enough—and had enough to drink with them—that they didn't seem so obnoxious anymore. That takes . . . some drinks, huh? You know that pair?"

"*What time,* Major?" asked Kennelly.

"Hey. You guys are serious. You got a problem. This is no casual inquiry. Is it?"

"Who left the bar first?" asked Deconcini. "You? Pettengill?"

Major William Deakins stared for a moment at his watch, as if it would suggest to him what time it had been when he left the Farragut. He was a bald, flushed-face, compact man whose credentials were graduation from West Point in 1937, followed by assignment to the War College, and now assignment to Plans and Operations at the Pentagon—with a distinct possibility he would never have a combat command.

"I, uh . . . I think I left first. But—but I'm not sure. Look, fellows, we were off duty and drinking. Let's see . . . okay. Those two were still at the table when I got up and left. And that was . . . a little before midnight."

"Deakins," said Kennelly sharply. "Where were you and those two at eleven-fifteen, eleven-twenty, and eleven-thirty? That's the critical question. Where were you from—"

"Hey! From eleven to half-past—In the Farragut. For damn sure. From half-past eleven to midnight—In the Farragut. Still there, for sure. After midnight . . ." He shrugged. "I left at twelve, maybe five minutes before. I left and returned to quarters. Okay? That it? That what you want to know?"

"What I want to know," said Kennelly angrily, "is where the two Navy officers were between half-past ten and midnight."

Deakins was running out of interest and patience. "And I'm your witness? Okay. Give or take ten minutes, I sat at that table with those two Harvard beauties from ten-thirty to midnight."

"Were you with them there, Major, at seventeen minutes past eleven?"

"Seventeen after eleven is between ten-thirty and mid-night, isn't it?"

"And Pettengill was there with you. For sure."

"*There . . . with . . . me.* Got that? With . . . me."

"Damn," muttered Kennelly.

"Hey! Is Pettengill suspected of something evil?"

"Not any more," said Deconcini."

"I should like to have the answers to a question or two, Captain Bunker," said the First Lady.

She had decided after dinner—while the President and his English guests returned to the Executive Wing for further meetings—to pursue her own line of questioning. Still wearing the white satin gown she had worn to the dinner for Lord Mountbatten and Ambassador Halifax, she had walked through the Executive Wing and out to the gatehouse that guarded the West Executive Avenue entrance to the White House grounds. The Army captain stood stiffly, almost at attention—a late middle-aged man with graying hair.

"What I am trying to find out, Captain," she said, "is how an intruder managed to get into the Blue Room last night. You are aware that an intruder did get into the Blue Room last night?"

"I am painfully aware of it, Ma'am," said the captain.

"You have been questioned on the subject."

"Yes, Ma'am."

"Then perhaps I will only be covering ground you have already thoroughly covered, with others; but even so I should be grateful if you would give me your conclusions as to how it may have happened."

"I'm sorry, but I don't know how it happened, Ma'am."

"Sit down, Captain Bunker," she said. "I will do the same." There were two little folding chairs in the guardhouse, and she sat down facing the nervous captain, who sat only reluctantly. "Now. I am not your superior officer. What is more, I can keep a confidence. So . . . if you don't *know* how it happened, give me your best judgment as to how it *may* have happened.''

''I've got twenty men on the grounds,'' he said. ''Inside the fence. There are also a few White House policemen on the grounds at night. My men are stationed mostly at posts, about half of them on the anti-aircraft guns. They don't patrol. The policemen do, but they patrol on schedule. Anyone who watched them a little would see the pattern and could evade them.''

''And anyone who knows where your posts are could avoid them, too,'' she suggested.

''Yes, Ma'am.''

''Any clever man could enter the White House in the middle of the night and assassinate the President,'' she said grimly.

''No, Ma'am.''

''Why not?''

''Security inside the White House is much tighter,'' said Captain Bunker. ''To get up to the private quarters is all but impossible. The Secret Service handles that.''

''And during the day?''

''During the day the security emphasis shifts to the Executive Wing. In fact, it moves with the President. Where he is, that's where it's tightest.''

''All right. Then how did the intruder get to the Blue Room last night?''

''Assuming he was not someone who was already inside the White House—that is, someone who had business there last night?''

''I believe we may assume that,'' she said. ''Otherwise, he was a policeman or one of your soldiers. So the first question is, how did he get onto the grounds?''

''Two gates are guarded all night,'' said Captain Bunker. ''This one and one on Pennsylvania Avenue. The others are locked.''

''How locked?''

''With rather sophisticated locks,'' he said. ''Also,

electric alarm systems would alert everyone if someone tried to break through."

"What about climbing over the fence? It's not so formidable, I should think, from the look of it."

"Actually, it is more formidable than it might appear, Ma'am. The ground just inside it is crisscrossed with hidden wires. Anyone who came over it would land on them and set off an alarm."

"Locks . . . Where are the keys?"

He nodded toward a cabinet mounted on the wall of the guardhouse. "Right there," he said. "The police have a set in their office inside the White House, and we have this set. They lock and unlock the gates, but we could lock and unlock them from here, if there were ever any need to."

"Are you confident no one could have obtained one of those keys?"

"I don't see how, Ma'am. This guardhouse is manned at all times, twenty-four hours a day, always by a man who knows what those keys are. No one is allowed to touch that cabinet or those keys."

"Last night?"

"I was on duty myself, Ma'am. I left the guardhouse once an hour, on the hour, to check my posts; but whenever I was out a man was here."

"Who was here, Captain?"

"Private McCloud, Ma'am."

"Can we speak with him?"

"Certainly, Ma'am. He's standing by the gate."

The Captain stepped outside to summon the private, but Mrs. Roosevelt rose and went out. The soldier stood just inside the gate, facing the guardhouse. He was a new recruit from the look of him, probably not more than eighteen years old—a boy with a cowlick lying on his forehead under his old, flat, World-War-I-type helmet. When Captain Bunker approached him, Private McCloud snapped his rifle to the present-arms position.

"At ease," said the captain. "This is Mrs. Roosevelt. She wants to speak to you."

Private McCloud's eyes turned toward the First Lady. He was conspicuously nervous, even afraid.

"When Captain Bunker went off to check his posts, you were responsible for this gate," she said. "Is that correct?"

"Yes, *Ma'am.*"

"For how long each time?"

"About ten minutes, *Ma'am.*"

She smiled. "Please relax, young man. I won't bite. Now—You would be facing the guardhouse, as you now are. Correct?"

"Yes, Ma'am."

"And no one could have passed through the gate or entered the guardhouse that you didn't see."

"No, Ma'am. No one could've."

"Did you let anyone through?"

"No, Ma'am. That is, not while Captain Bunker was away from the guardhouse."

"We keep a gate log," Captain Bunker explained. "If he had let anyone in, he would have written the name and time in the log."

"How would you know who to let in and who not to?" she asked.

"They carry passes, Ma'am," said the private. "If there's any question, my orders are to make them wait for the officer in charge—which last night would have been Captain Bunker."

"Did anyone approach the gate while you were here alone? Did you talk to anyone?"

"Only Sergeant Lee, Ma'am."

"Sergeant who?" asked the captain.

"Staff Sergeant Lee, Sir."

"Well, who—Who the devil is Staff Sergeant Lee?"

"Sir . . . Sir," stuttered Private McCloud. "Staff Sergeant Lee came here while you were out, Sir. About midnight, Sir. He said you'd sent him to check a name on the gate log, Sir. He went in the guardhouse for a minute or so, then came back out.''

''From what direction did he come, Private McCloud?'' asked Mrs. Roosevelt. ''From inside the grounds, or from the street?''

''From the street, Ma'am. He said he'd spoken to Captain Bunker through the fence on Pennsylvania Avenue. He said the captain had ordered him to come here and check the log. I'd never seen the sergeant before, but he had a regulation identification card.''

''Where'd he go when he came back out?'' asked the captain.

''Back along the street, Sir. Toward Pennsylvania Avenue.''

Mrs. Roosevelt smiled at the captain. ''Let's take an inventory of those keys, Captain,'' she said.

She changed her clothes before she received Dom Deconcini and Captain Ed Kennelly in her office at about ten o'clock. She was wearing a comfortable old white dress that she favored, one she would not have worn had she been leaving the White House again that night. She had tied a white band around her loosened hair.

''I am sorry to ask you to meet with me so late.''

''We hadn't thought of giving up for the day,'' said Kennelly. ''The older an investigation gets, the less chance of getting results.''

She had ordered sandwiches and an assortment of liquor brought up from the pantry. If these men had to work such long hours, they deserved a drink. As they poured for themselves, she told them what she had learned at the west guardhouse.

''The key to the gate on East Executive Avenue was indeed missing from the cabinet. So, whoever 'Sergeant Lee' was, he had access to the White House grounds last night.''

''Could the private describe him?'' Deconcini asked.

''Brown hair, brown mustache, a rather tall man. Private McCloud admits that the man only passed his supposed identification card under the private's nose. Poor Private McCloud was so awed by rank that he didn't demand a closer look. I feel sorry for that lad. He couldn't be more than eighteen years old, and I am afraid Captain Bunker will load the blame on him to escape it himself.''

"There's no excuse for—''

Mrs. Roosevelt interrupted Deconcini. "Private McCloud insists he saw enough of the identification card to have recognized it as a regular Washington Military District ID card. I think that is significant.''

"Unfortunately,'' said Deconcini, "you caught only a glimpse of the intruder and don't know, I suppose, if he was a tall, brown-haired man with a mustache.''

"No, but I think I can testify that he was wearing khaki clothes,'' she said.

"Once he came in through the east gate—assuming that's what he did—no one saw him until you encountered him in the Blue Room,'' said Deconcini.

"Quite obviously, the man knew the White House,'' she said. "Even to knowing that Captain Bunker leaves the guardhouse every hour on the hour.''

"Pettengill,'' said Kennelly with annoyed emphasis. *"He* knows the White House. He knew the dead girls. He had motive. He—''

"He also has an ironclad alibi,'' said Deconcini. "Lieutenant Morris, Major Deakins, and the bartenders at the Farragut. We went over there this evening and asked around. Two bartenders agree with Morris and Deakins that Pettengill was in the bar when Peggy Shearson was killed.''

"Three-quarters of an hour before and three-quarters of an hour afterward,'' Kennelly agreed glumly.

"Let us look, then, to another question, gentlemen,'' said Mrs. Roosevelt. "Why do you suppose our intruder was in the Blue Room last night? Assuming it was the fictitious Sergeant Lee, why did he go to that trouble, take that risk? What was in the Blue Room that we overlooked

Friday night? And if there was something, did he get it? Or does it remain there?''

''Four men spent an hour searching the room today,'' said Deconcini. He shrugged. ''Nothing. They even dug around in the soil in the potted plants.''

''Was the intruder just a burglar, then? If so, what did he hope to steal from the Blue Room?''

Kennelly shook his head. ''Was it just a coincidence he was in there? No. I don't like coincidences. Don't believe in 'em.''

Mrs. Roosevelt reached for the bottle and poured herself a small glass of dry sherry. ''I am frustrated,'' she said. ''There *must* be an answer. We are overlooking something.''

''We've overlooked Mr. Marvin 'Marv' Ritchey,'' said Deconcini. ''I'm not sure just how to handle that one.''

''I've got a suggestion,'' said Kennelly. ''Neither one of you can afford to face him. I can. I'll do it in the morning. When Mr. Marv Ritchey comes off the air, I'll be there, playing my rough, tough act. I'll sweat the son of a—Well, you know what I mean.''

''Officially I deplore such an idea,'' said Mrs. Roosevelt. ''Unofficially and off the record, please do sweat the son of a . . . gun.''

Kennelly laughed. ''Count on it,'' he said.

''Was there anything unexpected in the autopsy report?'' she asked.

Kennelly shook his head. ''Peggy died between ten P.M. and midnight. The cause of death was skull fractures and damage to the brain. She was struck repeatedly—strong, heavy whacks with a blunt instrument, maybe a piece of pipe.''

''I'm curious about something,'' said the First Lady. ''You said her wrists were broken, as if she had tried to ward off the blows. Surely, she must have been screaming. Did no one in the neighborhood hear her screaming?''

''That's odd,'' said Kennelly. ''Every person living

within a hundred yards has been questioned. No one heard a thing.''

"There is something very wrong there, Captain Kennelly," said Mrs. Roosevelt. "A girl being bludgeoned . . . both her wrists being fractured by blows . . . and she did not scream? A summer night. Windows open. And no one heard her scream?''

"My guys knocked on every door in the neighborhood," said Kennelly. "Nobody heard a scream, no time, all evening, all night.''

"Is there any possibility she was killed elsewhere and her body moved to that alley?''

"Her blood was all over the place," said Kennelly. "On the gravel of the alley pavement, on a board fence. Samples were checked for type. It was her type.''

"It is impossible, I suppose, that she was killed elsewhere, her blood gathered in a glass or bottle, and . . . No. Impossible.''

"Impossible is a big word, Mrs. Roosevelt. I wouldn't say anything is impossible. But—''

"I'm groping," she admitted.

"One more piece of evidence," Kennelly said, reaching into his pocket and pulling out an envelope. "Unfortunately, it points to Pettengill again.''

He opened the envelope, and a brass button rolled out on the table. It was a button from a naval officer's uniform.

"In her room," he said. "In a drawer with some pictures and stuff. No fingerprints you could read, except her own. Where she got it, when she got it, how long she had it . . .'' He shrugged.

"Military insignia . . .'' mused Mrs. Roosevelt. "A pair of silver bars was found in Miss Ryan's desk. Now a naval officer's button is found among the possessions of Miss Shearson. A naval officer could wear a pair of silver bars on his suntan uniform. On the other hand, there is no way an officer of the Army could wear a naval button. The clues keep pointing toward a naval officer.''

"Pettengill, *Pettengill*,'' growled Kennelly.

"I judge from what you gentlemen have learned that we have to find another naval officer," said the First Lady. "I think it would be well if we stopped focusing on Lieutenant Pettengill. In some ways, he is not a very attractive young man, but . . ."

"But he has a perfect alibi," said Deconcini.

"For last night," grunted Kennelly. "For the Shearson murder. Not for the Ryan murder. He was in the White House Friday night. For that killing, he's as good a suspect as any."

Mrs. Roosevelt checked the President's bedroom. He wasn't there.

She was concerned about how he used his mental and physical resources. The war had already taken a toll of him, seen in the dark rings around his eyes, in the lax tone of his muscles, in the graying of his complexion. If he was to continue to function effectively, he had to pace himself better. The Molotov visit, followed now by the Mountbatten visit, to be followed in two weeks by another Churchill visit . . .

Worse than that, the burden of decision . . . Could the Allies afford to give the Soviet Union some measure of relief by making a feint, at least, across the English Channel? Should the prospective invasion of North Africa be scrapped to make such a feint? How many lives would be lost in either case?

For some time, rumors had been coming in that Hitler and his fellow criminals were beginning to exterminate the Jews of Europe. *Exterminate!* Surely the rumors exaggerated the fact. Yet, they continued to come, one after another, accumulating evidence that something horrible was happening in Europe. And what could the United States do about it? What could the President of the United States do about it?

What if . . . ? What if the German armies defeated Russia, as Molotov insisted was possible, even likely? What if the Germans then turned against Great Britain with all their massed fury, crossed the Channel and conquered the British islands? What if the Japanese conquered Australia? India? Could the United States, left alone, prevail against the Axis when it controlled all the world outside the Western Hemisphere?

These were not fanciful questions. It was all possible.

And now, tonight, what was left of United States naval power in the Pacific was about to face a Japanese battle fleet of almost unparalleled strength.

She knew where the President was. He was in his situation room on the ground floor of the White House.

During his visit in December, Winston Churchill had described to the President his situation room, where on huge maps on the walls his staff marked every movement of every kind of force, anywhere in the world. Geography, Churchill had insisted, was the key. A commander in chief had to know precisely what was happening, everywhere, and to relate what was happening anywhere with what was happening somewhere else.

The President had established his own situation room in the big ground-floor room immediately to the west of the ground-floor oval room—under and to the west of the South Portico.

There she found him. With General Marshall again, and Admiral King, and—granting an extraordinary privilege—Lord Mountbatten.

"Fine job of navigation," Mountbatten remarked as Mrs. Roosevelt entered the situation room.

"Weather's foul," said Admiral King gravely. "Can't see anything. Can't fly reconnaissance. *Foul!*"

"Even so," said the President calmly, "everybody reached Point Luck and made the rendezvous."

Admiral King—tall, gray, gaunt, somber—nodded and said, "All we have to do now is hope Point Luck isn't a thousand miles from anywhere the Jap fleet plans to go."

Two lines across the map of the Pacific were suggestive—suggestive of certainty about two Japanese task forces, one heading toward the Aleutian Islands and so threatening Alaska, the other moving directly from Saipan and Guam toward Midway.

The third line was the important one. It represented the main battle fleet—and the line ran only as far as the last report of its position: not far from the Japanese home islands. On the American side, no one really knew where it was.

Four or five carriers. Battleships. Cruisers. Hundreds of planes. At large in the Pacific.

''Your chaps have done extremely well,'' said Mountbatten. ''I mean, in deciphering their code, getting a reasonably certain idea of where they are going.''

''They are going to Midway,'' said the President. He looked up at Mrs. Roosevelt, as if he were taking notice of her presence for the first time. ''They are going to Midway. And heaven help us if they are not.''

9

Captain Edward Kennelly crushed his Lucky in the ashtray on the receptionist's desk and followed her back into the complex of offices and studios of the radio station. Mr. Ritchey, he had been told, saw no one without an appointment; but when he had showed his shield as chief of the detective bureau, D.C. police, the receptionists had acknowledged that there was an exception to the rule.

He had never been inside a radio station before, and he was interested in the way it was laid out. It had to be one of the most cluttered places he had ever seen, more cluttered even than the detective bureau's warren of tiny offices. Most of the people worked in dinky, dusty rooms, at little desks, where stacks of papers seemed invariably topped with coffee cups and balled wax paper that had once wrapped doughnuts and sandwiches.

The broadcast studios were not much different, and they were distinctly unlike the tidy, gleaming radio studios seen on the movie screen. He could see into them through the double-glass windows that separated each one from the corridor. The studios were bigger than the offices, though just as cluttered. A heavy wooden table sat in the middle of each. The microphones sat on that table. Three of the four studios had just one microphone. The fourth had several, situated around a larger table—apparently so the station could broadcast interviews.

Two of the studios were equipped also with phonograph turntables. Since whatever was on the air was piped through speakers on the walls, Kennelly could hear what was being broadcast at that moment—a singing commercial for Chase & Sanborn coffee. He could also see where it originated. A man in one of the studios attended a turntable on which a record maybe fourteen inches in diameter spun at seventy-eight revolutions per minute. The commercial was on a band on that record, and as the jingle ended the man lifted the tone arm.

"Ed Kennelly! Nice to see you. I hope."

Kennelly turned, surprised, then grinned as he recognized the man who had spoken: Arthur Godfrey, one of the most popular radio personalities in Washington.

"Here strictly for a social visit, I hope," said Godfrey.

"Here to get some information, that's all," said Kennelly.

"Uh-oh! Isn't that what you guys always say, just before you break out the rubber hoses?"

"Come on now, Arthur. Us redheads gotta stick together."

This had been a joke between the two men for several years. Although Kennelly's hair was white now, it had been red; and Godfrey, though he was known for his voice and manner by tens of thousands of people who had no idea what he looked like, was an elfin redhead, with freckles on his pink face, and a ready smile.

"Didn't come to see me, did you? I go on the air in—" He glanced at the clock in the nearest studio. "Four minutes."

"No, I didn't come to see you. Everybody knows you never go near any kind of trouble."

This, too, was a joke. Arthur Godfrey, almost alone of radio performers, had a reputation for slipping controversial ad libs into his show from time to time. A less popular man would have lost his job long ago. More than one sponsor had dropped him for departing from the script of a commercial, only to find that listener protest cut into their sales and forced them to renew his contract.

"I'm pure as the driven snow," said Godfrey.

"How 'bout Ritchey? He's the one I'm here to see."

"Uh-oh. Here to beard the lion? A formidable man, Marv Ritchey. What you need to see him about, if it's not confidential police business?"

"It's confidential police business, and I'll ask you a question, Arthur," said Kennelly.

"Shoot. I've got three minutes."

"Between you and me. Strictly. A young woman got herself murdered last week. We have reason to believe Ritchey had been dating her."

"That make him a suspect?"

"No, not really. But he may have information we can use."

Arthur Godfrey glanced toward the studio a little farther along the hall, where Ritchey was broadcasting—his voice, in fact, had been coming through the speakers since the coffee commercial ended. "Good luck, Ed. You'll need it."

"Luck's not going to have anything to do with it," said Kennelly. "But what do you figure? Does Ritchey date girls?"

Godfrey smiled. "He's married. But . . . well, he has the name around here for engaging in a little—How should we say? A little extracurricular activity. I don't have any details. So listen, I gotta run. I'll be on the air for two hours. If you're still around, let's go to lunch."

"I appreciate the invite, but I don't think I'll be here for two hours. God forbid, in fact."

Arthur Godfrey slapped Kennelly lightly on the arm and hurried into a studio. Kennelly watched him for a moment as he settled earphones on his head and began to talk into the microphone; then Kennelly went on along the hall and looked in through the glass at Marvin Ritchey.

Ritchey sat at a table the same as the tables in the other studios, facing a big, diamond-shaped microphone. He was an imposing man, bulky and muscular, with a long, lined face, hard, squinting eyes, loose jowls, and a tall forehead that had been abandoned by his white hair. The hair he had left lay across his head in a thick white blanket, held in place by a generous application of a fragrant hair tonic. He smoked a cigarette as he spoke into the microphone, and from time to time, as a sort of nervous gesture apparently, he shoved his earphones this way and that, as if seeking a more comfortable position for them. His voice was deep. It came up from his chest.

The final words of his morning newscast echoed from the speakers.

. . . a hundred more alphabet agencies, with no purpose anyone can see, except to provide comfy jobs for ten thousand more bureaucrats. And so it seems our Presi-dink means to run the war the way he runs everything else—by taking more and more dollars out of the pockets of the American people and putting more and more unemployed Democrats on the federal payroll. Marv Rrr . . . *Ritchey*! Washington. Good . . . morning!

The secretary from the outer office, who had led Kennelly back into the studio corridor opened the door and spoke briefly to Ritchey.

Ritchey looked up and glanced through the glass at the man he'd been told was a Washington police detective. He shrugged.

The secretary came out and by gesture invited Kennelly into the studio.

As Kennelly entered the room, Ritchey pulled off his earphones. Without standing, he reached across the table and shook Kennelly's hand. "Something I can do for you?" he asked.

"Maybe," said Kennelly. He opened a big manila envelope and handed Ritchey an eight-by-ten enlargement of a morgue photo of Emily Ryan.

The man winced. The photograph was ugly, and even Kennelly had difficulty looking at it without tensing in the stomach. After a second, Ritchey turned his eyes away from it and shoved it across the table.

"Emily Ryan . . ." said Ritchey.

"That's right."

"What happened to her?"

"That's what we're trying to find out. She was murdered."

"When? Where?"

"The usual ground rules, Mr. Ritchey, are for the police investigator to ask the questions."

"Oh, is that so? Okay. I'll go along. Ask questions."

"You knew her, I suppose."

"If you didn't know the answer to that question, you wouldn't be here."

"Where did you meet her? And when?"

"In a bar," said Ritchey. "It was .. uh, the Farragut, I think."

"How'd you meet her? Somebody introduce her? Or did she introduce herself?"

Ritchey shrugged. He reached for his package of Raleighs and shook one out and lit it. "I don't remember for sure," he said. "I imagine somebody said, 'Hey, meet Emily' or something like that."

"When did you first take her out?"

"Who says I ever took her out?"

"I have information that you did. So . . . ?"

"I took her out the night I met her," said Ritchey. "Look. I'm sure you know this. Emily was a tramp. Yeah, I took her to a hotel and took her to bed. And I may not have been the first guy who did that night, or the last."

"Did you pay her?"

"No. She wasn't a hooker."

"Did you know where she worked?"

"Yeah. She worked at the White House. For Steve Early, Roosevelt's press secretary."

"How many times did you take her out?"

Ritchey turned down the corners of his mouth, drew a deep breath, and seemed to be counting in his mind. "Say, a dozen times," he said.

"Take her to bed every time?" asked Kennelly.

Ritchey allowed a smile to spread over his face. "Yeah. Every time. No problem."

"Where?"

"You know the Cardinal Hotel? I have a special relationship with the night manager and can always get a room for a couple hours."

"When was the last time?"

"Uh . . . Say, three months ago, about. Say, middle of February."

"Who broke it up?"

"I hate to admit it, but she did. Said she had the hots for another guy and was going to be faithful to him."

"What about Peggy Shearson?" Kennelly asked.

"Peggy . . . Hey, wait a minute! Didn't I see her name in the paper? Murdered Monday night in an alley. You mean, did I know *her?* No, I didn't know her. Anyway, what's the connection?"

"They were roommates in the same boardinghouse," said Kennelly. "Emily Ryan and Peggy Shearson."

A look of knowing skepticism came over Ritchey's face. His eyes narrowed. He lifted his chin high. "A guy in my business watches the news," he said. "I read that Peggy Shearson was murdered. But nothing about Emily Ryan. I didn't even know she was dead. And she worked in the White House. Is there some angle in this? Don't play games with me, Kennelly. I got a voice that everybody hears. Maybe it's time we switched roles, newsman conducting interview. Then *I* get to ask the questions, and you get to answer them."

"I never answer questions," said Kennelly. "I'm an old-fashioned cop."

"Tough guy, huh?"

"You better believe it."

"Well, you've given me my lead story for tomorrow. White House secretary's murder hushed up!" He nodded. "Quite a story. Tomorrow morning."

"That is, if you're broadcasting tomorrow morning," said Kennelly.

"What's that supposed to mean?"

"You might be in the District jail, held on suspicion of murder."

"You got nothing on me!"

"A married man, prominent radio personality, who had a love affair with a girl who's just been murdered? She broke it off, so damaging his ego? Or maybe she was blackmailing him. I got nothing on you? I got enough to hold you on suspicion."

"All you got in mind is gagging me!"

"Or let's say I just have the vice squad pick you up for adultery," said Kennelly. "Also for using a false name when you checked in at the Cardinal Hotel. Or did you use your real name? And suppose I have them haul in the night manager at the Cardinal, for running a hot-sheet operation. After all, the girl you took to the Cardinal a dozen times has been murdered. Routine investigation requires me to—"

"Okay, okay! I keep my mouth shut."

Kennelly smiled. "I think that'd be wise, Ritchey. I think that'd be wise. Now I'm going to need from you a detailed statement about where you were at certain times—with the names of witnesses who can verify your story. If you don't mind, I'll be taking a few notes."

"Knox won't do a thing," said Mrs. Roosevelt to the President. "I discussed the problem with him yesterday morning, and all he did was smile tolerantly and mumble about difficulties."

"I suppose it is difficult," said the President.

She had asked him for fifteen minutes alone in the Oval Office, whenever he could find the time; and he had called for her in the middle of the morning.

She had met yesterday with Secretary of the Navy Frank Knox and had presented to him some unhappy facts about racial discrimination in the armed forces, particularly in the Navy.

"To begin with, there is the Marine Corps," she said. "They will not accept Negro enlistees. There is not a single Negro in the Marines. Then there is the Navy itself. Negro men are permitted to serve only as mess boys and in no other capacity. In the Army, Negroes are strictly segregated."

"There are a lot of southerners in the forces," said the President. "If we tried to mix the races, violent incidents would happen."

"The local office of the NAACP arranged for me to speak by telephone yesterday afternoon with a young Negro army officer. His name, is, uh—" She paused to check her note. "His name is Lieutenant Jackie Robinson. He told me a number of things. In the first place, he himself is from California and was never before in his life compelled to ride in the back of a bus or denied service in a restaurant. He is an officer in a Negro company, and the soldiers in that company are denied use of the post exchange. Franklin, that is unconscionable."

"Babs . . ." said the President patiently. "Right now I have to concentrate all my attention and energy on the *winning* of this war—something that is by no means certain, let me tell you. The next President of the United States may be Hank Wallace, and I need hardly tell you that he will be as interested in this problem as you are."

"But will he say, as you are saying, that attention to *this* problem will have to be deferred until some other, even greater problem is solved? It seems that a reason can always be found for postponing an effort to do something about this disgraceful injustice."

"Suppose I just issue an executive order. 'Racial prejudice and segregation in the armed forces are prohibited.' Will that solve the problem?"

"You know it won't," she said.

"No."

"Lieutenant Robinson asked me to give you a message. Ask the President, he said, if he thinks the bullets the Japs and Germans will be firing at us will be marked 'for white only' and 'for colored only'?"

"Persuasive," the President murmured.

"Yes. He told me one of his soldiers had observed that they were about to be shipped thousands of miles to fight for democracy, when a hundred feet away there was a post exchange where they couldn't even sit on the stools at the bar and drink a beer."

The President pressed a button under his desk. The door opened immediately, and Grace Tulley entered, carrying her shorthand pad.

"Sit down, Duchess," said the President. "Two memos, same text. F.D.R. to H.S. and F.D.R. to F.K. 'Race segregation in forces unreasonably pervasive. Devise plans to phase it out. Let me know progress.' "

Dom Deconcini and Ed Kennelly met with the First Lady in her office later in the morning.

"Ritchey can't account for himself in any satisfactory way, either for Friday night or Monday night," said Kennelly after he had described the rest of his interview with the newscaster. "I'll tell you something more about him. He's an air-raid warden, and guess what he wears for a uniform."

"I guess khakis," said Deconcini.

"Right. With an armband and a white helmet. Khakis. Now—Put a set of staff sergeant's chevrons on that khaki shirt and what you got? 'Sergeant Lee.' Or maybe. A possibility."

"A new world's record for jumping to conclusions," laughed Mrs. Roosevelt.

"He called the girl a tramp," said Kennelly. "No one else has."

"Mr. Ritchey is no gentleman," said she.

"What motive?" asked Deconcini.

"She threw him over, by his own admission," said Kennelly.

"If that angered him so much as to motivate him to kill her, then I doubt he would have admitted the matter to you," said Mrs. Roosevelt.

"Who knows what motive?" asked Kennelly. "She was in a position to embarrass him."

"Precisely when was it that she was seeing Mr. Ritchey?" asked Mrs. Roosevelt.

"January and February," said Kennelly.

"Ah-hah! That does raise an interesting possibility."

She lifted her telephone, dialed a number, and asked to speak to Press Secretary Stephen Early. When Early came on the line, she asked him to come to her office—now, if convenient.

Five minutes later the press secretary entered the office.

"I appreciate your interrupting your morning, Steve," she said. "You know Mr. Deconcini and Captain Kennelly, of course."

Early nodded toward the two men and sat down.

"Steve," said Mrs. Roosevelt, "do you remember the incident in January when Mr. Ritchey broadcast the story of General MacArthur's appeal for the transfer of major naval forces from the Atlantic to the Pacific?"

Early nodded. "I thought the Boss was going to have me kicked out the back door."

She smiled at him. "The matter was never that serious. But let's review that incident both to refresh my memory and fill in Mr. Deconcini and Captain Kennelly."

"Well, the general was screaming for help. He knew he was going to lose the Philippines. The Boss knew it, too. There was no way we were going to get enough stuff out there in time to prevent it—even if we'd had what MacArthur wanted, which we didn't."

"So you prepared a news release," said Mrs. Roosevelt.

"The Boss was afraid MacArthur would go public. So we sat down and worked out a carefully worded statement, trying to prepare the American public for the loss of the Philippines, still trying not to tell the Japs too much. As it turned out, MacArthur didn't leak his appeal, but somebody in the White House leaked our news release. Or so it appeared; maybe it didn't really happen. Anyway, this damned Marv Ritchey character broadcast a story, saying the President was prepared to accept the loss of the Philippines. It could have been a coincidence."

"Would you have been so ready to think it a coincidence," the First Lady asked, "if you had known Miss Emily Ryan was sleeping with Mr. Ritchey?"

"She *what?*"

"It appears," said Deconcini, "that your secretary Emily Ryan was involved in a torrid affair with Marvin 'Marv' Ritchey."

"I thought she was involved in a torrid affair with Lieutenant Don Pettengill."

"She seems to have been involved in several torrid affairs," said Mrs. Roosevelt with a small, tight-lipped smile. "Some in succession but apparently others simultaneously."

"She worked on that damned news release," said Early. "She typed it. I can't believe she took a carbon out of the White House."

"Maybe that's just what she took," Kennelly suggested. "The carbon paper—and gave Ritchey the reverse image."

"A leak!" complained Early. "God knows what else she—"

"I am very curious about something," Mrs. Roosevelt interrupted. "Just what advantage was Miss Ryan getting out of this? Do you follow my line of reasoning? She was accompanying Mr. Ritchey to a hotel two or three times a week and—Well . . . we know what she was doing. And she gave him—or *apparently* gave him—access to a confidential document. Now. In return for that, what did Miss Ryan receive? Money? Or what?''

"Nothing," said Kennelly. "And she demanded something, and he killed her."

Deconcini shook his head. "Too easy. Why, then, did he kill Peggy Shearson? I'm not willing to buy the idea that the death of Peggy is a coincidence."

"Did it occur to any of you," Early asked, "that maybe what you've got is a rapist running loose? Two good-looking girls living in one boardinghouse—"

"Steve . . ." Mrs. Roosevelt interrupted. "Miss Ryan was killed in the White House."

"Okay. Some such motive could still account for Peggy Shearson."

"Neither girl was sexually molested," said Kennelly. "The medical examiner—"

"Not all sexually motivated crimes actually involve rape," said Early.

"I've thought about that pipe-smoking old busybody Clyde Merck," said Deconcini. "You know, Ed. The old boy who sits on the porch at the boardinghouse and never misses a thing. But he sure wasn't in the White House Friday night."

"Or in the Blue Room Monday night," said Mrs. Roosevelt.

"I'll tell you what I'm going to do," said Steve Early. "I'm going to go through a file I keep about real or imagined leaks from government agencies to the press. Mr. Marv Ritchey has a record of broadcasting things he's not supposed to know, right up to the edge of leaking war secrets. Maybe his secret is . . . well. You know."

"Tonight," said Kennelly, "I'm going to sweat the night manager at the Cardinal Hotel."

"I suppose you are aware of—if not amused by—my habit of reducing things to charts," said Mrs. Roosevelt to Deconcini and Kennelly after Early had left. "I am just thinking of making matters perhaps a little easier to understand."

She had a big pad of paper mounted on a tripod, and she began to write a list of questions.

How did Miss Ryan gain access to the White House? To the Blue Room?

Why was she carrying a revolver?

Whose are the initials engraved on the Ronson lighter?

Who provided the money for Miss Ryan's funeral?

Who was threatening Miss Ryan (as the pawnbroker says she told him)?

Who was in the Blue Room Monday night?

Why was someone in the Blue Room Monday night?

Why did Miss Shearson not scream as someone struck her repeatedly and broke both her wrists?

What relationship, if any, is there between the death of Miss Ryan and the leaks of confidential information to Marv Ritchey?

What is the relationship between the deaths of Miss Ryan and Miss Shearson?

"I've got one more question," said Kennelly wryly. "When are we gonna come up with an answer to any of these questions? I haven't very often been in an investigation that just kept coming up with more questions, and never any answers."

After lunch Mrs. Roosevelt walked over to the Executive Wing and to the offices of Steve Early. As she had hoped, she found Alicia Robinson busy typing in the little room she had shared with Emily Ryan. The red-haired young woman snatched off her wire-framed glasses, pushed back her chair, and stood.

"Sit down, Miss Robinson. Be comfortable. I shall sit here. I just want to review one or two things with you. About Miss Ryan, of course."

"It is still hard for me to believe she's gone," said Alicia Robinson.

Alicia Robinson had not adopted the wartime custom of wearing slacks to the office, but she was wearing her skirts at the "patriotic" length, Mrs. Roosevelt noted. When she crossed her legs, they were exposed four or five inches above her knees.

"Miss Robinson, what do you know about the relationship between Miss Ryan and Mr. Marvin Ritchey?"

Alicia Robinson's chin dropped. Her mouth fell open, and she shook her head. "He's not a very nice man," she said.

"He says Miss Ryan was a tramp," said Mrs. Roosevelt.

"I'll lose my job," said Alicia Robinson dully.

"Why?"

"Because I didn't tell what I saw," the secretary said.

"And that was . . . ?"

"I saw her save her carbon paper," said Alicia Robinson. "Not just once. Many times. Do you know what I mean? She would type something . . . making copies with carbon paper. Ordinarily, you can use carbon paper several times, five or six at least, before you need to replace it. Emily would pull out her carbon paper after she used it *just once* and save it in a box. She could only have had one reason for doing that."

"To keep copies of the documents she typed," said Mrs. Roosevelt.

"If you have typed on a sheet of carbon paper only once, it has a readable copy of the document on it," Alicia Robinson agreed.

"And you suspected she was giving these copies to Mr. Ritchey?"

"I don't know for sure. But what else could she have been doing?"

"Perhaps *selling* the copies," said Mrs. Roosevelt. "Not giving."

"To Ritchey . . . He is a dreadful man."

"Do you *know* she was giving them to him? Or are you just guessing?"

"I don't know she was. I know she went out with him for a while. She talked about him—about how she was dating the famous radio news broadcaster."

" 'Dating,' " said the First Lady quietly. "I believe Ritchey suggested the relationship was something rather different from a date."

"He called her a tramp. She *wasn't*," said Alicia Robinson emphatically, and she began to cry.

"Is there something else you haven't told?" Mrs. Roosevelt asked gently.

Alicia Robinson nodded. "I didn't want to make trouble for Don Pettengill," she said. "But Emily thought he was going to marry her. She was really changing. For him. Quit going out with a lot of guys. She started saving herself for Don."

"You didn't want to cause trouble for him?"

"Well . . . it makes it look like he had a reason to kill her. And he was in the White House that night. Working. You know, it looks like *An American Tragedy*. I mean, that's the first thing that came to my mind."

"In the Theodore Dreiser novel," said Mrs. Roosevelt, "the young woman was pregnant."

"Emily thought maybe *she* was."

"She wasn't. The medical examiner—"

Alicia Robinson covered her face with her hands and wept.

Mrs. Roosevelt waited a minute or so, until the young woman stopped sobbing, then said—"Also, in the novel the young man was engaged to be married to a girl of higher social standing."

"So's Don," said Alicia Robinson.

"Oh? I didn't know that."

"He's engaged to Barbara Lowell," said Alicia Robinson.

"Barbara . . . Lowell?"

"Boston. His mother was a Cabot, you know; so a Cabot is marrying a Lowell."

"How perfect," said Mrs. Roosevelt dryly.

10

Mrs. Roosevelt had a two o'clock appointment at a Victory Garden in the southeast quarter of Washington. Informally dressed in flat shoes suitable for walking through a garden, with the rugged khaki skirt and jacket she had worn to Fort McNair when she inspected the amphibious jeep, she left her car and strode purposefully into the middle of the big vegetable garden.

Some commentators scoffed at the Victory Garden program. They were wrong, as she knew. Already in that first summer of war, hundreds of thousands of amateur gardeners were cultivating tens of thousands of acres of land that would not otherwise have been planted with food crops; and by the end of the summer they would harvest an immense amount of food.

This garden was a shared project, established by the tenants in a housing project occupied almost exclusively by blacks. The gardeners—mostly women, since the men in the project were either serving in the armed forces or at work in defense plants—stood around their garden,

shyly, yet proudly, and talked to the reporters and cameramen who had gathered in anticipation of the visit by
the First Lady.

In early June only a few vegetables were ready for harvest—radishes mostly, and a few peas—but the long, neat
rows of other crops were in place, and the plants looked
healthy.

Two of the women had pulled big red radishes from the
ground and washed them for the wife of the President of
the United States. As the newsreel cameras whirred, Mrs.
Roosevelt accepted a bunch of radishes from the hands of
a plump, beaming woman.

"They come along real good," the woman told the First
Lady. "We never knew we could grow stuff like this."

Mrs. Roosevelt plucked one of the smaller radishes from
the bunch and bit it in two. "Uhmm . . ." she murmured
as she chewed. "Tasty. There is nothing so good as fresh
garden vegetables."

"You should have a little salt on that," said the other
woman.

"When it's as fresh and good as this, it doesn't need
salt," said Mrs. Roosevelt, and she popped the rest of the
radish into her mouth.

An elderly man stepped forward. "We have cucum-
ber," he said gravely. "We have bean—lima and string.
Them 'ere going to be pole bean. And we've got corn and
onion."

"Don't forget the tomatoes," a woman said, pointing
to scores of staked tomato plants growing some distance
from where they stood.

"Tomato . . ." the old man agreed. "You want know
how I l'arn to plant and cultivate, Miz Roosevelt? I l'arn it
in *slavery,* Ma'am. I am eighty-six years old, and as a boy
too young to work in the field I was l'arned to make garden. We have melon and squash. And dere—You know
what that plant is?" He grinned, showing he had but two
front teeth left. "I bet you don't know what that crop will
be."

She smiled. "I'm afraid I don't," she said.

"That will be our gumbo," he said.

"What folks call gumbo is okra," a woman explained.

A woman stepped forward. "I'll be teaching them to preserve these foods," she said. "Canning, mostly. It's an ironic thing about the war, Mrs. Roosevelt. Many of our families will eat better this winter than ever we have before. Victory Garden. It may be a long time before we see victory and the boys come home. But a little victory has been won here, already."

Back at the White House, the First Lady telephoned Steve Early and asked him to come once again to her office. He told her it would be inconvenient until perhaps five o'clock but that he would be there then.

She spent an hour or so reading and answering correspondence. Then Early came in.

"Steve, a thought has come to mind," she said after he was seated. "I've been wondering if a clue as to who murdered Miss Ryan might not be found by reviewing instances when confidential information escaped us and reached Mr. Ritchey."

"The story about MacArthur is the only leak I've had from my office in years," said Early.

"Precisely," said Mrs. Roosevelt. "But I was wondering if Mr. Marvin Ritchey didn't obtain other information from Miss Ryan. If she went out with Congressman Dirksen, if she had drinks with Harry Hopkins in at least two bars, if she was regularly dating a naval officer assigned to the White House . . . Do you see? I wonder if we could identify any unauthorized disclosures of information *they* might have given her. And, more to the point, can we identify any other men she went out with by matching them to leaks of confidential information?"

"A little far-fetched, Eleanor," he said.

"You said you keep a file of real or imagined disclosures," she said. "Have you checked to see if Mr. Ritchey came into the possession of any other information he wasn't supposed to have?''

"I've identified one other incident," said Early. "That was in January, too. Ritchey broadcast a story about our efforts to get Chile to go along with the unanimous action of the Inter-American States and declare war on Germany. He talked about some economic pressure we might put on the Chilean government. That was strictly off the record. We wondered where he got that.''

"Where *might* he have gotten it, Steve?''

"From the office of the Coordinator of Inter-American Affairs,'' said Early.

"Mr. Nelson Rockefeller?'' she asked.

"He's the Coordinator of Inter-American Affairs,'' said Early. "And he runs the office like a little fiefdom. He insists he reports directly to the Boss—not to the State Department, not to anyone else. Anyway, that was an embarrassing leak. And Chile still hasn't declared war.''

"I wonder if . . .'' she mused.

"He's a Rockefeller, don't forget.''

"Yes. Unfortunately, I seem to have a question to ask of a Lowell, too.''

Dom Deconcini had made inquiries about Barbara Lowell. He reported to Mrs. Roosevelt late that afternoon.

"She's here in Washington,'' he said. "Leases a house in Georgetown. If you really want to know about her, you should ask Alice Roosevelt Longworth.''

"I shall,'' said the First Lady. "But by telephone only.''

She had the White House operator place the call. Whether Deconcini knew it or not, there was bad feeling between the Oyster Bay Roosevelts and the Hyde Park Roosevelts. Alice, who was of course the daughter of Theodore Roosevelt, was a lifelong Republican and had made no secret of her opposition to the New Deal. What was worse, she had often expressed personal scorn for the President and Mrs. Roosevelt, neither of whom she considered quite her social equal. Her acid jibes had so irritated the President that he had once refused to appoint her to a minor and mostly honorary position on a commission, remarking that he wanted nothing to do with "that woman."

Relations between Mrs. Roosevelt and her cousin Alice were a bit more cordial, so she was not surprised when she heard the familiar voice on the line.

"Eleanor. How nice to hear from you. How is everything with you?"

"I am well," said Mrs. Roosevelt. "So is Franklin."

"I am pleased to hear it," said Mrs. Longworth.

"I've telephoned to ask you a question, Alice."

"By all means. What is the question?"

"I have been given reason to believe that one of the naval officers employed here in the White House is engaged to be married to a Miss Barbara Lowell, of Boston I believe. I was wondering if you know the girl, or know if it is true there is such an engagement."

"Bobbie Lowell! Of course! Don Pettengill is marrying Bobbie Lowell. It will be a marriage made in heaven, Eleanor! Or, better yet, made by the Four Hundred."

"It mates standing and money, I suppose," said Mrs. Roosevelt dryly.

Alice Roosevelt Longworth laughed. *"Old* money, dear. Old, old money. With which, of course, goes standing."

"What can you tell me about the girl? I understand she lives in Washington."

"High spirited," said Mrs. Longworth. "She wanted to be in Washington, which she said is the center of the world these days. She has a nice little house, where she entertains. She does a lot of volunteer work, too. A perfectly splendid girl, Eleanor."

"What do you know of Lieutenant Pettengill?"

"They were not engaged, I believe, before she came to Washington. They were old friends, though, and here in Washington they renewed their friendship and . . . And, well, friendship ripened into love. It's quite romantic."

"Lieutenant Pettengill has done a good job here, so far

as I know," said Mrs. Roosevelt. "On the other hand, I know nothing of his personal life. Do you?"

"A fun boy, I hear," said Mrs. Longworth. "He rowed for Harvard. I've heard it said that he is a little inclined to sow his wild oats. You know—secretaries, waitresses, and the like. Nothing serious."

"I see," said Mrs. Roosevelt soberly.

"The very finest families," said Alice Roosevelt Longworth. "The Lowells especially, of course, but the Pettengills, too. The wedding will be the event of the season."

"What season?"

"The first one after the war ends, I believe. I understand they've agreed to wait until after Don is discharged from the Navy. They'll live in Boston, of course. He'll be with the bank."

"Well, thank you, Alice. I appreciate the information."

"Is it anything terribly significant?" asked Mrs. Longworth.

"Probably not," said the First Lady. "Thanks again . . . and good-bye."

"I am honored indeed," said the tall young man with the oddly square-jawed face and wide, thin mouth.

"I am grateful to you for coming, Mr. Rockefeller," said Mrs. Roosevelt. "My call was short notice. Please sit down. The President and some others will be joining us shortly, and I should like to ask you a few questions whilst we are still alone."

Nelson Rockefeller sat down on a couch in the sitting hall in the family quarters of the White House. She had invited him to join her and the President for the evening cocktail hour—after ascertaining from the President that he had no objection and would not be coming up from the Executive Wing much before seven.

Rockefeller glanced around. He had been in the White House many times but never before in the private quarters on the second floor. He knew that the doors he faced led directly into the bedrooms of the President of the United

States and his First Lady. He was probably surprised at how modest the quarters were. The space was limited, and the furnishings, provided by each First Family for itself, were, in this administration, anything but luxurious. Most presidential families, someone had remarked, lived better at home than they could in the White House.

"If you enjoy martini cocktails, Mr. Rockefeller, you will please my husband, who loves to mix them. He considers himself something of a connoisseur of martini cocktails."

"So I have heard," said Rockefeller.

He was well dressed, as she had expected of a man worth many millions of dollars—in a gray pinstriped double-breasted suit, white shirt, striped necktie, and highly polished shoes. He also seemed to possess the self-confidence she supposed was characteristic of a man as secure in his life as any Rockefeller of this generation was.

"The questions I have to ask you are of a somewhat personal nature, Mr. Rockefeller," she said. "Also, they are distinctly of a confidential nature. I shouldn't ask them except that they are important. That is, the answers are important."

"I shall answer to the best of my ability," he said in a somewhat dry, flat voice.

She was a little reluctant to do what she did now, but Captain Kennelly had insisted that it was an effective and wholly legitimate way of breaking through the self-assurance of a person about to be interrogated. She handed him a manila envelope.

"Please look at what is inside," she said.

Rockefeller pushed back the flap of the envelope and reached inside to pull out the photograph. He stiffened and gasped. It was one of the morgue photographs of Emily Ryan, one graphically showing the wound to her head that had caused her death.

"I believe you knew the young woman," said Mrs. Roosevelt.

Rockefeller frowned over the picture, as if he were not certain he knew her or not. Then he nodded.

"How would you describe your relationship with her?"

He drew a deep breath. "I think I'd rather not describe my relationship with her," he said.

"It was a private matter."

"Yes."

"It is a little difficult, Mr. Rockefeller, for a relationship to continue to be respected as private when one of the parties to that relationship has been murdered."

"I've heard that she was murdered," said Rockefeller. "I have also heard where and when. I can account for my time that evening."

"I didn't expect to ask you if you had murdered her. I think it is all but impossible that you did. It may be, on the other hand, that you know something about the motive that drove her murderer."

He frowned. "I doubt very much that I can contribute anything whatever to the investigation into her death."

"Look at *this* photograph," said Mrs. Roosevelt, handing him a second envelope, this one containing a morgue photograph of Peggy Shearson.

He grimaced over the ugly picture. "I don't believe I know this girl," he said.

"Very well. Now. I should be grateful if you would tell me something about your relationship with Miss Ryan."

"She was an excellent stenographer and typist," he said. "I have to keep track of some private business, you know, in spite of the fact that I'm working in Washington; and Emily Ryan did some work for me, evenings."

"What kind of work, Mr. Rockefeller?"

"Well . . . she took letters and typed them."

"Where?"

"In a suite I keep at the Mayflower—where I do my private buisness."

"She . . . took letters in shorthand and then typed them for you?"

"Yes, exactly."

"I see," said Mrs. Roosevelt, frowning thoughtfully. "Uh . . . Did she ever type any *official* documents for you?"

He shook his head. "I have staff for that. She did only my private work."

"Can you give me the approximate dates when she began to do this kind of work for you, and when she stopped?"

Rockefeller grinned. "She began working for me in . . . oh, December. And after about the first of February, I stopped calling her. To be frank, Mrs. Roosevelt, the girl made too many mistakes."

"Yes," said the First Lady. "Let me tell you a mistake she made. She carried confidential information from her White House office to a news broadcaster. We have identified at least one document of which she supplied a copy to this broadcaster."

"I find that hard to believe," he said.

"It's true," she said. "Now, there was an improper disclosure of confidential information from the office of the Coordinator of Inter-American Affairs about the time when she was working for you."

"The Marv Ritchey thing," said Rockefeller. "Chile. We concluded that was a coincidence, a lucky guess on his part."

"An unlucky guess, I should call it," she said. "But it may not have been a guess. Mr. Ritchey has acknowledged that he had a meretricious relationship with Miss Ryan. Though he hasn't acknowledged that she brought him at least one confidential document from the White House press office, we know she did. Could she, by any chance, have seen a confidential document of yours, perhaps lying on a table or desk?"

"Maybe she went through my briefcase," he said somberly. "I sometimes left her alone, working."

"Transcribing," said Mrs. Roosevelt.

"Yes. I dictated letters and memoranda to her, and she typed them."

"So it is not impossible that she read something and carried the information to Mr. Ritchey?"

"I'm afraid I can't say that is impossible. I am embarrassed. Do you suspect Ritchey of murdering her?"

"Not for the moment," said Mrs. Roosevelt. "In any event, I appreciate your cooperation." She glanced at her watch. "The President will be here any minute. If you will excuse me for a moment, I have a brief telephone call to make from my office."

The President did indeed arrive within a few minutes. His valet Arthur Prettyman pushed the wooden wheelchair off the elevator, and from there the President propelled it with his strong arms, into the sitting hall where Rockefeller sprang to his feet.

"Ah! Rockefeller. My wife said she'd ask you to stop by. Good to see you. You've met Ambassador Halifax, of course. And Admiral Lord Louis Mountbatten?"

"I haven't had the pleasure of meeting Lord Mountbatten," said Nelson Rockefeller, as he extended his hand to Mountbatten.

Edward Wood, First Earl of Halifax, was a tall, taciturn man with a broad, open face that gave an impression of complete calm and total honesty. He wore a London suit, handsomely tailored but of wool too heavy for a Washington summer. His white shirt had an old-fashioned round collar, and one suspected he owned two dozen dark-blue ties with discreet white dots.

Mrs. Roosevelt emerged from her office and sat down beside Rockefeller.

"I asked Lord Mountbatten to bring some photographs with us," said the President.

Mountbatten began passing big enlargements to the First Lady. "These," he explained, "are the reconnaissance photographs from the Saturday-Sunday raid on Cologne— just flown over for the President and General Arnold to see. For the first time in history, more than one thousand bombers have struck one target on one night. Another raid by a thousand machines went over to Essen last night. I think you can see from the pictures that London is being avenged."

The pictures were difficult to decipher, for one not accustomed to looking at that sort of thing; but Mountbatten showed her that two photographs showed a Cologne tire factory before the raid and after. She could see that what had been a sprawling factory complex of a dozen or more buildings had been reduced to burned-out, shattered wreckage.

"It is Winston's hope," said Halifax quietly, "that the United States will match the RAF in this effort, that we may bring Germany under more or less constant air attack. Indeed, Air Chief Marshal Harris thinks the war can be won this way."

"An alternative to the Second Front," Mrs. Roosevelt suggested.

"I'm afraid not," said Halifax. "The Wehrmacht won't withdraw divisions from the Russian front to confront our air attacks. Strategic bombing makes its effect felt only in the long run, by reducing the enemy's ability to produce the materiel of war. We shall have to bomb heavily for a year or more before we begin to see results at the battle fronts."

The President began to measure the ingredients for a pitcher of martinis, from the table of necessaries set up for him by Arthur Prettyman. "The third front," he said. "The overhead front. I think Bomber Harris has a good idea. We'll follow up on it. That's confidential, of course, Rockefeller."

When they had finished their drinks—and this evening Mrs. Roosevelt joined them with two small glasses of sherry—the British visitors and Rockefeller left, and the President sipped the last from his glass and glanced around for his valet to wheel him to his bedroom and help him into his bath.

"Was there any particular reason for having Nelson Rockefeller here this evening?" he asked.

"I thought I might learn something," she said.

"And did you?"

"I did. I learned that the man doesn't always tell the truth. Having caught him in one lie, I wonder how many more he's telling."

Dom Deconcini accompanied Ed Kennelly into the refrigerated vault of the morgue.

The white-uniformed attendant tugged on a door, and a drawer rolled out, bearing the corpse of Peggy Shearson. It was wrapped in a rough white sheet, and he pulled the sheet away from her face.

"I want to see the whole body," said Deconcini.

The attendant shot him an odd glance, but he pulled the sheet away until the ghastly, pallid corpse was exposed naked.

"Has she been washed?" Deconcini asked.

The attendant shook his head. "Only some of the blood off her head. Otherwise, no."

The legs were an odd, unnatural tan color. Deconcini knew why. Since nylon stockings had disappeared from the stores, some girls had taken to simulating stockings by painting their legs with a water-soluble tan paint. Some even used soft pencils and drew lines up the backs of their legs, to look like seams in stockings.

Deconcini sighed. "It's like I remembered. Something that bothered me whenever I had time to think about it. Look at her hands and knees, Ed."

Kennelly frowned closely over the hands and knees. The knees were abraded and discolored. So were the palms of the hands. Tiny bits of sharp gravel had penetrated the skin at a few points and remained imbedded.

"So what is it that bothers you?"

"The alley is paved with gravel—gravel lying loose in mud and dust. She's attacked. She falls heavily to her knees on rough gravel. If she were a kid, we'd say she skinned her knees. Okay. But look at her hands. The same thing. She fell on her knees, then forward on her hands. She threw her hands out in front of her as she fell, so she wouldn't slam her face into the gravel. Right?''

"Right. Go on."

"Our scenario of the murder," said Deconcini, "holds that she threw her hands up to protect her head and face against the blows that would kill her. The first blows hit her on the arms and broke both wrists. Then she was hit on the head and fell. Now—Would the instinct to protect her face hitting the gravel have been strong enough to cause her to throw out her hands and land on them . . . *with two broken wrists that had to be in agonizing pain?*''

"A damned good question," said Kennelly. "But what conclusion follows?"

"And she didn't scream," said Deconcini.

"Meaning . . . ?"

"Meaning this thing didn't happen the way we visualized it."

"Is it going to make any difference?" asked Kennelly.

"I don't know. But if her wrists weren't broken that way, then how were they broken?"

"And why?" asked Kennelly.

"And why?" Deconcini agreed.

The Cardinal Hotel was on G Street. Ed Kennelly went there alone.

It was a modest small hotel and had been, until the past few months, a politicians' hotel, an offbeat place where congressmen of both parties met men and women they were not quite afraid to be seen with, yet didn't want to be seen with in the most public rooms in town. Mrs. Roosevelt had never been there and was hardly aware it existed.

Like most such places, it featured a smoky lobby with a white tile floor and big oak-and-leather chairs where men smoked cigars, drank, and read the newspapers. One side of the lobby was dominated by a news and tobacco stand,

selling local and out-of-town newspapers, cigars, cigarettes, and pipe tobacco. A small gas flame burned at the
end of a pipe that protruded through the counter, affording
customers a handy light for their cigars. The hotel desk
dominated the other side of the lobby. Two young women
sat in chairs beside the bell captain's station. Only the
most naive didn't understand that they were prostitutes,
waiting for trade.

Kennelly went to the counter. He showed his badge to
the clerk and said he wanted to talk to the night manager.

The clerk turned without a word and spoke into the
office behind the desk—"Hey, Mike, there's a cop out
here."

A voice answered. "Tell 'im I'm busy. He'll have to
wait a few minutes."

The clerk smiled at Kennelly and shrugged.

"Now!" barked Kennelly.

Startled, the clerk turned and spoke again through the
door—"He says now."

"Tell 'im to wait, dammit."

Again the clerk shrugged.

Kennelly grabbed the hinged part of the counter that
made a gate, threw it over, and let it bang down. Everyone
in the lobby stared as he stalked through the opening and
into the office. He grabbed the office door and slammed it
shut.

"Hey! Who the hell you think you are?"

"Captain Ed Kennelly, chief of detectives, District police. Sit down."

"Why? What's—"

"You don't want to talk here, we can talk at headquarters," said Kennelly. He reached into his jacket pocket
and pulled out a pair of handcuffs. "Your choice. For the
moment."

The man sat down behind a desk. He was rather small.
He wore a black mustache and round gold-framed
glasses. His black hair grew only to about the tops of his

ears, and his bald dome was shiny. He was in shirtsleeves, his collar was open, and his necktie hung loose.

"What's your name?" Kennelly asked.

"Michael Marks."

"You're the night manager?"

"Right."

"Since when?"

Marks shrugged. "Six years. Seven."

"You here every night?"

"Six nights a week."

"You don't sit back here, I suppose. You're out behind the desk most of the time, aren't you?"

Marks nodded. "Out behind the desk. Dummy out there can't make change."

"Okay," said Kennelly. "I want to show you some pictures. All I want to know is, have you ever seen any of these people."

For this, Kennelly and Deconcini had obtained photographs of the living Emily Ryan and Peggy Shearson. The picture of Emily Ryan Kennelly now handed to Marks was copied from a photo in her White House personnel file. It had something of the appearance of a mug shot, but it did represent her as she had been before Friday night.

Marks looked at the picture and turned up the palms of his hands. "Am I supposed to know this broad?"

"Do you?"

He shook his head.

Kennelly handed him a picture of Peggy Shearson, copied from a snapshot that had been among the things taken from her room.

"Don't know this one either," said Marks.

Kennelly handed him a picture of Marvin Ritchey, the broadcaster.

"Never saw this guy either."

Kennelly handed him a picture of Lieutenant Donald Pettengill, and Marks shook his head, turned down the corners of his mouth, and shrugged.

"Never saw any of them, huh?"

Again Marks shook his head. "You gotta understand, I stand out there behind that desk and look at the faces of hundreds of people every night. I coulda seen any of these people. But I don't remember any of them. I don't know who they are."

Kennelly had left the handcuffs lying on the edge of Marks's desk, and now he picked them up and said, "Okay, buddy. Lemme have your hands."

"Hey! What for?"

Kennelly grabbed Marks's left wrist and quickly locked a cuff on it. Then he locked the other cuff on the right. "Let's go," he said curtly.

"Wait a minute! What is this? What you charging me with?"

Marks remained seated behind his desk, staring in disbelief at the handcuffs. Kennelly had stood.

"Let's start with lying to a police officer investigating a murder," said Kennelly. He pointed to the pictures, which still lay on the desk. "That's good enough for a start. I can make some other charges against you if I need to."

"Lemme take another look," said Marks hoarsely, reaching for the photographs.

Kennelly sat down again and waited while Marks feigned a close study of each of the photographs. Marks separated them. He put aside the picture of Pettengill. The other three he spread out and stared at.

"Yeah. Okay. I guess I do know these three."

"You *guess?*"

"I know 'em," Marks conceded.

"Talk."

With his two chained-together hands, Marks shoved the Pettengill photo back toward Kennelly. "Him I never saw. I swear. This guy here is Marv Ritchey, the news broadcaster. This broad"—pointing at the picture of Emily Ryan—"is a girl he used to shack up with here in the hotel. The other little broad is another girl a guy used to bring in. I don't know their names. They were registered as 'Mrs. Smith' or 'Mrs. Jones.' You know."

Kennelly nodded. "Let me tell you something, Marks," he said soberly. "Both these girls have been murdered. So I have to know who brought them here and when."

"You wanta look at the registers?"

"Probably. Later. Right now, you just tell me the story."

Marks pushed the picture of Emily Ryan toward Kennelly. "I haven't seen her for four, five months. Ritchey brought her in. He brings lotsa girls in. He registers every time as 'Mr. and Mrs. Robert Smith.' No matter who the girl. She came in a few times with another guy. You won't believe what his name was. He could buy the hotel out of the money he carries around in his pockets."

"What *is* his name?"

"Rockefeller. I mean, one of *the* Rockefellers. A grandson of old John D., I think. He brought this girl in the hotel."

"How did he register?"

Marks grinned. " 'Mr. and Mrs. Harold Douglas.' "

"Okay. What about the other girl?"

"She's been here a few times. I don't think she's a hooker. In fact, I don't think either one of 'em was. They were just . . . modern girls. Wartime modern girls. This one . . . this blonde, she came in here with a congressman a couple times."

"Which congressman?"

"I don't know. I swear I don't know his name. If I looked at pictures of a lotta congressman, I could probably pick him out."

"Anybody else? I need names."

Marx managed a weak smile. "Well . . . Rockefeller brought her in, too. 'Mr. and Mrs. Harold Douglas.' "

"When did you last see this girl?" Kennelly asked.

"Saturday night."

"*Saturday* night? With who?"

"Rockefeller."

11

While Ed Kennelly was at the Cardinal Hotel, Dom Deconcini was back at the Farragut Bar. By now the bartenders were aware that he was a Secret Service agent, and when he suggested that one of them take a few minutes off work to talk to him, the others filled in and made it possible.

They knew in fact that he was investigating the murder of Peggy Shearson, as was the gruff Captain Kennelly. The murder had become the talk of the establishment. Customers stepped back and gave Deconcini elbow room when he pressed up to the bar.

One of the bartenders was named Sam Lawson. He was a fiftyish man, heavyset and pink, with thin sandy hair and little round eyeglasses. He wore black pants, a white shirt, and a tiny bow tie made of black leather.

Deconcini ordered a Scotch and soda. "You know what I have to talk about," he said to Lawson.

Lawson nodded. "Wish I could tell you something that would help. An awful thing, that murder. Awful."

"I gather she was a regular in here."

"She was. But let me tell you something. She was no hooker. The boss won't stand for hookers hanging out in here. If he's got the least suspicion about a girl, he puts her out."

"Emily Ryan the same, I suppose," said Deconcini.

"For sure. She was a fun girl, too, but it had to be strictly innocent. Listen, I've seen girls thrown out of here just for being a little pushy. I mean, those girls' dates brought them in here. Or met them here. The boss won't stand for girls getting picked up in here. Listen, I saw both those girls tell guys to go away. If you didn't know 'em, you couldn't pick 'em up."

"Okay. Peggy was murdered after she left here last night. So when was the last time she'd been in before last night?"

"She was here Monday night."

"With anybody?"

"With Pettengill. They stood here at the bar for a while, until they could get a table; then they went over there and sat and talked. And they left separately. I mean, she left, and he stayed here."

"What time did she come in?"

"Well, you know she works—that is, she did. So it was like nine-thirty."

"And left?"

"Oh . . . maybe eleven."

"Were they alone?"

"Part of the time. That other young Navy officer was with them part of the time. Morris, I think his name is."

"It's damn important to know who else she dated," said Deconcini. "Pettengill was here when she was killed, so he couldn't have killed her. I mean, you and too many other people agree that he was sitting at that table over there at the time. So, who else? Any ideas?"

"She came in with Morris once or twice," said Lawson. "Aside from him . . ." He shrugged. "Others, sure. But nobody I could name."

"Emily . . ." said Deconcini. "When was the last time she was here?"

The bartender scratched his head. "You say she died Friday night? She hadn't been in here for a week before that. She'd been coming in once in a while, sort of looking around, then leaving without having a drink."

"But she used to meet Pettengill here?"

"Oh, yeah. For a while. They looked like they were pretty close. Then they weren't anymore. I figure he changed his mind and decided he liked Peggy better."

"One witness has told us she said somebody was threatening her," said Deconcini. "Did you ever see her having hard words with anybody?"

Lawson frowned thoughtfully and shook his head. "No. Both those girls were always *fun* girls. Guys like them. Maybe what did 'em in, huh? Too many guys liked them too much."

"I could hardly ask you," said Mrs. Roosevelt, "to meet with me so late if I didn't offer a light refreshment."

The light refreshment, served in her office just before midnight, was a platter of cheese, an assortment of the fresh vegetables given to her at the end of her visit to the Victory Garden—radishes and scallions, plus some very small carrots—with bread and crackers and a tray of bottles from which the two men could mix drinks. Also, there was a pot of coffee and some cookies.

"You have been busy," she said. "And so have I. Let us compare notes. May I begin? I caught Mr. Nelson Rockefeller in a lie. He said he employed Miss Ryan to take shorthand notes and transcribe them. Steve Early was most emphatic that she did not take shorthand."

"A Dictaphone machine took up most of her desk," said Deconcini.

"I can add something to that," said Kennelly. "Nelson Rockefeller checked into the Cardinal Hotel several times with Emily Ryan. But—a lot more important—he checked in Saturday night with Peggy Shearson."

Deconcini objected. "*We* saw her Saturday night."

"Checked in after midnight. Left by six in the morning. 'Mr. and Mrs. Harold Douglas,' which was the name he used when he spent the night there with Emily Ryan."

" 'Harold Douglas . . .' " Mrs. Roosevelt murmured.

" 'Harold Douglas. H . . . D. Where have we seen those letters? Do you remember?"

"H . . . D . . ." muttered Kennelly.

"On the Ronson cigarette lighter," said the First Lady. "Remember? H.D. and E.R. Harold Douglas and Emily Ryan?"

"Yes, and remember the symbols, too," said Deconcini. "Engraved on the lighter."

He reached for a sheet of paper and drew the symbols

$$\male + \female = \heartsuit$$

"Forgive my frankness, Mrs. Roosevelt," he said. "It means, the male plus the female, joined, equals love."

"Surely," she said, "Mr. Rockefeller was not suggesting there was a love interest between him and Miss Ryan."

"The way he used the word," said Kennelly bluntly, "that's exactly what it meant. I'm sorry, Ma'am, but 'love' is some things to some people and other things to others."

"I am well aware of it, Captain Kennelly," she said.

Mrs. Roosevelt rose from her chair and stepped to the window. She parted the blackout curtains just enough to give her a quick look at the dark city and country beyond. Surely a German bomber would not spot this brief show of light?

"It doesn't solve anything," she said. "All it tells us, really, is that Mr. Rockefeller is a rather libidinous man. He didn't murder Miss Ryan. It is almost impossible that he murdered Miss Shearson. He—"

"On the other hand," said Kennelly, "he is a *vulnerable* man. We can maybe sweat out of the grandson of John D. Rockefeller some information that will help us put our hands on the killer."

"Do you really think so, Captain Kennelly?" asked Mrs. Roosevelt.

"Ma'am," he said. "Experience tells me that solving a mystery is a matter of learning everything you can, including a lot that turns out to be entirely beside the point, and matching fact to fact in a lot of odd ways. I—But I'm not telling you anything you don't know. This isn't the first murder mystery you've worked on."

The First Lady smiled and reached for the bottle of Tio Pepe, the very dry sherry the stewards always made sure was available when they suspected she might share in the drinking. She poured a splash into a tiny wineglass.

"We have something more to tell you," said Deconcini. He told her what he and Kennelly had observed about the corpse of Peggy Shearson—that the knees and hands equally were bloodied by hard impact on sharp gravel. "It doesn't fit what we have assumed about how she was murdered," he said. "Do you see my point?"

Mrs. Roosevelt frowned. "Mr. Deconcini," she said. "You may have come up with the most significant fact so far produced in this investigation. Suddenly the thing is beginning to make sense to me."

"Enlighten us," said Deconcini.

She smiled. "You have worked with me before. If I tell you my idea, it may close your mind to other alternatives. I would much prefer that you came to the same conclusion through independent investigation."

"We may not come to the same conclusion," said Kennelly.

"So much the better," said she. "Different conclusions, supported by facts and reasons, may come to a better result. I am not, gentlemen, infallible; and my idea may not be as good as yours."

At that hour of the night of June 3 and 4, 1942, Task Force 16, under the command of Admiral Spruance, and Task Force 17, under the command of Admiral Fletcher, were racing toward a rendezvous at "Point Luck." An immense joint Japanese task force was steaming toward Midway.

A Japanese fleet had been sighted by PBY scout planes, and nine B-17 bombers had tried to damage that fleet by high-altitude bombing. They had scored no hits. What was worse, they had seen no carriers, so the Navy still did not know the location of the main enemy battle fleet.

At midnight in Washington, it was but six P.M. at Midway. The forces on the island were braced for what promised to be an overwhelming assault.

In Hawaii, a Japanese landing seemed inevitable. All forces were on alert. There was no confidence that the forces available were sufficient to forestall invasion and capture of the islands.

In California, word of the Japanese naval advance across the Pacific seemed to presage a major amphibious landing somewhere on the coast. California Attorney General Earl Warren was preparing to declare martial law.

The next twenty-four hours would determine whether the Japanese or the United States of America would control the Pacific Ocean.

In Washington the President had gone to bed. He had no choice but to place confidence in Admiral Chester Nimitz. He had given the admiral every bit of help and support within his power.

In Washington, too, Lieutenant Donald Pettengill was sitting over brandy and coffee in the Georgetown house rented by his fiancée, Miss Barbara Lowell. Decency required that he leave by midnight—everyone understood that young ladies did not receive young men after that hour—but he remained, sipping Rémy Martin and subtly pressing his case. Barbara was his affianced, but he had never been to bed with her. He was carefully suggesting that he would like to remain with her overnight.

Marvin Ritchey was in bed at home. His wife was indifferent. He had slept so many nights away from home that she no longer cared where he slept.

Nelson Rockefeller was not in bed. He was in his office,

rummaging through his files, looking for any piece of paper he should destroy. So far he hadn't found anything.

Lieutenant Foster Morris sat on a stool at the bar in Farragut's. He had drunk far more than he should have. Staring into his last Scotch, aware that the bar was about to close and he would be asked to leave, he reviewed for the fiftieth time every word that had been spoken, every gesture that had been exchanged, between Don and Peggy last night, before she went away to be murdered. He was sure Don had had nothing to do with it. But somebody had, and he couldn't believe it was coincidence that Peggy had encountered her murderer in an alley an hour after Don left her at home at her boardinghouse.

Alicia Robinson lay in bed alone. She, too, pondered the murders. She only wished that Don was there with her. The chance, however remote, of marrying that man had to be every girl's dream. He had everything. Money. Prestige. Class. And . . . well, whatever it was that made a man a man.

"I hate to do this at this hour, but I'm going back to the boardinghouse," said Kennelly. "There's no end of it. That's where some part of the answer is."

"I cannot but agree," said Mrs. Roosevelt. "I would go with you, but—"

"You can't."

"Can I not?" she asked, suddenly animated. "I went to Mr. Gully Balzac's striptease nightclub with you, when we were investigating the murder of Philip Garber. I went incognito, and no one recognized me."

"Mrs. Roosevelt, please . . ."

"Seriously," she said, "you've told me you always interview people on the front porch. Surely it's not very light there. I can dress so—"

"Sooner or later," said Kennelly glumly, "I'm going to get in trouble."

* * *

They arrived at the boardinghouse half an hour later, driven by Kennelly in a D.C. police car. Mrs. Sophia Bartlett, the owner, sat on the porch, relaxed, drinking beer and idly contemplating the street—dressed as usual in a flowered dress that hung over her ample figure like a tent. She fit into a great wicker chair as though she and the chair had been molded for each other.

Mrs. Roosevelt wore one of the pairs of slacks that had been sent to her after she mentioned slacks in her newspaper column. It was a slack suit, actually, with a matching jacket. The color was khaki. The slacks themselves were loose and floppy, with wide cuffs. She also wore a blue-and-white polka-dotted bandanna tied and pinned to cover her head and confine her hair. Finally, the disguise was completed by a pair of old round green sunglasses she had kept from the days when she went on the beach at Campobello.

"Don't laugh, please," she had said when she came out of her bedroom and confronted the waiting Kennelly and Deconcini; but the three of them had joined laughing.

"Who are you supposed to be?" Kennelly had asked.

"Well . . . your sister perhaps," she had said. "You are driving me to my shift at a factory."

And so he introduced her—"My sister Rose. Gas is so short I try to drop her off anytime I'm going out that way. Too hot to ask her to wait in the car."

Sophia Bartlett regarded the odd-looking woman with unconcealed skepticism. By gesture she suggested the woman sit in the porch swing, and Mrs. Roosevelt sat there.

"You're not here for a social visit, I suppose," she said to Kennelly.

"No."

"Well?"

"I want to be sure of something," said Kennelly. "You said Peggy left here about eight-thirty Monday night. Right?"

"Right."

"She was killed at eleven-seventeen. We also know she left the Farragut Bar about ten. We can't account for that hour and seventeen minutes. You said she was not back here, but are you sure?"

"Either I was on this porch or Clyde was," said Sophia Bartlett. "And I asked Clyde if I was right in saying she didn't come back. He agrees she didn't."

"She was killed in an alley," said Kennelly. "Could she have come in the back door and up the back steps?"

"She never did before."

"Well, there was something odd about Monday night," said Kennelly.

"Nobody saw her," said Mrs. Bartlett.

"What about your other boarders?" asked Deconcini. "What about the two girls I met on this porch the first night I came here?"

"Phyllis and Betty? They're upstairs if you wanta talk to 'em."

"Why not?" said Deconcini.

Mrs. Bartlett went just inside the door and yelled up the stairs.

Mrs. Roosevelt had been studying the handsome old front porch of what had been a stately family home. Having been born and reared in Manhattan, she had never known the pleasure of sitting on a shady front porch on summer evenings, and the pleasant aspect of this one had momentarily distracted her from the questions the two men were asking the keeper of the boardinghouse.

"Do you think she suspects who I am?" she asked while Mrs. Bartlett was inside and could not hear her.

"God knows what she suspects," laughed Deconcini, "but I think we can be confident she doesn't suspect the truth."

The two girls—the ones gossipy old Clyde Merck had called "khakiwacky"—came out. Mrs. Roosevelt was surprised to see how young they were, to be living on their own in a boardinghouse. She judged neither of them was more than eighteen years old. Both were barefoot. One was wearing a pair of white shorts, the other a singularly short skirt. The one in shorts wore a halter, the one in a skirt a man's ribbed vest undershirt. Neither costume was modest. Neither was, in fact, quite decent. The two girls leaned against the porch rail, confronted Kennelly and Deconcini and seemed hardly to notice the strange woman sitting in the porch swing.

"You two are roommates, as I understand," said Deconcini.

"Is there anything wrong with that?" asked the one in the skirt and undershirt.

Kennelly rose abruptly out of his chair and stepped within a foot of the girl who had spoken. "As it stands right now," he said in her face, "you girls are in no trouble at all. We just want the answers to a few questions. But if you want to play games, I can take you in, lock you up for the night, and we can ask the questions in the morning."

The girl turned up her palms. "Wha'd I say?"

"What's your name?" asked Kennelly.

"Phyllis Anderson."

He glanced at the one in shorts. "That makes you Betty Howard. Now, the question is, are you two roommates?"

"Yeah."

Kennelly sat down.

"Okay," said Deconcini. "And your room is where, related to the room that Emily Ryan and Peggy Shearson had?"

"Next room down the hall," said Betty Howard. She shook a cigarette from the pack she had carried down with her. It was a Chesterfield, and she lit it with a match. "Next-door neighbors, you might say."

"All right. Where were you Monday night when Peggy was killed?"

The girls exchanged glances, then Betty Howard said, "I was home. In the room. Listen' to the radio." Like Al Smith, she pronounced it "raddio." "An' Phyllis was out. Had a date."

"All right. If Peggy came up to her room between, say, ten or ten-thirty and went out again a little later, would you have known it?"

"Maybe. But not for sure."

"So *did* she come in?"

Betty Howard shook her head. "Didn't hear her. 'Course . . . maybe I wouldn't've."

Deconcini sighed. He looked at Kennelly as if looking for a suggestion.

"Ed . . . " said Mrs. Roosevelt quietly. "Why don't you ask if all these girls were good friends."

Startled to have been called by his first name by the First Lady, Kennelly jerked his head around and frowned. Then he went along. "Oh, sure, Sis. Good idea. Thanks."

Mrs. Roosevelt smiled. Mrs. Bartlett stared at her with new curiosity.

" 'Kay. You heard the question. Were you girls good friends with Emily and Peggy?"

Betty Howard answered. "They thought they were better'n us."

"Meaning?" asked Kennelly.

"Well, they were older, you know. They had high-class kinds of guys for dates. They had jobs and were makin' some money. They figured they were pretty good kinds of girls."

"So you weren't good friends?"

"Well . . . not really."

"Ed . . ." murmured Mrs. Roosevelt. "Were Emily and Peggy good friends to *each other?*"

"Yeah, girls. Were they good friends to each other?"

"Sort of," said Phyllis Anderson. "They had differences."

"Like what?"

"Well . . . they dated the same guys sometimes. Emily had her way of getting around and making deals with good guys. By 'good guys' I mean guys a girl might think of marryin' sometime. I mean, not just—You know what I mean. Emily made deals with good guys."

"Okay," said Kennelly impatiently. "So . . . ?"

"Well, Peggy pushed in on the same guys. Like rich guys. You know. And Emily didn't like it, her buttin' in that way."

Betty Howard intervened. "You know how it was with Peggy. She could date any guy she wanted. She had her ways. You know what I mean."

"Which has to do with what?" asked Kennelly.

"Well, they argued about it sometimes," said Betty Howard. "I mean, they had *fights* about it."

"Specifically . . ." said Deconcini.

"They fought over that Navy guy," said Phyllis Anderson. "It got pretty tough between 'em on that subject. Emily was goin' to marry him. Peggy—Well, you know what Peggy did. Emily'd like to kill her."

"Pettengill?" asked Deconcini.

"Yeah, him," said Betty Howard. "They really had it out about him. Emily said she'd treated Peggy like a sister and Peggy was stealin' her love."

"When did this argument happen?" asked the First Lady.

Phyllis Anderson looked into the shadows where the woman in the slack suit was now asking questions. She looked at Kennelly and raised her eyebrows. "Last week," she said. "If I didn't know it was impossible, I'd think one of those girls killed the other. But Emily couldn't have killed Peggy because—And the other way . . . no. It wasn't that bad between 'em."

"You heard this kind of argument, between your two rooms?" asked Mrs. Roosevelt.

Betty Howard nodded. "They had it out pretty bad sometimes."

"Tell me something," said Deconcini. "Did either of them think she was pregnant?"

The two girls exchanged glances.

"Talked about it sometimes," said Betty Howard.

"Which one?"

"Well . . . Both of 'em, sometimes."

"Lately?"

"I guess Emily thought she maybe was," said Phyllis Anderson. "Anyway, she was really in love with the guy she thought it might be."

"Who was . . . ?"

"The Navy guy. Pettengill."

"Uhm," grunted Kennelly. "It always comes back to Pettengill. Well . . . Anything else?"

"Ed," said Mrs. Roosevelt quietly. "Have you seen the room?"

Kennelly took the hint. "Uhh . . . Yeah, but—Let's have one more look."

"You know where it is," said Sophia Bartlett. "Tomorrow or the next day, I'm going to clean their things out of it. I've got to rent it to somebody else, you know."

Glad that they were allowed to go up to the room alone, Mrs. Roosevelt followed Kennelly up the stairs to the second floor. Kennelly had visited the room twice before and did know which room it was, as the landlady had suggested.

It was a big old bedroom, pleasant, with broad windows overlooking the porch roof and the street. It was furnished with a double bed Emily Ryan and Peggy Shearson had slept in together. They had shared one big old dresser and one closet. Their clothes still hung in the closet, Emily's to the left, Peggy's to the right. An assortment of cosmetics was laid out on a dressing table, these too separated into what was Emily's and what was Peggy's. There was a radio, a few magazines lying on a table by the window. The room said very little about the two young women who had lived in it.

Deconcini stood in the door, to assure privacy for Mrs. Roosevelt as she looked around the room.

"Tell me something, Captain Kennelly," said the First Lady. "Where did you find that naval officer's button?"

"In the drawer of the little night table," he said.

A big alarm clock on the night table had been allowed to run down. Apart from that, there was a lamp on the table. The drawer remained open. A Bible lay inside.

Mrs. Roosevelt frowned. "You found it when you looked through the room after Miss Shearson was killed," she said. "Was it not here when you looked through the room after Miss Ryan was killed?"

Kennelly, too, frowned; then he nodded. "You got a point," he said. "I looked in that drawer the first time I was in this room. That button got itself in there between the time Emily Ryan was killed and the time Peggy Shearson was killed. I'm not sure what that means, but—"

"I'm not sure what it means, either," said Mrs. Roosevelt, "but it's an interesting fact, isn't it?"

She began to look through the clothes the two young women had left behind. After a moment she stopped and spoke to Deconcini. "There is a distinctive odor in this closet, don't you think?"

She stuck her head in and sniffed. "Yes. Odd . . . I don't recognize it."

Kennelly sniffed. "I do," he said. "That's Wildroot Hair Tonic." He grinned. "One of the girls had a boyfriend who must love the stuff, judging by how much has got on those clothes."

"On what?" asked Mrs. Roosevelt.

She pushed hangers apart and came after a moment to a pink blouse which was saturated with the odor. Other blouses and a sweater smelled only faintly of it.

"Those are all Peggy's," said Kennelly. "Her side of the closet."

Mrs. Roosevelt shook her head. "Insignificant, I have to suppose," she said. "That brand of hair tonic is probably used by millions of men."

"Now that I think of it, I remember one who uses it," said Kennelly.

"Oh? Who?"

"Marv Ritchey," said Kennelly.

"It's not evidence," said the First Lady in a firm and cautionary voice.

"Every little bit helps," said Kennelly.

"Do I dare go to the Farragut Bar?" asked Mrs. Roosevelt as they drove away from the boardinghouse.

"No, *no*, no, no, *no!*" howled Kennelly. "In the first place, they wouldn't let you in, in that outfit."

"Why, Brother Ed," she laughed. "They wouldn't like my outfit?"

"They . . . oh, God!"

"What have we learned?" she asked.

"I'm tired of hearing about Pettengill," said Deconcini.

"So am I," said Kennelly. "I'd like to lay this thing on him. But I don't see how."

"At this point," said Mrs. Roosevelt, "I am troubled by one fact more than by any other. Why did Miss Ryan have a pistol in her handbag when she was killed? Other facts are beginning to fall into line, but I cannot imagine any explanation for that."

"Let's think of the chart you made," said Deconcini. "As I recall, it had ten questions on it. So far, we have answered only one—who was the H.D. engraved on the Ronson lighter. That was Nelson Rockefeller using his name Harold Douglas. And even that doesn't mean much, because—"

"Because Mr. Rockefeller didn't murder either one of them," the First Lady interrupted.

"I hate that Marv Ritchey," said Kennelly. "I'd like to lay it on him."

"He could have been 'Sergeant Lee,' " said Deconcini. "And he could have been in that alley Monday night."

"Did you inquire of Mr. Ritchey as to his whereabouts on Monday night?" asked Mrs. Roosevelt.

"No," said Kennelly. "He said he didn't even know Peggy Shearson, except that he knew she and Emily Ryan were roommates."

"One would be curious to know if he can account for his time that night."

"I'll check up on him first thing in the morning," said Kennelly. "I know he'll be glad to see me."

When Kennelly reached the White House, they had a moment's difficulty in entering, even though he was driving a marked District police car and the woman in the back seat was the First Lady. The soldiers at the gatehouse were newly cautious, and the First Lady looked nothing like their image of Mrs. Franklin D. Roosevelt.

Once inside, they went up to the second floor, to the family quarters, and to the First Lady's office.

Mrs. Roosevelt was glad to notice that the President's study was dark. Tonight, apparently, he had been able to go to bed at his usual hour, or something near that. She did wonder what was the situation with the Pacific fleet and the looked-for attack on Midway, and she would have liked to speak with someone from the Navy about it; but she was glad the President was not still up and worrying about it. At this point there was nothing the commander in chief could do. The battle was in the hands of the commanders on the spot.

She found a telephone message waiting on her desk. Nelson Rockefeller had called and said she could return his call, to his office, anytime before eleven. It was now after midnight.

"Curious," she said to Kennelly and Deconcini. "He must be worried."

"Maybe in the morning you can worry him a little more," said Kennelly.

"Yes," she said. "I think he has a great deal to worry about."

12

Although she had been up very late, Mrs. Roosevelt rose early as usual on Thursday morning, June 4, 1942. She did not begin her days by tuning in to Marv Ritchey news, but again this morning she switched on her radio and listened to his first newscast of the day.

He closed with this:

Earl Warren, attorney general of California, hinted last night that the state may be put under martial law before the end of . . . *today!* That big Jap fleet that's loose in the Pacific and hasn't been sighted for . . . *days* . . . may be only a few hundred miles off this country's West Coast.

Our Navy doesn't know where it is. Our Navy, made to steer this way and that by conflicting orders from armchair admirals and just plain bureaucrats in Washington, is searching frantically . . . so far without results.

How could we lose a fleet of fifty or sixty big ships? Well . . . the Pacific Ocean is a mighty big place . . . and sneaking is a Jap specialty. They sneaked up on Pearl Harbor, didn't they? So, if you on the West Coast were listening to yours truly . . . *last evening* . . . and suddenly your radio went silent, it was because all radio stations were ordered off the air to prevent the Japs from homing on the signals. That's how they found Hawaii, remember—by tuning their radio direction finders to Honolulu broadcast stations.

Marv Rrr . . . *Ritchey!* Washington. Good . . . day!

The First Lady's schedule for the day began with a breakfast for Senator Harry Truman of Missouri, with his wife. The President would meet with the senator in the Oval Office as soon as the breakfast was over, and Mrs. Roosevelt would take Mrs. Truman on a personal tour of the White House.

Senator Truman, who had been an obscure and not-terribly-successful politician, had come to Washington in 1934 under the cloud of having been tapped as a candidate by Kansas City's notorious political boss Tom Pendergast. He had established an honorable record as a senator. In 1940, when Truman had to run for re-election, Pendergast was convicted of income tax evasion, and the Missouri Democratic Party had tried to cast Truman aside, saying they could not afford to run a Pendergast errand boy. Senator Truman had had to run without party support or funds; but he had won and had returned to the Senate floor to a standing ovation from his fellow senators.

In 1941 he had proposed the creation of a Senate committee to investigate waste and corruption in armaments spending. He became the chairman of what was now known as the Truman Committee. The committee had been highly effective, and Senator Truman had a nationwide reputation as an indefatigable and incorruptible watchdog over defense spending.

The President, who had at first been inclined to dismiss Truman as everyone else did, as a Pendergast man, had learned to respect him. He was meeting with him this morning to review several spending projects, to explain to the senator just what they were for.

The breakfast was being served in the Private Dining Room, and as Mrs. Roosevelt went down to join the Trumans her mind was distracted by half a dozen urgent problems—not least of which were the two murder cases, in which the trail seemed to be growing colder and colder.

For Captain Edward Kennelly it looked cold, too. He had no great confidence that he was going to achieve anything by once again interrogating Marv Ritchey. Still—It was his philosophy of criminal investigation—if he could be said to have a philosophy—that you solved crimes by gathering as much information as you could and then trying to fit it together.

Something else. The fact that a man lied *was* information.

Ritchey lit a cigarette and glowered at Kennelly. He had a way of glowering. He could frighten some people just by staring hard at them, Kennelly had no doubt.

"You've moved up a step on the list of suspects," said Kennelly. He, too, lit a cigarette. "That's why I'm back so soon."

"I didn't know I was on a list."

"Maybe you can get yourself off it," said Kennelly.

Ritchey shrugged and blew cigarette smoke over the microphone that sat before him in the radio broadcasting studio. The smoke did not overpower the scent of Wildroot on his hair. He looked up at a secretary who was trying to signal him through the glass and shook his head at her.

"Let's start off with you telling me where you were Friday night," said Kennelly.

"Friday . . . What time?"

"Make it the whole evening."

"The whole evening. Okay. Friday . . . I had dinner at Reardon's, with Senator Tom Connally. The senator from Texas? I suppose you know—"

"I know who Tom Connally is," said Kennelly. "What time?"

"My last news show is at six-thirty. I'm out of here at

six-forty-five. I suppose it was seven when I made it to the restaurant. Then . . . drinks and dinner. I suppose it was eight-thirty or nine when we left Reardon's.''

"A political interview?''

Ritchey nodded. "Senator Connally is a powerful man in the Senate. I count a number of powerful men among my friends.''

"So do I,'' said Kennelly dryly. "Now—Where did you go after you left Reardon's?''

"I went home. I drove home. I live in Georgetown.''

"What time did you get home?''

"Well it was—what?—nine-thirty, quarter to ten.''

"Was anyone there who can confirm that?''

"I have a daughter ten years old. She was in bed asleep, as she always is by that hour. My wife was out playing bridge and came in about eleven-thirty.''

"You were alone from nine-thirty to eleven-thirty,'' said Kennelly. "Any telephone calls?''

"As a matter of fact, yes. I telephoned the vice president, Henry Wallace.''

"Let's talk about Monday night,'' said Kennelly.

"I was on duty as an air-raid warden. From sunset, about seven-fifteen, say, until 3:00 A.M.''

"Doing what?''

"Patroling my neighborhood, looking for blackout violations.''

"Can anybody confirm that?''

Ritchey shrugged. "If you want to know if I had time to run over to that alley and murder the Shearson girl, the answer is that I wasn't seen every half hour or every hour, especially later in the evening. But I didn't know the Shearson girl. I knew her name, but I never met her.''

"Suppose I tell you I've got some evidence that you did know her?''

"I don't give a damn what you've got, Kennelly. I never met the girl.''

"Your answers don't take you off the suspects list,'' said Kennelly.

"You can't sweat me," said Ritchey wearily. "You got evidence, show it."

"Just don't leave town, as we say," said Kennelly.

Senator and Mrs. Truman seemed to enjoy the simple summer breakfast Mrs. Nesbitt had put on the table— bacon and eggs, melon, juice, toast with butter and marmalade, and coffee.

"The President asked me to say he wishes he could join us for breakfast but that this morning's schedule would have to be described with no word short of 'oppressive.' He will, of course, meet with you as scheduled, Senator."

"I'm pleased when he can give me a few minutes any time," said Senator Truman in his nasal Midwestern voice. "I understand the burden he's carrying."

Though like the President she had not been at first impressed, Mrs. Roosevelt had decided she not only respected the senator from Missouri; she liked him. For her, he took a little getting used to, as did his wife; but when they had a chance they demonstrated a canny native intelligence, especially a facility for getting through to the core of things.

If she wanted to look for a fault in the senator, she found him a little too tightly wound, a bit bouncy. He was deferential to the President, as indeed he was to the First Lady, but could not conceal his innate self-confidence. His clothes did not fit him perfectly, and she had to suspect he went out in Virginia somewhere to find a barber who would cut his hair the way it was cut. She had heard, too, that he was a little too fond of the bottle for her entire approval.

If these were all the faults she could find in him, they were much outweighed by his merits, and there had developed between them a casual friendship that had proceeded a little beyond what the President had so far developed with the Missouri senator.

Mrs. Truman—Bess—was better educated than her husband, and Mrs. Roosevelt wondered how much influence the self-contained woman had on the senator. The quiet Mrs. Truman had the look of a farm wife, and maybe she had a farm wife's practiced sensitivity for nature and human nature, and perhaps the courage, too.

He had pleaded with her to address him by his first name. So she did—"Harry. As you investigate the defense industries, do you see good jobs being denied to our Negro citizens?"

"I know you are interested in that," he said.

"Look at it this way, Harry," she said. "Willing workers are a defense resource. If a man with the skill to run a lathe is condemned to sweep the factory floor, we lose the value of that man as a resource."

Harry Truman had a cup of coffee in his hand. He nodded as he put it down. "I am senator from a state where Negro children don't attend the same schools as whites. If I suggested they should, I wouldn't be nominated, much less re-elected in 1946. If I were a senator from Connecticut, I could call for equality in employment opportunities. As a senator from Missouri, I don't dare."

"If Harry were President, he could work for racial justice," said Mrs. Truman. "He would represent the nation, then."

The senator shrugged. "You see my problem?"

"What do you believe, Harry? In confidence?"

Senator Truman shrugged. "As a country boy back home, I believed what everybody else believed," he said. "I am a very fortunate man, Mrs. Roosevelt. I've been given the opportunity to learn better."

Mrs. Truman turned her eyes toward the ceiling and smiled. "I hope he will not tell you what else he learned as a boy and has decided not to believe anymore."

Half an hour later in the Oval Office, the President faced Senator Truman across his desk.

"Harry," he said. "I haven't very often, as President, asked anyone, especially a member of Congress, just to take my word for something and not look into a question any further. I'm going to ask you to do that now. You have every right to the answer to the question you've asked. But I will be very grateful to you if you could accept my word that the money you asked about is being spent wisely."

"Lots of money," said the Senator. " 'The Manhattan Engineering District . . .' "

"It's a code term, Harry," said the President. "And I'd be grateful if you'd forget you ever heard of the Manhattan Project. I can't deny you the information if you really want it. You're entitled to it. But, believe me, if I tell you, you'll be burdened with a secret you don't want to have to carry."

"I'll take your word for it, Mr. President," said Senator Truman.

"I'm grateful," said the President. "And when you do find out—as you ultimately will—what this and a great deal more money is being spent for, you will see why I did it; and I don't think you'll disagree with my decision to spend it, even if the project fails."

While Senator Truman was with the President, Mrs. Roosevelt escorted Mrs. Truman through the White House. She succeeded nicely in concealing her impatience to be back at work. The senator returned from the Executive Wing somewhat subdued. He thanked the First Lady for her hospitality. So did Mrs. Truman. A White House car took the senator to the Capitol and Mrs. Truman to their apartment.

In her office, Mrs. Roosevelt found that Nelson Rockefeller had telephoned again.

"Call him, Tommy," she said to her secretary Malvina Thompson. "Tell him I have time to see him if he wants to come over here."

Mrs. Roosevelt picked up her telephone and called Grace Tully. The President was available for a moment's conversation.

"What word from the Pacific?" she asked the President.

"The sun's not up at Midway," said the President. "Scouts sighted a major force of Japanese ships yesterday, and B-17s went out to bomb them. But they didn't see carriers. Their carriers may have slipped past our carrier task forces and could be on their way to Hawaii or even the West Coast—Well . . . all we can do is wait."

"If they find the Japanese fleet, are they strong enough to—?"

"No," said the President.

When Mrs. Roosevelt put down the telephone, filled with dread by the President's forthright statement, Tommy told her that Nelson Rockefeller was not at his office but that Dominic Deconcini and Captain Edward Kennelly were waiting.

"Somebody, sooner or later," said Deconcini, "is going to have to confront that redoubtable socialite Barbara Lowell."

"Why?" asked the First Lady. "What can she tell us?"

"Who knows?" asked Kennelly. "Faced with the news that her fiancé has been sleeping with at least three other girls that we know about, she might prove a flowing fountain of information."

Mrs. Roosevelt sighed. "We may be breaking up a pretty little romance for nothing."

"Two young women who slept with Lieutenant Donald Pettengill are dead," said Deconcini. "He has an ironclad alibi for the Peggy Shearson murder, but let us not forget he was in the White House and on the first floor the night Emily Ryan was killed. If I were Barbara Lowell and knew the relationships, I think I might become a little cautious."

"Very well," said Mrs. Roosevelt reluctantly. "I can't go see her. Who does?"

"Call her in here," said Deconcini.

"Very well," said Mrs. Roosevelt again.

"Now," said Kennelly. "I'd like to check up on the alibi given by Mr. Marvin Ritchey. He says he had dinner with Senator Tom Connally on Friday night. He left the senator early enough to have come to the White House and killed Emily, but he also says he telephoned Vice President Wallace from home about the time the murder happened.''

"How could Mr. Ritchey have killed Miss Ryan?'' asked Mrs. Roosevelt. "Access—"

"The same way he could have done it on Monday night," said Deconcini. " 'Sergeant Lee,' If the fictitious sergeant was in fact Ritchey, he's a man who knows a lot about the White House. I had personnel records checked. Ritchey worked in the White House for six months during the Hoover administration. It seems President Hoover felt he didn't come across well on radio and asked someone to come in and teach him the rudiments of speaking into a microphone. So—Marvin Ritchey. So, he was around here a while. The guy knows something about the White House.''

"It will be easy enough to check his alibis," said Kennelly. He looked to Mrs. Roosevelt. "I thought you might want to call Senator Connally and the Vice President.''

"From what you have said, the Vice President's testimony would be the most suggestive," she said.

"It would," Kennelly agreed.

She picked up a telephone and called the office of the Vice President. In a moment Henry Wallace was on the line, and she asked him to come up to her office. He said he would be there in five minutes.''

"Well . . .'' she said then. "Barbara Lowell.''

She asked Tommy Thompson to put through a call to Barbara Lowell and ask her to come to the White House for a meeting with the First Lady. Before Wallace arrived, Tommy returned to say that Miss Lowell had agreed to come immediately. She would need half an hour or so.

Henry Agard Wallace, Vice President of the United States, was a tall, horse-faced man with unruly hair and a ready, toothy smile. He was a former Republican, had been Secretary of Agriculture, and had been nominated only by a vociferously reluctant Democratic National Convention in 1940. He was grateful to the President for the office he now held, and was a committed internationalist and New Dealer. He was grateful also to Mrs. Roosevelt, whose speech to the convention may have won him a nomination the delegates had been in a mood to deny him.

"Oh, yes," he said. "I had a call from Marvin Ritchey the other night. Despicable man. But he called."

"We need to know when, Hank, if you don't mind. It is important to know at what hour you received that call."

Wallace turned down the corners of his mouth and frowned as he tried to recall the telephone call. "It was late," he said. "I mean, it was late to get a call from a news reporter. Let's say it was ten o'clock. Maybe ten-thirty."

Kennelly sighed. "Are you sure?" he asked.

Wallace nodded. "I could be off a few minutes either way," he said. "But it was close to ten-thirty."

Kennelly looked at Mrs. Roosevelt and shook his head. This confirmed Ritchey's statement and put him at home in Georgetown very close to the hour when Emily Ryan was killed.

"He telephoned you," said Mrs. Roosevelt, "at home about ten-thirty."

"Not from home," said Wallace. "Not from home, unless he runs a very funny home. I could hear automobile horns in the background . . . plus maybe the sound of a trolley car. No. He was calling from a pay station somewhere downtown. Well—I can't say downtown. But not from his home, for sure."

Kennelly grinned now. "Ah, so," he said. "Not from home. He *said* he called from home."

"Not from home," said Wallace. "From someplace where I could hear the sounds of traffic."

"Hank, you have been very helpful," said Mrs. Roosevelt. "Thank you, so much."

"For what, may I inquire?"

"Let us explain it later," said she.

* * *

Tommy Thompson reminded Mrs. Roosevelt that she had an appointment with the newsreel cameras at eleven. She hurried into her bedroom, changed clothes, and went down to the colonnade between the White House and the Executive Wing to make a statement on film.

The cameramen were set up and waiting. Though they never traded banter with her as they did with the President, they had learned that his First Lady was always a bright and cooperative subject, and most of them welcomed the chance to film her.

The subject of the statement to be filmed today was War Stamps. She held in her left hand a sheet of them and in her right a stamp book. She was to speak to the school children of America.

"Boys and girls, the fathers of many of you, the brothers of many others, have gone off to war—as in fact my four sons have done. I know that many of you ask, as my grandchildren ask, 'What can *I* do to help win the war? How can I help bring my daddy or brother home sooner?'

"Well, boys and girls, there is a way you can help. I am holding here a sheet of War Stamps. Each one costs ten cents, a dime, the cost of an ice-cream cone or two candy bars. Each dime you contribute to the defense effort by buying a War Stamp a dime is contributed to your country, to help us win the war.

"But it is not just a gift to the war effort, actually. It is an investment. As you buy your stamps, you stick them in one of these books. You can stick ten stamps on each page, and each book contains eighteen pages. When you have filled the book, you can exchange the filled book, plus seventy-five cents, for a twenty-five dollar War Bond. You buy the War Bond, thus, for eighteen dollars and seventy-five cents, and in ten years your government will pay you twenty-five dollars.

"You are not, then, just giving your dimes to your government to help pay the cost of airplanes and ships and guns and all the things our fighting men need. No. You are *lending* your government the money, and the government will repay you with interest.

"Boys and girls, War Stamps will be offered to you in your schools. Please buy them. The money you lend your country will be used to buy the things our soldiers, sailors, flyers, and marines need to fight this war. Almost every boy and girl can afford a dime a week. Most can afford more. Give up a candy bar or an ice-cream cone and help your country win the war.

"Remember. War Stamps. Your parents buy War Bonds. You can buy War Stamps and turn them in for War Bonds of your own. That is what *you* can do to help our country win."

Barbara Lowell arrived while Mrs. Roosevelt was filming this message, and Tommy Thompson led her out into the colonnade to watch. When the First Lady stepped away from the cameras, the young woman waited.

"Miss Lowell. You have arrived at lunchtime. May I ask you to join me for something light and a glass of iced tea?"

Barbara Lowell was capable of accepting an unexpected invitation to lunch at the White House, or lunch with the King of England, with equal aplomb. She said she would be pleased to stay for lunch.

"Mrs. Nesbitt," said the First Lady, "specializes in nutritious light lunches."

A call to the housekeeper quickly produced a table on the lawn adjacent to the rose garden and a lunch of tuna salad, raw vegetables, and iced tea. The tuna salad was composed of canned tuna that had been opened yesterday, plus celery that had gone limp, stirred with mayonnaise and sprinkled with pepper that had been ground a year ago. The vegetables were aging and limp. Mrs. Roosevelt hardly noticed. She cared nothing for food; anything that eased her hunger was good enough; and she sat over the unpalatable meal innocently contented.

Barbara Lowell concealed her surprise over what was served at a White House luncheon. She had been a 1940 debutante, and she was practiced at concealing her surprise at any gaucherie. She was a tall young woman, with a long face—a long jaw, chiefly, a jaw in fact so long that wags had suggested her generation of Lowells had chins like the Habsburgs. She had bulging blue eyes. Her light-brown hair was rigidly coiffed, in curls over her head and above her ears. Her rosebud lips remained pursed, mostly. She was not thought of as any great beauty; yet she made an overall impression of formal, restrained attractiveness.

For the first few minutes of their lunch Mrs. Roosevelt kept the conversation inconsequential. Then she felt compelled to go on to a distressing subject. "Miss Lowell," she said. "I believe you are engaged to marry Lieutenant Donald Pettengill."

Barbara Lowell nodded. "I am," she said.

"I should like to speak to you in confidence," said Mrs. Roosevelt.

"Of course," said Barbara Lowell calmly.

"Friday night," said the First Lady, "a young woman was murdered in the White House. I am not in possession of evidence that indicates that Lieutenant Pettengill had anything to do with her death. I am in possession of incontrovertible evidence to the effect that he, for a considerable period of time, was involved in a romantic relationship with her."

"Emily Ryan," said Barbara Lowell.

"You know?"

"Don told me."

"Ah . . . I see. Uh, did he tell you anything about his relationship with her?"

"It is not easy to tell you," said Barbara Lowell.

"Please do tell me, nevertheless."

Barbara Lowell pondered the request for a long moment. "Well," she said. "How does one answer? I, uh . . . Are you familiar, Mrs. Roosevelt, with the story by John Galsworthy in which the aristocratic young man developed an intimate affair with a pretty little farm girl and—''

"Megan," Mrs. Roosevelt interrupted. "I know."

"Well . . . It was like that. She was attractive. She made herself available. Don—Need I say more? Then she was murdered. And Don said to me that he might be suspected of her death, because of his intimate relationship with her."

"You are satisfied that—"

"I am satisfied that his affair with Miss Emily Ryan had nothing to do with his future and mine." The young woman raised her chin and regarded Mrs. Roosevelt with a confident smile. "Women like you and me, Mrs. Roosevelt—if you don't mind my making the comparison—live on a plane above most of the population, and things happen in our personal lives that the readers of romance magazines could never understand."

Mrs. Roosevelt frowned hard and glanced away from Barbara Lowell for a moment as she regained her composure. "Do you mean you don't mind that he— Forgive me, Miss Lowell, but I see no way to put it but to ask if you don't mind if he took advantage of a young woman."

" 'Took advantage,' " said Barbara Lowell. "Forgive me, but can it not at least as well be said that she took advantage of him?"

"Excuse me, but do I understand you to be suggesting that Miss Ryan should have been grateful for the opportunity to have an intimate relationship with Lieutenant Pettengill?"

Barbara Lowell shrugged. "Something like that. Don't women of our class allow our men—"

"Miss Lowell—No. Women of our class do not. Maybe you suggest that you and I are of a different class."

"A different generation, then," said Barbara Lowell.

The First Lady regarded the young woman with restrained indignation. She drew a deep breath. "Miss Lowell," she said. "Do you know where Lieutenant Pettengill was Monday evening?"

"Not really. I had a board meeting. I canceled a date with him to attend."

"Do you know the name Peggy Shearson?"

Barbara Lowell shook her head. "I never heard that name."

"Peggy Shearson," said Mrs. Roosevelt, "was also murdered. Monday evening. Within an hour after a pleasant interlude with her good friend Lieutenant Pettengill in a bar in Washington."

Barbara Lowell was at last dismayed. "You are saying that he had a . . . friendship with another girl who was murdered?"

Mrs. Roosevelt nodded. "I do not suggest he had anything to do with the young woman's death. Indeed, there is ample evidence that he did not. There is, on the other hand, evidence that he indulged in an intimate relationship with this young woman, too. And, in fact, Miss Lowell, I have the testimony of still another young woman that she engaged in an intimate physical relationship with Lieutenant Pettengill."

Barbara Lowell looked away from Mrs. Roosevelt for a moment. Then she lifted her glass of iced tea and took a sip. "May I assume the third girl has not been murdered?" she asked.

"No, she has not. And neither have you."

Barbara Lowell slammed her glass on the table. "Are you calling Don a murderer?" she asked, her voice breaking.

"Not necessarily a murderer," said Mrs. Roosevelt. "On the other hand, a man who may have knowledge that will lead us to a murderer."

Barbara Lowell's jaw trembled. "I . . . I will do anything necessary to clear his name," she said.

"The relationship between you is . . . ?"

"Mrs. Roosevelt . . ." said Barbara Lowell. "It is

wartime. The world is turned upside down." She hesitated, caught a sob in her throat and subdued it, and went on. "Traditional values are challenged. Traditional values *die*. I . . . I believe in the old values. But the man I am engaged to marry may go away to the Pacific any day. I mean, his service in the White House may end any day. You would know more about that than I. So, I—I . . ."

"You, in common with thousands of other young women," said Mrs. Roosevelt, "extend to your young men license you would not extend in peacetime circumstances. The war has not gone on many months, but it has changed standards. I do not approve, but I cannot condemn."

"We live together as husband and wife, in my home in Georgetown," said Barbara Lowell.

"Oh, my dear! And he . . ."

"As other husbands do, I guess," said the young woman.

Mrs. Roosevelt sighed heavily. "I suppose so," she said. "Can you, then, account for his whereabouts on Friday and Monday evenings?"

"No," said Barbara Lowell. "I must tell you, too, that for the sake of appearances he keeps his own apartment and sometimes goes there. Friday night . . . I thought he was on duty here in the White House. Monday . . . ?" He came to my place very late. I was already asleep. It could have been three in the morning."

"Your domesticity," said Mrs. Roosevelt. "Did it extend to caring for his clothes? Like, for example, sewing a button on his uniform?"

Barbara Lowell smiled wryly. "Odd," she said. "I am a debutante. More than that, I would have been a debutante of the silver rose and would have come out in Vienna if the Nazis had not taken over the city. Even so, my mother insisted I must know the domestic skills a woman was expected to have in—Well . . . wherever. Mrs. Roosevelt, I *can* sew a button on a

man's suit. I can make a pie crust. I can bake a cake.
I can—"

"But the question is," said Mrs. Roosevelt, *"did* you
sew a button on Lieutenant Pettengill's uniform?"

Barbara Lowell nodded. "Yes. I did. Sunday, I think it
was."

13

Looking down from her office window, Mrs. Roosevelt saw still another camera crew on the White House lawn. She was glad she did not have to go down and make a speech to this movie camera. It was filming a short feature on first aid, and the White House made a patriotic background for the actors playing injured patients and others playing men and women giving first aid.

Mrs. Roosevelt was reminded of a bit of doggerel that was going the rounds, poking fun at the earnest ladies solemnly practicing bandaging and the correct applications of tourniquets:

> *Lady, if you see me lying*
> *On the ground and nearly dying,*
> *Let my gore run bright and free.*
> *Don't attempt to bandage me.*

Idly, she studied the chart she had made, the list of unanswered questions in the two murders. She had been able to check off only one question as answered.

How did Miss Ryan gain access to the White House? to the Blue Room?

Why was she carrying a revolver?

√Whose are the initials engraved on the Ronson lighter?

Who provided the money for Miss Ryan's funeral?

Who was threatening Miss Ryan (as the pawnbroker says she told him)?

Who was in the Blue Room Monday night?

Why was someone in the Blue Room Monday night?

Why did Miss Shearson not scream as someone struck her repeatedly and broke both her wrists?

What relationship, if any, is there between the death of Miss Ryan and the leaks of confidential information to Marv Ritchey?

What is the relationship between the deaths of Miss Ryan and Miss Shearson?

Tommy Thompson came in. "Mr. Rockefeller is here," she said.

"Show him in."

The Nelson Rockefeller she had talked to yesterday evening was not the man she saw before her now. Yesterday's Rockefeller had been composed, even amused. This one could not conceal his tension and apprehension.

"It is good to see you again, Mr. Rockefeller," said the First Lady.

"It's good to see *you* again, Mrs. Roosevelt. I hope I'm not intruding on something urgent."

"Not at all. I just called the Oval Office for a report on events in the Pacific, and the President's secretary was able to give me the latest reports."

"Ah. What is happening, may I ask?"

"Midway Island is under attack by Japanese bombers," she said. "Obviously they are carrier-based, so that means the elusive Japanese carriers are somewhere in the central Pacific and not approaching San Francisco as was reported by some last night."

"In a sense that is good news, isn't it?"

"Yes, I suppose in a sense it is. Unless the attack on Midway is a feint. Those bombers could be flying off one carrier, while others do in fact approach the West Coast."

"The last news I heard was that American B-17s and PBYs bombed a Japanese fleet yesterday and again during the night," he said.

"Admiral Nimitz is convinced that is not the main force," she said. "Our pilots spotted no aircraft carriers. The admiral believes the force spotted and attacked yesterday and last night is the invasion force, carrying soldiers to be landed on Midway."

Rockefeller shook his head. "It's a hazardous situation."

"It is, indeed. But, in any event, what can I do for you today, Mr. Rockefeller?"

He sighed. "Mrs. Roosevelt," he said, "I am deeply sorry, but I withheld some information from you yesterday. I was embarrassed to tell you what I should have told you, and I am concerned about the conclusions you might reach if you learned the facts from other sources.''

"I see," she said quietly. "Well. Have you come to give me those facts now?''

"Yes, embarrassing though it may be.''

"You understand," she said, clasping her hands before her, "that I am not officially involved in the investigation into the deaths of Miss Ryan and Miss Shearson. You are under no obligation, really, to tell me anything.''

"But I want to," he said. "I want to be honest.''

"Very well. I shall listen.''

Nelson Rockefeller scratched the side of his face as he seemed to ponder about how to begin. "All right," he said. "I told you last evening that I employed Emily Ryan as a stenographer. That is not entirely true.''

Mrs. Roosevelt smiled. "I did think it a bit curious, in view of the fact that we knew Miss Ryan could not take shorthand.''

"Yes . . . She was an interesting girl, but I suppose great secretarial skill was not among her attributes.''

"Actually, she did quite well. She transcribed the cylinders off a Dictaphone, and since Steve Early seems to have had no objection to dictating into one of those machines, she did good work for him.''

Rockefeller nodded nervously, jerking his chin up and down so rapidly that his hair flew. "Yes," he said. "She told me she transcribed Dictaphone cylinders. Thinking back last night, remembering she had told me that, I realized I had told a stupid lie when I said I employed her as a stenographer. I hope you can understand my motive. I didn't want to admit, particularly to you, Mrs. Roosevelt, that my relationship with Emily had been anything but business.''

"Do you want to tell me what the relationship really was, then?''

His mouth twisted into a weak wry smile. "I wish I

didn't have to," he said. "The relationship was . . . well, I had an affair with her."

"For how long?"

"For a few weeks, only."

"You took her to a hotel," said Mrs. Roosevelt bluntly.

Rockefeller winced. Obviously he wondered how much more the First Lady knew. "Yes," he said.

"I can understand *your* motive. I find it a little difficult to understand hers. Did you pay her for her favors?"

"No. Never. Nothing like that."

"She knew you were married, of course. She knew you would not obtain a divorce and legitimize your relationship with her."

"Yes, she knew that."

"Then what, Mr. Rockefeller? What was Emily's motive? Was it by any chance to gain information from you that she could pass along to Marvin Ritchey?"

He turned down the corners of his mouth and shook his head. "I can't imagine that. How many exciting secrets could anyone get from the office of the Coordinator of Inter-American Affairs?"

"Oh, I don't know. Perhaps Mr. Ritchey has his tentacles out in all directions—all kinds of tentacles. He did get one story from you, presumably through Miss Ryan."

Rockefeller sighed. "A bit fanciful . . ." he said quietly.

"Mr. Rockefeller," she said briskly. "I want to show you a list of questions. Maybe you can offer a scrap of information that might lead toward an answer to one or two of them."

She handed him her little chart.

Rockefeller frowned hard over the paper. "I see you've put a check beside the question on the Ronson lighter," he said soberly. "May I ask why?"

"The lighter," she said, "bore two initials. 'E.R.' was of course Emily Ryan. The other set was 'H.D.' A romantic man, Mr. H.D. Unwilling of course to have his initials engraved on the lighter he gave to Miss Ryan, he had engraved a set of initials she would know and might remember with warm affection—that is, if she were romantic, too. H . . . D. 'Harold Douglas.' A more careful man might have used different names on different occasions.''

Nelson Rockefeller interlaced his fingers. He squeezed, and his knuckles turned white. "I really rather cared for the girl," he said. "For a while, anyway. I never gave her money. But the lighter was only one of the gifts I gave her. I bought her clothes. A purse. I—"

"Did 'Harold Douglas' take other girls to the Cardinal Hotel?"

"How do you know about the Cardinal Hotel?" he asked.

"Captain Edward Kennelly is a dogged investigator, Mr. Rockefeller," said the First Lady.

Rockefeller sighed. "Yes . . ." he admitted. "I have taken other girls to the Cardinal Hotel."

"The management is . . . circumspect there," she suggested.

"Definitely."

"Very well. Is there a question on the list for which you can suggest an answer? Or if not an answer, an approach?"

Rockefeller shook his head. "I had a love affair with the girl who was murdered. I suppose she may have taken information from me and given it to Marv Ritchey." He sighed. "That's quite bad enough, isn't it? I'm glad I came and told you. I'm sorry for the circumstances that made me come and tell you."

"Yes. I am sorry too, Mr. Rockefeller," said Mrs. Roosevelt.

"And I . . . I'm awfully sorry Emily was killed. She was a lovely young woman . . . in many ways."

"Mr. Rockefeller," she said. "I am, tentatively, arranging a meeting at about five o'clock. I am calling together everyone who might have something to contribute to this investigation, and I am hoping that we can put our heads together and, if we don't solve the mysteries, then at least we will contribute something. Will you be so kind as to make yourself available at that time?''

He nodded. He was unhappy about it, but conceded that he would be present.

As Nelson Rockefeller hurried out of the private quarters, his dissatisfaction with his interview showing on his face and in his nervous pace, Lieutenant Foster Morris arrived on the elevator. Although a Harvard man and of good family, he was awed to find himself in the White House. An usher had led him through the first floor, where he had gaped at the formal rooms, then up on an elevator to the private quarters of the President of the United States, to meet with the formidable First Lady in her office.

Dressed in his whites, he carried his cap correctly under his left arm. He was just twenty-one years old, and he had not had time to telephone his father in Boston for instructions on how he should talk to the woman who had been so intemperately condemned around their breakfast table that he was almost embarrassed to confront her. His father had thought ''We Don't Want Eleanor Either'' had been the cleverest political slogan of 1940. For the President, they had used only one term. He was *"That Man."*

She was surprisingly tall. He had not expected that. Dressed in a summery white dress with buttons all the way down from her throat to the hem of her skirt, she was not the unattractive woman he had expected, either.

''If you would like,'' she said after their initial words of greeting, ''I can have you taken on a full tour of the White House when we are finished here.''

''I would appreciate that,'' he said.

''In fact, Lieutenant, I may ask you to stay. I am beginning to think we will have a little meeting this afternoon, involving many of the people who knew Miss Ryan and Miss Shearson. I understand you knew both of them.''

''I did, Ma'am, but I don't know how they got killed.''

''No, I don't suggest you do. But I am sure you understand that I am pursuing information. Captain Kennelly, who is an experienced criminal investigator, says the best way to solve a mystery is to accumulate as much information as you can, then see how it fits together.''

"Excuse me, Ma'am, but I would like to know if Lieutenant Pettengill is regarded as a suspect.''

"Well," said Mrs. Roosevelt gently, "we do have to take into consideration the fact that he had an intimate relationship with both of them, whilst at the same time being engaged to marry Miss Lowell. That is a circumstance we cannot overlook, I believe you will agree.''

Morris smiled. "Don has always had a way with girls.''

"Do you know Miss Lowell?''

Morris's smile widened. "Yes. That marriage will be . . . perfect. Don—Lieutenant Pettengill—is not only a Pettengill; he is a *Cabot*—his mother was a Cabot. And marrying a Lowell!''

"Who do Morrises marry, Lieutenant?" Mrs. Roosevelt asked dryly.

The young man blushed. "Forgive me. I am a snob. It shows.''

"You could be something worse," she said. "Now. I understand you regard yourself as so close a friend of Lieutenant Pettengill that you are reluctant to disclose any facts that might tend to suggest he—''

"Ma'am," the young man interrupted. "I cannot be a snitch. But . . . on the other hand—''

"On the other hand, a criminal investigation is in progress," she said. "Two young women are dead. What can you add to the statement you made to Captain Kennelly and Agent Deconcini?''

"Ma'am . . . I don't think I can add anything.''

"Something that might tend to exonerate Lieutenant Pettengill? After all, I am at least as interested in exonerating him as in finding evidence against him.''

"I might say this, Mrs. Roosevelt. I dislike disparaging the character of a girl as much as I dislike snitching on a friend, but I must tell you that Emily Ryan had a foul temper. She was jealous. She was alternately worshipful and scornful of Don's family and educational background. To be altogether frank with you, Ma'am, it is my impression of Emily Ryan that she was . . . How shall I say it? That she was *unhinged.*''

"Go on, Lieutenant. I think you have more to say."

The young lieutenant drew a breath and clearly demonstrated that he wished he hadn't said as much as he had. "She . . . she was ambitious. Mercenary. I—I'm afraid I'm not helping Don."

"Be specific, please."

"Mrs. Roosevelt, she was jealous. She was jealous of Barbara Lowell. She was jealous of the attention Don paid to Peggy. I can't believe she was so foolish as to think she had any kind of permanent relationship with Don, but she acted as though she might."

"How did she manifest her jealousy, Lieutenant?"

"Angry words, Ma'am. Bitter words. I once heard her tell Don she wanted to kill him."

"Kill him?"

"Yes, Ma'am."

"And how did Lieutenant Pettengill react to that?"

"He laughed at her."

"Oh . . . well, Lieutenant Morris—I am interested also in the death of Miss Shearson. I believe Lieutenant Pettengill was with you at the time she died."

"So I am told," said Morris. "I was told she died at . . . What was the exact minute? Eleven-seventeen? Well, I can tell you for certain, without any possibility of error, that Don was at the Farragut Bar with me from about ten-thirty until midnight."

"I am interested in Miss Shearson's mood during that time," said Mrs. Roosevelt. "Do you recall any suggestion of fear on her part? Dread? Apprehension?"

Morris shook his head. "I'd say she was pretty well drunk by the time she left the Farragut," he said. "She'd swilled a lot of beer. A *lot* of beer."

"More than usual?" asked Mrs. Roosevelt.

Morris shrugged. "Well—Peggy was a beer drinker."

"But that night—?"

Morris grinned. "That night Don got her involved in a game of chug-a-dunk. Have you ever heard of it?"

"I'm afraid not."

"Well, it's kind of silly. The two players bet on how much beer they can drink without stopping—how much they can chug, in other words. But there's so much laughing, hardly ever can anyone get down more than a couple of gulps before they lose."

"What do they bet, Lieutenant Morris?"

"Uh—Well, this sounds sillier yet. The 'chug' in chug-a-dunk is the drinking. The 'dunk' is that the loser has to dunk something in whatever beer is left in the glass, then drink the rest of the beer with that in there. It's usually nothing much—a few coins, a cigarette lighter. If it's paper money, that makes the beer that has to be chugged pretty icky. Anyway, the drinker has to put the bet on the table. Whatever it is, money, lighter, even eyeglasses, goes in the beer."

"What went in the beer that evening?"

Morris chuckled. "Well, Don bet his fountain pen once, and it leaked ink into the beer as he drank it. Don dared Peggy to bet her wristwatch. She was a little upset when she drank. She was afraid the beer would leak into her watch and ruin it."

"But of course, it didn't," said Mrs. Roosevelt. "It was still running when—"

Morris nodded, grinning. "Don ran back to the men's room with it and washed the beer off it before it could leak in. He brought it back and shoved it up to her ear so she could hear it ticking. Both of them had a good laugh over that."

"And shortly they left," said Mrs. Roosevelt.

"Shortly they left," Morris agreed. "And shortly Don came back, a little annoyed he couldn't take her home for the night. And . . . And we never saw her again."

"Well . . . thank you, Lieutenant. You have been most

helpful. Please let me send you on a tour of the White House. I should be grateful if you were here at five o'clock. If there is need, I will call your office and confess that I am detaining you here.''

"No need," said Morris. "My commanding officer knows where I am.''

"You lying son of a bitch, I ought to haul you out of here in handcuffs," said Kennelly to Ritchey.

"A man's gotta—''

"A man's got something to hide," said Kennelly.

"Okay, I tried to keep something from you. Okay? But I didn't kill that girl. Whichever one you want to pin on me. I . . . What you want to do, arrest me?''

"Maybe later," said Kennelly. "Right now I want you to come to the White House for a meeting. We're having a meeting of all the guys who ought to know something about the murders of Emily Ryan and Peggy Shearson. You're on the list, kiddo.''

"I'll miss my six-o'clock broadcast," Ritchey protested.

"Maybe you'll miss the next six weeks' broadcasts if you say no to me, Marvin.''

Ritchey sighed and reached for his pack of Raleighs. "I come with you," he said wearily. "Under protest.''

Barbara Lowell returned Mrs. Roosevelt's call. Surprised to hear from the First Lady so soon again, she agreed to return to the White House—"Though I really have no more information to give.''

Alicia Robinson broke into tears when told she was summoned to a meeting where the murder of Emily Ryan was being investigated. "I've told all I know," she wept. "I have now. I didn't tell everything at first, but I have now. What do they want of me?''

Michael Marks, night manager of the Cardinal Hotel, was asleep in his roominghouse when the District detec-

tive knocked on his door. He disentangled himself from
sweat-damp sheets and went to the door in his underpants.

"Five o'clock? The *White House?* Hell, man, they won't
let me in the White House."

"The word for you from Cap Kennelly is, come to the
White House and tell the truth. They'll let you in. But you
tell anything but the truth, the whole truth, and nothin'
but the truth—you may never see the streets again. Got
it?"

Marks squinted at his alarm clock that was ticking away
loudly on the table beside his bed. "Five—How'm I gonna
cover the desk at the hotel if . . . ?"

"Your problem, fella. I got your promise you'll be there
on time, I go on about my business. I don't, I take you."

"Thanks," said Marks. "Nothin' like havin' a choice.
So I'll be there."

Mrs. Roosevelt smiled up at Lieutenant Donald Pettengill, who stood by her desk.

"I'm hoping we will resolve the case of the murder of
Miss Ryan, maybe even that of Miss Shearson. Your cooperation will be valuable, Lieutenant. I hope I may count
on your being present."

Pettengill stood stiffly, as if at attention. "Of course,
Ma'am," he said. "Of course I will be there, if you want
me."

"I do, Lieutenant. I think you may be in possession of
facts that will prove very helpful."

"I want to be helpful," he said. "I will be present."

Tommy Thompson interrupted Mrs. Roosevelt just as
she reached for the telephone to place a call.

"I'm sorry. I know you are as busy as busy can be,"
said Tommy, "but Ambassador Litvinov is downstairs and
has asked to see you."

"Litvinov? Whatever—? Very well. I can hardly refuse
to speak with the Soviet Ambassador, can I? So. Well . . .
tell them to bring him up."

The chubby, ruddy, puffing ambassador glanced around her office as if he were afraid someone were hiding somewhere. The departing Tommy Thompson closed the door, leaving him alone with the First Lady. Litvinov took the chair she suggested by a gesture of her hand.

"My dear lady," he said in his accented English. "I am glad you could give me the time."

"I shall always have time for the ambassador from the Soviet Union," she said.

"I am grateful."

"You perhaps understand that the President is—"

"I did not come to see the President," he said. "I came to see *you*."

"Ah . . . Well, then?"

"I wish to speak to you on a matter of confidence," he said. "It is, shall we say, a matter of awkward to both of us. You do not wish to speak of the matter. I do not wish to speak of the matter. I have communicated nothing of it to my government. I do not wish to. Of it, I think the President knows little. Of it, I imagine you know more."

"And the matter is . . . ?"

Maxim Litvinov drew a deep breath. "My dear lady," he said. "When my foreign minister was here during the weekend, a horrible crime was committed in the White House."

"A crime?" she asked cautiously.

"Indeed," he said solemnly. "In the White House, while Mr. Molotov is dining with you and the President, not far from the dining room there has been committed a murder."

Mrs. Roosevelt raised her chin. "Yes. But there was no threat to the safety of the foreign minister."

"Of this he was convinced," said Litvinov. "It was, he said, a personal matter, the cause of this murder, and was in no way directed at him."

"That is true."

"Yet," said Litvinov, "I believe one of our personnel has been regarded as possibly the author of this murder."

"Not really," she said.

"Vasili Aleksandrovich Potapava," said Litvinov. "He was about on the first floor of the White House when the brutal murder has been committed. His name has been listed informally among the suspects, I should think, and for diplomatic reasons has been discounted. In fact, Mrs. Roosevelt, I have to wonder if the investigation has not been suspended in the thought that poor Vasili Aleksandrovich is the murderer, who cannot be apprehended and condemned, and so the question of the murder has been left . . . How do you say? Up in the air?"

"Ambassador Litvinov," said the First Lady. "The investigation has by no means been suspended. I *know* who killed Miss Ryan. And it was not Mr. Potapava. Indeed, we never really suspected your secret police agent. Not really."

"You know who killed the unfortunate young woman?"

"I do," she said. "Not to an absolute certainty. But to a sufficient certainty that I expect to confront and accuse the killer this afternoon."

"Then perhaps the evidence I wished to give you is of no consequence."

"I am sure it is of consequence, Mr. Ambassador, and I shall be glad to have it."

"Then, Mrs. Roosevelt, I will tell you what the unhappy and badly frightened Vasili Aleksandrovich saw."

Her last visitors for the afternoon were Dom Deconcini and Ed Kennelly. They sat down with her in her office, drank iced tea, and heard her report of the conversations she'd had during the afternoon. She did not tell them of her talk with Maxim Litvinov. She did tell them what she believed was the solution to the murders of Emily Ryan and Peggy Shearson.

"I hope you will disagree with me if you see fit," she said. "If you see any hole in the logic, please say so."

"I'd say the case is pretty tight," said Kennelly.

"I have arranged to use the Cabinet Room," she said.

"I know the President won't be needing it this evening. We have quite a few people for our meeting. Also, I have arranged for a courtroom stenographer to be present and record everything that is said. So . . . Gentlemen, are we ready?"

They were ready. But before the three of them could leave the office and start down to the first floor and to the Executive Wing, the telephone rang, and Tommy Thompson suggested to the First Lady that she should take the call.

"It's the President."

"Yes, Franklin?"

"We have word from the Pacific," said the President. "Our carrier planes have found the main Japanese battle fleet. We're sending out torpedo bombers, dive bombers, fighters . . . everything we've got. It's still morning there. The battle is on."

"I shall be in the Cabinet Room," she said quietly.

14

The people invited—or summoned—to the meeting in the Cabinet Room were prompt. When the First Lady arrived, with Deconcini and Kennelly, at a few minutes past five, all the rest were there, as was the stenographer. They were standing around nervously, some of them reluctant to talk to each other. A sharp exchange of angry words between Lieutenant Pettengill and Barbara Lowell was interrupted by the appearance of Mrs. Roosevelt.

"Well, ladies and gentlemen, please take seats around the table," she said. "We shall try to be brief."

She sat at the head of the table. The others found places along the table. When they were in place, they were seated like this:

Kennelly   Pettengill   Lowell   Morris

Mrs.
Roosevelt

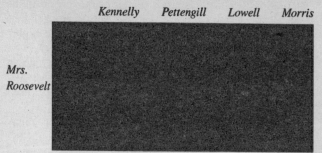

Deconcini   Rockefeller   Ritchey   Marks   Robinson

The stenographer, a young woman in a short black skirt and a white blouse, sat at a tiny square table to Mrs. Roosevelt's left and would take a record of the proceedings on her stenotype.

"I am grateful to all of you for coming. This is a rather unusual kind of meeting, and of course you all know why I called it and that it is apt to become a somewhat painful sort of meeting."

Marv Ritchey pulled a package of Raleighs from his shirt pocket, then a lighter; but Kennelly frowned hard at him from across the table and shook his head. Ritchey took the signal and reluctantly returned his cigarettes to his pocket. The others, too, understood; and several of them shifted uneasily in their seats.

"You all know the purpose of our meeting, too," Mrs. Roosevelt continued. "It is to identify the person or persons who murdered Miss Emily Ryan and Miss Peggy Shearson. Let me explain that my own role in the investigation is entirely unofficial. You have met Captain Kennelly of the District police and Agent Deconcini of the Secret Service. They represent the official investigation."

"Is somebody going to be accused before this meeting is over?" asked Marv Ritchey.

"We shall see," said the First Lady.

"I am reluctant to discuss a matter of this nature in the presence of a radio reporter," said Nelson Rockefeller. "We could come out of this meeting with some highly embarrassing things broadcast to the whole country."

"I've got a feeling," said Kennelly, "that there's going to be enough embarrassment to go around and that Mr. Ritchey's going to keep what he hears pretty much to himself."

Everyone turned and for a moment stared at Ritchey. He glared at Kennelly, then turned away.

"It may be," said Mrs. Roosevelt, "that not everyone present knows exactly what we are investigating. Let me state it briefly, if you don't mind.

"Last Friday evening, May 29, Miss Emily Ryan was murdered in the Blue Room here in the White House. Miss Ryan had no reason to be in the White House that evening, and we don't know why she was there—or, specifically, why she was in the Blue Room. We believe we know how she got into the White House, which is to say that she climbed in a window, one she had unlatched earlier when she came into the house to deliver a document.

"She was killed by a heavy blow to the head, struck with a heavy candelabrum from a mantel in the Blue Room. No one heard her scream. She was struck from the front. Those circumstances suggest she was struck by someone she knew—though certainly that fact is not proved.

"At the time of her death, Miss Ryan was carrying a loaded revolver in her handbag. The bag was open, and she seemed to be grasping for it when she died—though, once again, that is suggested by the appearance of the body and is not proved.

"Miss Shearson, who was her friend and roommate, claimed Miss Ryan's body and provided her with a funeral that must have cost a year's wages for a secretary, which Miss Ryan was, or a waitress, which Miss Shearson was. The funeral was paid for in cash.

"The funeral was Monday—that is, June 1—and on that

evening Miss Shearson was murdered also. She, too, was bludgeoned to death, though she was struck repeatedly, not just once as was the case with Miss Ryan. This occurred in an alley on the route between the Farragut Bar, where Miss Ryan had earlier been drinking with Lieutenants Pettengill and Morris, and the boardinghouse where the two young women had lived. There are some circumstances relating to Miss Shearson's death that I will leave for later discussion.

"That same night—actually, very early in the morning of June 2—an intruder entered the White House, in fact the Blue Room. Whether that intrusion has anything to do with the murder committed there three nights before, we don't know. In fact, we should be curious to know why the break-in occurred. Was the intruder looking for something? If so, what?

"That is a quick review of what has happened. I hope we shall know a great deal more before this meeting closes."

"Obviously," said Ritchey, "you think one of us killed one of them—or knows who did. Otherwise we wouldn't be here."

"That is correct," said Mrs. Roosevelt.

"Then are you going to tell us?" asked Nelson Rockefeller. "Why don't you end the suspense and tell us."

"I could be wrong," she said. "I want to examine the facts and see if someone won't add to those facts the final, conclusive piece of evidence that proves the case."

"But you *do* think you know who killed those two girls?" asked Barbara Lowell.

"Yes. I think so."

"And you think whoever did it is in this room," said Ritchey.

Mrs. Roosevelt nodded. "I believe so, Mr. Ritchey."

They exchanged anxious glances, all of them. Alicia Robinson began to cry. The hotel man, Marks, pulled a toothpick from his pocket and focused his attention on picking his teeth.

"Confession is good for the soul," observed the First Lady. "Does anyone have anything to confess? Perhaps something less than the murder of either of the two unfortunate young women."

Except for Mrs. Roosevelt, Dom Deconcini, and Ed Kennelly, all of whom glanced around the table, waiting for an answer, everyone took the moment to stare at the surface of the tabletop, or at their clasped hands, or at a window.

"Does the presence of Mr. Marks, the night manager of the Cardinal Hotel, suggest an admission anyone might like to make?" asked Mrs. Roosevelt.

Nelson Rockefeller slapped the table. "All right," he said, annoyed and testy. "Frankly, Mrs. Roosevelt, I think you might have told me privately that someone had interrogated Marks. And you, Marks, you might have called and told me you'd been questioned. I—"

"You and Peggy Shearson checked into the Cardinal Hotel Saturday night," said Kennelly gruffly. "As 'Mr. and Mrs. Harold Douglas.' Right?"

Rockefeller threw up his hands. "So?"

"It wouldn't be a matter of any particular moment," said Mrs. Roosevelt, "except for the fact that you denied you had ever met Miss Shearson."

"It's embarrassing," said Rockefeller. "I'm being embarrassed—no, humiliated—right now."

"Men who spend a lot of nights in hot-sheet hotels usually get embarrassed and humiliated, sooner or later," said Kennelly.

"Was the relationship between you and Miss Shearson anything but what the facts make obvious?" Mrs. Roosevelt asked Rockefeller.

He looked at her for a moment, then shrugged. "A little more," he said. "Sure, I knew Peggy. Emily introduced us. I dined one evening at the Mayflower, with my wife. Peggy was our waitress. She said hello but was respectful . . . distant. But when my wife went to the ladies room, Peggy made a blunt suggestion. Well—She was attractive.

So—What? Four or five times. She didn't want money, but she wanted presents. I gave her a wristwatch. The last thing she asked me for was the money for Emily's funeral. She didn't just ask for it; she demanded it, with the implication that she could embarrass me if I didn't give it. *I* paid for Emily Ryan's funeral and burial. I handed her the money Saturday night in our room at the Cardinal. So . . . that's it. That's my confession. That's all of it.''

"Thank you, Mr. Rockefeller," said Mrs. Roosevelt. "That is helpful. It does, of course, leave the chief questions unanswered. But—Thank you, anyway. Now. Does anyone else have anything to tell us?''

"Ma'am," said Pettengill. "You know that I had a relationship with both the girls. You know that, so what can I add?''

"I don't know, Lieutenant. What *can* you add? Anything?''

Pettengill settled his eyes on Barbara Lowell. "It is more than a little embarrassing," he said.

"How about you, Brother Ritchey?" asked Kennelly. "Your soul need any improving?''

Marvin Ritchey would have been in a mood for defiance, but finding himself in a room where he couldn't smoke a Raleigh every ten minutes, he was rapidly losing composure. He drew a deep breath, sighed loudly, and shrugged.

"Emily worked for me," he said. "She was an ambitious girl, wanted whatever she could get. I'd look for a bank account in another name, if I were you. Nobody had to pay for *her* funeral—except for somebody who didn't know where she had her loot stashed. And she must have had some stashed. Yeah, she brought me information from the White House, from Steve Early's office. Trouble was, the President doesn't seem to put much trust in Steve Early. What Emily typed and brought me was nothin' much. And you—'' He turned and scowled at Nelson Rockefeller. "Sex is gonna get you in trouble some day, partner. A smart girl can take you to the cleaners.''

Ritchey turned directly to Mrs. Roosevelt. "I didn't kill Emily Ryan," he said. "Why should I? And that's all the confession you're gonna get from yours truly."

"Very well," said Mrs. Roosevelt. "Anyone else?"

No one spoke.

"Then we can begin reviewing the evidence," said the First Lady. She paused, glanced at Kennelly and Deconcini, and looked, too, at the stenographer to see if she was getting everything.

The placid young woman sat pressing her keys in the various combinations that printed a coded tape, containing a word-for-word transcript of the meeting.

"The murder of Miss Ryan," said Mrs. Roosevelt, "might have remained an unsolved mystery but for the murder three nights later of Miss Shearson. Quite obviously, there were only a few people who *could* have killed Miss Ryan—that is to say, people with access to the White House that evening. That of course includes you, Lieutenant Pettengill. It includes you, Mr. Ritchey—"

Ritchey shook his head firmly.

"Oh, yes. You could have entered the grounds and the White House. We know how. Maybe you didn't. But you could have."

"How—" Ritchey began.

"Also," Mrs. Roosevelt interrupted, "the murder could have been committed by one of the Soviet agents who were in the White House that evening. One in particular was on the first floor, prowling about. One of the ushers could have killed Miss Ryan. A White House policeman. A Secret Service agent. Or . . . Well, who knows? The evidence tended to point in one direction, but it did not prove who killed her. We might never have been able to prove it."

"Then Peggy . . ." said Deconcini grimly.

"We know who killed Miss Shearson," said the First Lady. "Uh . . . once again, would anyone like to confess?"

No one spoke. No one lifted eyes from the polished surface of the cabinet table.

"Then let's look at the facts," said Mrs. Roosevelt. "Miss Shearson left the Farragut Bar at approximately ten o'clock Monday evening. She left in the company of Lieutenant Pettengill who had offered to walk her home. Lieutenant Pettengill returned to the Farragut at approximately ten-thirty and remained there until midnight. Miss Shearson's body was found much later, with her wristwatch—probably the one you gave her, Mr. Rockefeller—smashed and stopped at eleven-seventeen. Lieutenant Pettengill could not be suspected—as he otherwise surely would have been—because he was in the Farragut Bar at eleven-seventeen in the company of Lieutenant Morris and Major Deakins. Besides that, he was seen by the bartenders and others. He *was* in the Farragut Bar at eleven-seventeen."

Pettengill listened intently, nodding solemnly, his blue eyes fastened all but hypnotically on the First Lady.

"I believe the term for the situation is an airtight alibi," said Mrs. Roosevelt.

"Or an ironclad alibi," said Kennelly.

"Yes," she said. She lifted her chin. "But with a flaw."

"What are you suggesting?" asked Barbara Lowell breathlessly.

Mrs. Roosevelt shook her head. "I'm sorry, dear," she said. "It's much more serious than—"

"Wait a minute!" Pettengill interrupted. "Are you accusing *me?"*

"I haven't accused anyone," said Mrs. Roosevelt. "Yet."

"Calm down, Pettengill," said Kennelly. "If you didn't do it, you got nothin' to worry about. Right?"

"Please," said Mrs. Roosevelt. "Let us review facts. When the body of Miss Shearson was found, both her wrists were broken. Her wristwatch was shattered and had stopped at eleven-seventeen. The obvious: Being attacked by an assailant who was beating her with a blunt instrument, such as a length of pipe, she raised her arms and hands to try to protect her head and face, resulting in her wrists being broken and her watch shattered. That's the obvious explanation for the observed facts.''

"Which my detectives accepted," said Kennelly.

"But," Mrs. Roosevelt continued, "two sets of facts are inconsistent with the obvious explanation—and they are persuasive.''

"I can't broadcast any of this, I suppose," muttered Ritchey.

"If you do," said Deconcini, "you will be prosecuted for bribing a government employee to obtain defense information. I believe that carries a ten-year sentence.''

Mrs. Roosevelt paused for the interruption but ignored it. "Facts," she said. "Miss Shearson was beaten to death in an alley between two streets, where people's houses were open against the summer's heat. People lay in bedrooms with open windows. People still sat on porches. A young woman was attacked. We are to suppose both her wrists were broken before her attacker got through to her head and delivered the fatal blows. And we are to suppose that she did not cry out in fear and agony. We are to suppose she did not scream." The First Lady shook her head. "No," she said with absolute finality.

"Good for you," said Nelson Rockefeller. "I wish I'd never heard of this pair of murders, but I'm glad so astute an investigator is on the case.''

"Oh, Mr. Rockefeller! I am not an investigator. I only try to help the professionals with a few insights.''

"Sure," said Rockefeller wryly.

" 'Sure,' '' echoed Kennelly.

"Additional facts," said Mrs. Roosevelt, hurrying on. "Examined in the morgue, the body of poor Miss Shearson proved to have abraded hands. I mean the palms of her hands. The skin of her palms was torn, and bits of gravel were even found imbedded in her flesh. *In the palms of her hands*. And we are to suppose that this young woman, in agony, with her wrists broken, threw her tortured hands and wrists out ahead of her to break her fall—

instead of drawing them back to avoid the excruciating pain of falling on her broken wrists.''

''It makes a persuasive case,'' said Ritchey. ''But what does it prove? Okay, I can't broadcast it. But it also proves *I* didn't do it. Right?''

''Not necessarily,'' said Mrs. Roosevelt. ''But—'' She allowed herself a faint smile. ''Yes, Mr. Ritchey. I suppose it does tend to exonerate you of the murder of Miss Shearson.''

''The point, please,'' said Nelson Rockefeller. ''I admire the chain of logic, which seems beyond argument, but—''

''The point,'' said Mrs. Roosevelt somberly, ''is that poor Miss Shearson did not raise her arms in a vain attempt to protect her head and face from the fatal blows of a lead pipe, or whatever it was. She was struck *first* on the head. She dropped to her knees, stunned—as the abrasions on her knees suggest—then threw out her hands to avoid falling on her face in the gravel of an alley, and her hands were abraded by the rough pavement. She didn't scream, because she was barely alive. She shook her head, probably, on her hands and knees on the gravel of that alley—and then the final, fatal blows fell. And, within seconds, she was dead.''

''The wrists . . . the watch?'' asked Lieutenant Morris.

''I believe you know the answer, Lieutenant,'' said Mrs. Roosevelt.

''Ma'am, I don't. I swear to God I don't.''

The First Lady glanced at Deconcini, then at Kennelly. ''The blows to the wrists,'' she said to Morris, ''were struck after Miss Shearson was at least unconscious and probably dead. As she lay on the gravel in that alley, her murderer, then, and only then, struck her on the wrists and broke the bones—and made it a point to smash the watch. And I believe you know why, Lieutenant.''

Morris suddenly turned on Pettengill. He leaned over the table, to confront him past Barbara Lowell. *''You ly-*

ing, murdering son of a bitch!'' he screamed. Then he broke into tears and dropped his head to the table.

"Shall I continue, Lieutenant Pettengill?" asked Mrs. Roosevelt. "Or would you like to take up the narrative?"

Pettengill sneered. "The lawyers my family will employ will be amused by your speculations," he said.

"Let us go on, then, with facts," she said. "In the Farragut Bar, you and Miss Shearson played a game that involved drinking beer and paying a penalty—such as dropping your wristwatch in the beer—if you lost."

"Chug-a-dunk," said Barbara Lowell dully.

"Yes, that's what it was called," said Mrs. Roosevelt. "That night you saw to it that Miss Shearson's wristwatch, which you knew she rather prized, was dunked in a mug of beer. You offered to take it to the men's room and wash it. Which you did. While you were in the men's room, Lieutenant Pettengill, you set Miss Shearson's watch ahead an hour. She'd been drinking and probably wouldn't notice it. In fact, she didn't. And that is why, in that alley, you made such a point of breaking her wrists and smashing her watch—so the watch would stop at a time one full hour later than the time it actually was. When Miss Shearson's watch stopped at eleven-seventeen, the time was ten-seventeen or thereabouts. When you returned to the Farragut Bar, Miss Shearson's body lay in a dark alley, not likely to be discovered for some time. In fact it was not discovered for several hours. And when it was, the watch stopped at eleven-seventeen threw everyone off."

Pettengill laughed. "Prove it," he said.

"We shall," said Mrs. Roosevelt.

"You were a busy boy that night, Pettengill," said Deconcini. "Let's don't play around. Isn't it time you told the truth?"

"Would you know it if you heard it?" asked Pettengill scornfully.

"Okay, we'll put together the rest of it," said Decon-

cini. He opened a small envelope and tossed a naval officer's uniform button in the center of the table. "Been
looking for that?" he asked.

Barbara Lowell gasped. She stiffened, drew down the
corners of her mouth, and stared coldly at Pettengill.

"It wasn't in the Blue Room," said Deconcini to Pettengill. "We found it in Peggy's room at the boardinghouse. Evidence? Let me improve on the evidence it
represents. You didn't appear in navy blue at the White
House the morning after the murder of Emily Ryan. Why
not? Because you were short a button."

"Which I sewed on, Don," growled Barbara Lowell.
"You picked up a replacement button and brought it to
me. Let's hear an explanation, Mister."

"I'll follow it up," said Deconcini. "You didn't lose
the button in the quick, short struggle with Emily in the
Blue Room. So you didn't have to come back Monday
night looking for it. Where it had gone was into the handbag of Peggy Shearson, whom you had the gall to meet
with an hour or less after you murdered Emily. She snipped
it off your uniform as the two of you snuggled in a booth
at the Farragut. Which was it, Pettengill? Did she ask for
it, for a souvenir? Or was it Peggy's insurance? She knew
how to take care of herself."

"You are now suggesting," said Pettengill with a smirk,
"that I committed two murders—Peggy's in an alley where
I never was, and Emily's in the . . . in, for God's sake,
the Blue Room!"

Mrs. Roosevelt intervened. "Let us not jump to that
conclusion, Lieutenant Pettengill," she said. "This conversation *has* gone rather much against you. You will certainly have—initially here, in a court later—every chance
to demonstrate your innocence."

"You may regard yourself as under arrest, Pettengill,"
said Kennelly. "When we search your rooms, as we'll be
doing this evening, will we find the stuff you used to
darken your hair and make yourself into 'Sergeant Lee'?

If you were smart, you got rid of it. If you're as cocky as I figure you are, you kept it."

"Sergeant Lee?" Pettengill sneered. "Who the hell is Sergeant Lee?"

"Let's see if we can find out," said Mrs. Roosevelt. "Captain Kennelly—"

Kennelly got up and went outside. In a moment he returned with a tall, pink-faced young soldier.

"Private McCloud," said Mrs. Roosevelt. "You've nothing to fear, young man. We only want to ask you a question."

"Yes, Ma'am," said the young soldier hoarsely.

"You were on duty at the gate Monday night when a man who identified himself as Sergeant Lee entered the gatehouse for a few minutes. Isn't that right?"

"Yes, Ma'am."

"Now, I want you to look at the people sitting around this table and tell us if any of them is Sergeant Lee. Let me explain to you that the man may have disguised himself in some way, such as by wearing an artificial mustache, wearing a wig, or some such thing. Take your time. You may see Sergeant Lee here, or you may not. Don't tell us you recognize the man unless you are sure you do."

Private McCloud blushed bright red as he stared at the men and women seated at the cabinet table. For a long moment he stared at Nelson Rockefeller, and Rockefeller stared back hard, almost threateningly. The young soldier glanced quickly over Morris. Then his eyes stopped on Pettengill. Pettengill, too, stared back. Then the young man nodded.

"That's him," he said. "I can tell by the eyes. Nobody else has got eyes like that."

Barbara Lowell watched Kennelly close the door after Private McCloud. Then she turned to Pettengill and said, "If you had the least class or courage, you'd tell the truth."

"He hasn't," said Morris sullenly. He fastened an angry stare on Pettengill. "I looked up to you. I was a fool."

Pettengill glanced around the table, as if looking for sympathy. "Circumstantial evidence . . ." he mumbled.

"Both of them loved you," sobbed Alicia Robinson, who had been crying softly most of the time. "That's what's so bad. They both loved you."

Pettengill shook his head. "No," he said. "They . . . they wanted something."

"Emily loved you," said Alicia Robinson. "She knew she could never hope to marry you, but she loved you. She couldn't believe you'd throw her over for Peggy. She could understand"—She pointed at Barbara Lowell—"her. But, *Peggy?* That was betrayal, Don. That was real betrayal."

"The two of them fought over you, Pettengill," said Deconcini.

"Emily loved you as much as a girl could love a guy," said Alicia Robinson.

Pettengill shook his head. "She tried to kill me," he said.

"What?" asked the First Lady.

He sighed loudly. "That's why she had the pistol that night. She came into the White House to kill me."

"I don't believe that," said Kennelly. "She told the pawnbroker where she bought the pistol that she'd been threatened."

"Of course," said Pettengill. "A girl buying a pistol in a pawnshop. What else would she say . . . if she thought she had to offer some explanation."

"You think she bought it specifically to kill you?"

"You've been worrying about why she had a pistol," said Pettengill. "Well, that's why. She climbed in a window on the ground floor. She knew her way around the White House and came up to the first floor. She knew I was assisting the President that night and would be in the hallway outside the state dinner. In fact . . . in fact, I'd told her myself that's where I'd be."

"You told me, too," said Alicia Robinson. "You like

to brag about how close to the President your job made you.''

Pettengill glanced at Alicia Robinson but did not respond to her. "I was outside the private dining room, where I would be available if the President wanted me for anything. Emily was in the Blue Room. She stepped out and called to me. I shook my head at her. I meant, I can't come in there! She pulled the pistol and pointed it at me. I . . . went to the Blue Room. She closed the door. I . . .''

"Go on," said Mrs. Roosevelt quietly.

"She had put the pistol back inside her purse, but the purse was open, so she could pull it out in an instant. She was wild, hysterical. She slapped me. She clawed at me. Then she stepped back and jammed her hand in the purse. I knew she was going for the pistol, so I grabbed what was within reach, which was the candelabrum. I hit her with it. It was self-defense. I swear that. I hit her to prevent her from shooting me."

"I am prepared to believe that," said Mrs. Roosevelt.

"It's the truth," said Pettengill.

"Then what will your plea be when you are charged with the murder of Peggy Shearson?" asked Kennelly.

"I was able to walk out of the Blue Room, leaving Emily lying there," said Pettengill. "I took up my station outside the dining room again. When the President and his party left for the Executive Wing, I was relieved of duty. I went to the Farragut Bar, as I usually did evenings. Peggy was there. I sat down with her, and I told her Emily was dead. I didn't say I killed her, of course, but I told her someone had murdered Emily in the White House that evening. It was a mistake. I shouldn't have told her. But I was shaken. I . . .''

"There is always that compulsion to talk," said Kennelly. "A man who's committed a crime feels an awful pressure on him to talk about it. Not to confess. Just to talk. Normal. Typical."

"Peggy accused me of killing Emily. Immediately. She said Emily had told her she was pregnant, carrying a child of mine, and that she was going to confront me and demand I marry her. Peggy said she'd testify to that. She said she'd call the police and tell them I had gotten Emily pregnant. I begged her not to. I—'' He stopped and sighed. ''I guess I tried every way to argue her out of doing anything like that. Finally I asked her why she thought I'd thrown over Emily in the first place. I told her it was for *her*. I—''

''You had in fact been seeing Peggy instead of Emily,'' said Kennelly. ''Why? What was the attraction, really?''

''No demands,'' said Pettengill. ''No delusions. All Peggy wanted was a good time.''

''Then why did you kill her?'' asked Kennelly.

Pettengill shook his head sadly. ''No demands, no delusions until she decided she was in a position to . . . to—''

''Blackmail you,'' said Deconcini.

Pettengill nodded. ''That button . . . I guess now she must have snipped that off my uniform as we sat there drinking in the Farragut. I wonder what she meant to do with it.''

''And so you were 'Sergeant Lee,' '' said Mrs. Roosevelt. ''You returned to the Blue Room to look for the button.''

''She had clawed at me, like I said. When I discovered the button was missing, which I didn't until Sunday, I supposed she'd pulled it off. Obviously it hadn't yet been found, but if it was somewhere in the Blue Room, it *would* be found sooner or later. I thought I had to go back and look for it. Getting into the White House was no great problem. I could have searched that room for two hours . . . except for the horrible coincidence that you, Mrs. Roosevelt, just happened to come in at that time.''

''Returning to the story of the death of Peggy Shearson,'' said Mrs. Roosevelt, ''why don't you tell us the rest of it?''

Pettengill sighed again. ''To calm her down Friday night, to stop her from going to the police with some kind of story, I told her I loved her. She wasn't sure whether or not to believe me, but it did slow her down. She asked me if I loved her enough to marry her. I said I did. What could I do? I said yes. She still didn't believe me. But she wanted to talk about it. Where would we live? What would we have and do when we were married? I sat there with her and . . . spun stories.''

"You bastard," said Barbara Lowell.

"I was supposed to see her Saturday night, after she got off work. She called me from the Mayflower and told me not to come, that the cops were there—as she put it.''

"Then she called me," said Nelson Rockefeller. "She demanded I meet her at the Cardinal Hotel—but quite late.''

"I saw her Sunday," said Pettengill. "She said she didn't want to live in Boston. Couldn't we live in Washington? And how many children would we have? How soon would we be married? When could she quit her job?''

"An innocent child, planning her wedding," said Rockefeller scornfully.

"Yes. Innocent," said Pettengill. "Behind every one of these questions, behind the whole conversation, there was the implied threat. It was in her voice. She thought she had me . . . where she wanted me. She was sarcastic, too. She asked me what she should call my parents. Mom and Dad? Or Mr. and Mrs. Pettengill?''

"You had no choice but to kill her, did you?" asked Deconcini.

Pettengill's chin jerked up. "Of course I did," he said. "I didn't have to kill her. I could have married her. Couldn't I? By now. By today. By today, Peggy Shearson could be Mrs. Donald Pettengill.''

"It was a little bit clever, the way you did it," said Marvin Ritchey dryly.

"We had walked down that alley before. Going through the alley on the way from the Farragut to her boarding-house gave us dark places where we could . . . kiss. I walked through on my way to the Farragut that night. I had picked up a hammer earlier, a simple ball-peen hammer. I'd wrapped the handle with cloth, so as to leave no fingerprints. I stashed the hammer between two trash cans, where I could pick it up when I walked her through the alley."

"The bit with the watch was what I thought was clever," said Ritchey.

"Oh, yes," said Pettengill to Mrs. Roosevelt. "You could have made that stick with a jury, with Morris's testimony. But you are wrong. I did take her watch back to the men's room and rinse the beer off it. But I didn't reset it then. After all, I couldn't have planned on a chance like that—and this was planned. What was more, she might have noticed it and set it back. No. I reset the watch after she was dead. I wiped off the fingerprints with the cloth from the hammer handle. Then I smashed the watch and broke her wrists, like you guessed. Clever?" He shrugged. *"Too* clever. But it was the best I could come up with in the time I had."

"What you didn't count on," said Kennelly, "was that a shrewd and dogged investigator like Mrs. Roosevelt would be looking into the case."

"I blush," said the First Lady. "But the mystery would have been solved in any case. I have withheld a bit of information that came to me only this afternoon. It seems there was an eyewitness to the murder of Emily Ryan. Well . . . he didn't see the murder, but he saw Miss Ryan enter the Blue Room, he saw Lieutenant Pettengill enter, he heard something of the struggle, he saw Lieutenant Pettengill leave the Blue Room, and he looked in and saw the body."

"Who?" asked Pettengill. "Not that it makes any difference."

"One of the security agents assigned to the protection of the Soviet foreign minister during his visit here," she said. "He was badly frightened. He thought *he* might be accused. He wasn't certain the murder wasn't part of a plot to harm the foreign minister. He reported the matter to Mr. Molotov. Mr. Molotov communicated the information to Ambassador Litvinov—with, however, an injunction against disclosing it until Mr. Molotov was back in Moscow. This afternoon Ambassador Litvinov came to me with the information.''

"Which drives the cork into the bottle," said Kennelly.

Kennelly put handcuffs on Pettengill. The others, stunned and exhausted by the emotions of the meeting, remained in their chairs. Rockefeller and Ritchey looked grim. Foster Morris spoke under his breath to Barbara Lowell, who wiped tears from her eyes but did not cry.

Mrs. Roosevelt picked up the telephone. The President, she knew, was in the Situation Room that had been established on the ground floor. There, with Admirals Leahy and King, and with General Marshall, he was taking reports of the Battle of Midway. He accepted her telephone call. She listened to his account of the reports received. She thanked him and put down the telephone.

"Ladies and gentlemen," she said solemnly, "I believe you all know that a major naval battle is raging in the Pacific. I have just spoken with the President. It appears that our Navy is in the process of winning a major victory. *Three* large Japanese aircraft carriers have been sunk. Our losses, in planes and men, are heavy; but only one of our carriers has been damaged, and it appears that it will survive and return to Pearl Harbor. A very great deal was at stake in this battle. And we have won.''

EPILOGUE

By the next day, Friday, June 5, the White House had a more complete report of the Battle of Midway. The number of Japanese carriers sunk was four, not three. The American carrier, the *Yorktown*, did not in fact survive. American losses of airplanes and crews were indeed heavy. But the victory was complete and was the greatest naval victory since Trafalgar. Never again would a Japanese fleet threaten Hawaii or the West Coast.

Lieutenant Donald Pettengill was indicted only for the murder of Peggy Shearson. His plea that he had killed Emily Ryan in self-defense could be accepted in view of the fact that he was subject to a charge of murder in the first degree in the Shearson case.

On Thursday, August 6, he entered a plea of guilty, on the understanding he would not be sentenced to death. He was sentenced to life in prison. In 1967, when he had served twenty-five years, he became eligible for parole. Considering the brutal nature of the murder he had committed, the parole board refused to parole him on his first hearing. On his second hearing, in 1972, he was granted parole, having served thirty years in prison.

He had inherited the Pettengill family fortune during his imprisonment, and on his return to Boston he reopened the family home on Beacon Hill, which had been closed but kept in good repair in anticipation of his coming back to live there. His money and property had been managed for him by a bank, and when he went to the bank in person for the first time, the president of the bank invited him to go to lunch at the Commons Club. Shortly, he was invited to join that club. He went to the Harvard Yard on commencement day and was welcomed by his classmates, most of whom had no idea where he'd been all those years. He bought a small sailing boat, took up golf again, and settled comfortably into the life of a wealthy Bostonian.

In 1945 Commander Foster Morris was wounded during a Kamikaze attack on the aircraft carrier *Franklin*. No longer fit for sea duty, he was sent back to Washington, to a job at the Navy Department. That fall, just after the war ended, he and Barbara Lowell were married. Morris went to law school and became a successful corporation lawyer in a big old firm.

Not long after Pettengill returned to Boston, he invited the Morrises to his home for dinner. They declined.

They were much criticized. "After all," said one of Barbara's sisters, "what else could he have done? Obviously he couldn't have married the girl."